Harbour

A Blackbridge Novel

Claire Boston

BANTILLY
PUBLISHING

First published by Bantilly Publishing in 2020 as book 3 of the Blackbridge First Response series.

Harbour: The Blackbridge Series 7

EPUB format: 978-1-925696-56-1
Mobi format: 978-1-925696-57-8
Print: 978-1-925696-58-5
Large Print: 978-1-925696-58-5

Cover design by Lana Pecherczyk
Edited by Ann Harth
Copyedited by Teena Raffa-Mulligan

About the Author

Claire Boston fell in love with romance and romantic suspense at eleven when she discovered her mother's stash of Nora Roberts novels. Like Nora, she writes series set around families or groups of friends with a guaranteed happy ending.

She loves travelling and learning about new cultures and interesting vocations which she then weaves into her writing.

When Claire's not at the computer typing her stories she can be found creating her own handmade journals, swinging on a sidecar, or in the garden attempting to grow something other than weeds.

Claire lives in Western Australia with her husband, who loves even her most annoying quirks and is currently learning how to knit.

You can find her complete book list on her website www.claireboston.com/books. You can connect with Claire through Facebook and Twitter, or join her reader group (http://www.claireboston.com/reader-group/).

Also by Claire Boston

Romance

<u>The Texan Quartet</u>
What Goes on Tour
All that Sparkles
Under the Covers
Into the Fire

<u>The Flanagan Sisters</u>
Break the Rules
Change of Heart
Blaze a Trail
Place to Belong

Romantic Suspense
<u>The Blackbridge Series</u>
Nothing to Fear
Nothing to Gain
Nothing to Hide
Nothing to Lose
Shelter
Shield
Harbour
Protect

Non-fiction
<u>The Beginner Writer's Toolkit</u>
Self-Editing

Dedication

To all Marine Rescue volunteers.

Chapter 1

Alyse Wilson laid the candle wick on the beeswax sheet she'd made earlier in the week and carefully rolled it up, loving the sweet scent drifting to her nose, and the soft waxy surface which moisturised her fingertips. Using all the products her bees produced made her feel responsible, like she was doing her bit to reduce waste—plus she loved using the candles she made.

"Alyse, where the hell are you?" Mark's bellow sent a shiver down Alyse's spine and her muscles tensed.

Her gaze swept the small work room. Nowhere to hide. The shelves along the walls were filled with her latest products, and Mark would easily see her underneath the large table in the middle.

His footsteps pounded closer, and she jammed the headphones into her ears so she could pretend she hadn't heard his call. Her hands shook as she added the candle to the shelf, waiting for him to arrive. What had she done? These days he only sought her out while she was working if he needed something or was angry.

A hand on her shoulder yanked her back and she stumbled into Mark's hard chest. She grunted and removed the headphones, using the time to calm herself and make sure her tone wasn't accusatory. "Mark, you startled me."

"I've been calling you for the last ten minutes," he growled, towering over her like a behemoth. He filled the whole doorway. Broad chest, broad arms and legs, built to play rugby but Blackbridge was an Aussie Rules town. His dark eyes glared at her and she froze. Many years ago she'd thought his eyes warm and sweet like the chocolate he used to buy her regularly for no reason other than he loved her and had been thinking about her. Now all she saw were the eyes of her jailer. How had she ever found him attractive?

Alyse stepped back, giving herself space to move. "Sorry, I was listening to music." She pasted on a smile, trying for super helpful. "What do you need?"

"Don can't go out on the boat with me. You have to come."

Terror crashed through her and her skin turned to ice. She retreated until her back slammed against the shelves on the opposite side of the room, shaking her head. "You want me to go on a boat?"

His eyes were pits of derision. "That's what I said. Time to get over your stupid fear." He dragged her out of the work room and through her large metal shed towards the door.

She was halfway across before her brain pushed her fear aside and she dug her heels in to resist. Mark tugged harder and her arm nearly came out of its socket. She winced at the pain. "I can't go." She hated the tremor in her voice. "I have work to do."

"This is more important."

Alyse grabbed onto the edge of the doorway. "I won't."

Mark whirled around. "You'll do as I say." He paused, his jaw tightening, before it relaxed again and he caressed her cheek, sympathy on his face. "Princess,

I know you're scared, but I need you. I'm not as mobile with my broken leg. You don't want to disappoint me, do you?"

Her stomach clenched, and she fought not to show her revulsion. If only the compassion was real, but this side of Mark only came out when he wanted something these days. She shook her head as his fingers travelled down her arm to the hand still clinging to the doorway.

With a jerk, he pried her fingers off and growled, "Get in the car." He flung her towards the black ute parked outside the shed, the silver dinghy already hitched to it.

Alyse's throat closed over. The boat was tiny, maybe three metres long, with sides that didn't sit far out of the water. Wind buffeted her towards the car and she opened the door almost automatically, her obedience well beaten into her. She had to get out of this. There had to be someone else.

Impossible. Mark would have chosen anyone else before he put up with her hysterics.

Across the property the trees shook like a boogie-monster warning her to stay inside. The ocean would be far worse. "Mark, it's too rough. Please, can't this wait until a calmer day?"

"No. They won't wait."

No wonder he needed her. His options were limited to those people in town privy to the illegal things he did and there were fewer of them as the police found and arrested them. She'd kept her head down, not asking questions, not going near the shed he'd deemed his man cave. What she didn't know couldn't hurt her. What she didn't see, he couldn't beat her about.

She strapped herself in as Mark drove out of her property. Her hands clenched together and her chest tightened.

Nausea rose so fast she wrapped her arms around her stomach hoping to keep it at bay. The weather was far worse than it had been that day…

They arrived at the deserted boat ramp far too quickly. Waves pummelled the shore and the salty smell made her throat close over, cutting off her breath. Beyond the break, the ocean rose and fell in a swell far too big for the little dinghy. Mark backed expertly down the ramp and then climbed out, pulling a plastic bin bag over his moon boot and tying it off. When he'd fallen off the roof a couple of weeks ago, Alyse had hoped the broken leg would slow him down, but it hadn't.

He slammed the door and prepared the boat for launching. For a split second Alyse considered getting behind the wheel and taking off, driving anywhere else, somewhere far from here. The thought vanished almost as quickly as it arrived. She had nowhere to run, no money, no one she could call to help her. And no matter where she went, he'd find her. He always knew where she was and what she did.

She'd got herself into this no way out situation. The small voice with a little fight left declared she wasn't leaving her apiary, wasn't letting Mark have her family home.

"Alyse!"

Mark's bellow made her flinch again and she didn't dare ignore him this time. He'd be keeping count. She leapt out of the car and hurried down the damp ramp to where he held the rope of the dinghy. He thrust it at her and returned to the car.

Alyse shivered and hugged her arms around her, glad the shed had been cold enough to warrant wearing her thickest jacket. The dinghy bobbed up and down like a manic merry-go-round horse and the waves washed over Alyse's feet, soaking her work boots and the bottom of her jeans. Her breath caught. No sane person would go out on a day like today. Not in such a tiny boat, not without at least logging the trip with Marine Rescue.

If the boat capsized, no one would know. Where were the life jackets? Mark's father had bought them for Mark for Christmas, along with an EPIRB and flare gun. Without a jacket she'd be left struggling to stay above the waves, swallowing gallons of sea water, fighting to survive as she had that evening three years ago.

She couldn't do it.

Alyse dropped the rope, turned and ran smack into Mark's chest.

He grabbed her arm, bruising fingers digging into her skin. "Get in."

She shook her head. "I can't," she squeaked, hating the fear battering her. "Mark, please. Don't make me. I can't do it." She'd promised herself she would never beg him for anything again, but this was different. She physically couldn't move towards the rocking death trap.

He swore and lifted her as if she weighed nothing, pinning her arms against her sides, and carried her to the boat. She kicked and shrieked, "No, no, no."

Her vision blurred with tears, terror trapping the air in her lungs. He dumped her at the front, on the cold metal seat and shoved the bow around so she faced out to sea.

Alyse froze, eyes on the sandy brown swirling, rough water waiting to drag her under.

Behind her the engine roared to life and the boat made its way through the choppy seas, the salt water splashing over the bow and soaking her. The smell, the salt, the damp, took her straight back to that day.

Except the sun had been shining that morning.

Her parents had been eager to leave the apiary behind and go deep sea fishing. They all needed a break and it had been fun until Marine Rescue reported a change in conditions. A summer storm was coming in.

Even now Alyse couldn't believe how fast the weather had turned. The clouds appeared on the horizon and only minutes later they were right above them, turning the bright day dull and bringing a wind that morphed the gentle waves into giant towers.

Her father had handed out the life jackets and radioed Marine Rescue to let them know they were heading in but caught in the storm.

That one call had saved Alyse's life.

The next thing she knew, a wave had swamped the boat, turning it over and she'd been flung into the heaving ocean, fighting desperately to reach the surface, but not sure which way was up. Her life jacket had grown firm under her arms, buoying her in the right direction and when she finally breached the water, gasping for breath, she'd frantically searched the ocean for her parents.

Water slapped Alyse in the face and she blinked, coming back to the present and the sea swirling in front of her. She slid off the seat into the hull and huddled, shaking, tears streaming down her face. She couldn't do this. Fear vomited from her, running into the bottom of the boat. The smell turned her stomach further and she retched and retched until nothing else would come. Mark swore. Her brain screamed at her to go back, to run, to get off the waves, but she was frozen. She squeezed her eyes shut before the claws of hysteria ripped her skin.

She wasn't on a boat, she was on a bucking bull ride in the middle of a showground and if she fell, she'd land on soft pillows below.

Another spray of water coated her face, soaking her jacket, and she tasted the salt. No amount of pretending would alter the truth.

She would die out here. The ocean hadn't claimed her last time, but it was coming for her now.

Maybe it was for the best. Dying was the only way she would ever be free of Mark. Perhaps she should give in to the call and throw herself overboard. She opened her eyes a crack. The dark water mocked, called to her, threatened. She remembered the pull of the water, the way the weight of the boat dragged her under, and she retched again, her stomach and throat straining.

No. If she had to die, there were better ways to go. She wouldn't let the ocean take her as well.

Mark shouted something but she didn't turn. Couldn't move.

Seconds later he grabbed her, twisting her around, almost unbalancing the boat. Her heart leapt to her throat.

"Get a grip," Mark snarled. "When we reach the yacht, you help me lift the package on board, got it?"

She nodded though she didn't think she'd be able to stand, let alone have the strength in her arms to lift anything. He released her and sat by the engine.

Alyse huddled back into a ball. Mark's interruption had been enough to cut through some of her fear, to switch gears. What was Mark smuggling—drugs, guns, people? No, he'd said *package* so not people, and the boat wasn't big enough for more than a couple anyway. Her hand slid to the mobile phone in her jacket pocket. Now wasn't the time to be brave and film his activities. Plenty of better opportunities at home that wouldn't make her an accomplice. She was already far more involved than she wanted to be. If Mark went to jail, she'd be going as well. He'd made sure of it.

A huge wave crested in front of them and Alyse's heart stopped. The engine roared as Mark accelerated, but he was too slow. He cut through the middle of the wave and water flooded the boat.

No. Not again.

This couldn't be happening.

The boat was low, close to the surface, full of water, barely able to make it over the oncoming waves.

Mark shoved a plastic bucket at her. "Bail it out."

Her hands shook as she threw bucket after bucket of water out of the boat. Mark continued to steer at the helm, taking them further and further out to sea. He was insane.

The dinghy laboured in the waves and Alyse kept bailing, moving as fast as she could, her arms aching, her breath coming in pants from the effort and the fear. She didn't want to die like this. Why didn't Mark have life jackets? This time nothing would make her take it off.

Not like last time.

Last time she'd had to remove the jacket to dive under the overturned hull to find her parents. Her father was caught on something around the steering wheel and her mother was trying to free him. She'd looked for a knife, but all their gear was at the bottom of the ocean.

Then the boat shifted, tilted down and began to sink in earnest. Terror had gripped her and they'd all fought to free her father, but it wasn't possible. She'd taken a deep breath just before the last air pocket disappeared and struggled to get away from the hull. When she'd reached the surface, she was alone. She'd waited and waited for her mother to appear, but she never did.

And the life jacket Alyse had removed had long since vanished in the waves. She was alone in the middle of the ocean, uncertain which way was land.

Mark's yell made her blink. He pointed to a large yacht. Their destination. At least they could soon go home.

She stayed huddled on the seat until they were close enough for the person on board to throw them a rope. She wrapped it around the cleat at the front of the dinghy to help hold the boat in place, fighting with the waves that tossed them about.

Mark and the man spoke, but the wind whisked their words away and then two men brought a big black crate to the edge of the yacht. It looked heavy and too wide to fit on the dinghy.

"Alyse." Mark prodded her. He stood, ready to receive the cargo.

It meant she had to stand too. Stand in this little metal boat that was rocking like crazy. And somehow they had to lift the huge box on board without overbalancing and falling overboard.

"Get up," Mark growled.

She knew that tone. If she didn't move now, she would regret it when they got home. If she made it home.

Slowly she stood, her legs shaking. She wanted to vomit all over Mark. It would serve him right. Instead she reached for one side of the black plastic case and prepared herself. When the two men on the yacht let go, the true weight hit her and it was more a controlled fall to the bottom of the boat. Whatever was inside weighed a tonne.

The dinghy rocked and dipped lower in the water. Going back would be far more dangerous than coming out. She wanted to push the case overboard right now so they would get back to shore alive.

She sat as Mark concluded his business and then she unhitched the rope and they drew away from the yacht. The boat was more sluggish, but the waves pushed them now. Her hands stung in the cold and she tucked them under her arms as the wind blew through her wet jeans. She stamped her soaked feet to get some warmth into them.

The hills near the boat ramp appeared on the horizon, but still so far away.

Then the engine stuttered and stopped.

Alyse whirled around, eyes wide as Mark pulled the rip cord and nothing happened. He checked the petrol tank, tried again. Still nothing. They were adrift. It was getting darker and in only an hour it would be night. Fear bubbled inside her.

"Mark, why isn't it working?" Her voice was shrill.

"Give me a minute. I'll fix it."

No, he wouldn't. He liked to think he was good with anything mechanical, but he wasn't, and she'd long since stopped asking him for help. But it would take him a couple of hours before he'd admit defeat—if he admitted it at all. And she had no intention of still being in this boat after dark.

She slipped off her seat onto the hull and made herself as small as possible. Mark was busy looking at the engine so she retrieved her phone. She hesitated. He'd hear her if she dialled Marine Rescue. She flicked her phone to silent and texted them instead. *Our boat has broken down near the Southpoint boat ramp. About a kilometre from shore.*

The response was instant. *Alyse?*

Her heart beat faster. Only one guy at Marine Rescue knew her phone number. Kim On. *Yes.* He knew about her fear. *Please hurry.*

Mobilising now. How many on board?
Two. Don't tell Mark I contacted you.
Be there soon. Hold tight, Aly.

Her heart squeezed at the nickname she hadn't heard in three years. Kim had been the one person she could turn to before her life went to shit. Her one confidante before her parents died. But then they'd fought about Mark and she'd pushed him away.

So stupid.

She stuck her phone back in her pocket. Hope warmed her. Kim would come, he would save her.

Mark swore at the engine. He would be furious if he discovered she'd contacted Marine Rescue, especially with the cargo on board.

The boat rocked, dipping low in the water, and she clenched the sides, her heart in her throat. No life jackets and, although land was in sight, she wasn't certain she was fit enough to swim to shore. She slid back up to the seat. It was more exposed, but at least there was little chance of getting caught on something and drowning if they capsized.

A wave splashed over the boat and she shrieked, squeezing her eyes closed, praying they wouldn't sink.

"Shut up," Mark growled. "It's just a bit of water."

She gritted her teeth. He knew it wasn't the water. He'd met her at the hospital on the day her parents had drowned, when Marine Rescue had finally found her struggling to stay afloat, and she'd told him everything. Those days he'd still pretended to care and was attentive and lovely. He'd soothed her and let her cry.

She'd avoided even looking at the ocean for ages afterwards. But eventually he'd manipulated her into going fishing with him. She'd climbed into the boat and sat still while he'd cast off, and before they'd been more than ten metres from the boat ramp, she'd broken down in hysterics, begging to go back.

He'd hit her.

Slapped her right across the face, telling her to pull herself together. Not even the pain had been enough to cut through her fear and eventually he'd headed back to shore. She'd vowed never to go on a boat again.

Her hands shaking, she picked up the bucket and bailed out the water sloshing in the bottom of the dinghy. The movement helped distract her, made her feel she was preventing a catastrophe. When she was done, she scoured the shore. Where were Marine Rescue? Shouldn't she see their bright yellow boat by now? It was growing darker by the minute and they had no lights on board. None that Mark would light at least.

Her teeth chattered and she shook. "What's wrong with it?"

Mark had the engine casing off and had some engine part in his hand. "Filter's gummed up."

Probably because he hadn't done a second of maintenance on the boat since he'd bought it. Anger stirred in her, but it dissipated as a huge wave crested right behind them.

They were going to drown.

Chapter 2

Impatience swirled through Kim as he waited for his team to arrive. Beyond the inlet the waves were rough and Mark's dinghy wasn't all that big. Alyse had to be terrified.

Mark must have forced her into it. There was no way she'd be out there on a day like this, if she had a choice. His hands clenched around the canopy.

The sun glowed on the horizon underneath the grey clouds. They had maybe forty minutes before dark, and finding the boat would be much more difficult.

Where the hell was his team?

Footsteps thudded on the wooden planks of the jetty as two volunteers ran towards him. He fired up the engine, waiting only long enough for them to climb aboard and untie the ropes before he was off. As he accelerated, Tamara asked, "What have we got?"

"Boat breakdown. Alyse Wilson is on board."

Tamara's eyes widened. "But she doesn't go near boats."

The thing about a small town like Blackbridge was everyone knew everyone's business. He nodded. "I'm guessing it was Mark."

"Someone has to do something about that prick," Quentin said.

Kim said nothing, but he agreed. Alyse had shied away from the community and turned from her friends since her parents died. When Mark moved in, she'd become a recluse, not even playing basketball anymore. Kim had tried to tell her he was there for her, but she'd pushed him away, pushed everyone away.

It hurt more than he cared to admit.

The boat banged through the waves, and he concentrated on the ocean and his task. The radar glowed but no hits. Alyse hadn't given any GPS coordinates, so they would have to search their way in.

"Where were they?" Tamara came to stand by him.

"About a kilometre off the Southpoint boat ramp."

She scoured the waves. "Why on earth would they go out in this weather? It's been crappy all day."

He shook his head. No use questioning the dumb things Mark Patton did; they'd be there all day. Kim flicked on the floodlights. They might reflect off the boat or show Alyse they were on their way. After they left the inlet, he increased their speed, the bow cutting through the waves as it was designed to do.

Where were they?

A blip appeared on the radar. He steered towards it as Tamara and Quentin continued to scan the water. "See anything?"

"The waves are too big," Tamara complained.

It was in the right direction. He pushed the boat as fast as he dared, the dot on the radar coming closer and closer. Finally, the waves dipped and the little silver dinghy appeared. Kim swore. It was so low to the waterline it was almost submerged. What the hell did they have on board?

Alyse waved her arms. Mark covered the box in front

of him with a tarp and shoved Alyse so she stopped waving. Kim growled.

"Easy, Skipper." Tamara rested a hand on his arm. "Let's get her safe first."

He slowed the boat, coming up alongside them.

"Got trouble?" Quentin yelled.

"No, we're right. Just about fixed it," Mark yelled back. Was he serious?

Alyse shook her head frantically, eyes begging for help.

"Get Alyse on board," Kim murmured to Tamara.

"Alyse, you look about frozen," Tamara called. "Why don't you come over here? We have blankets."

"I said we're fine," Mark called.

Kim manoeuvred the boat next to the dinghy and Quentin held the two boats together while Tamara held out her hand. "Come on."

"Stay here, Alyse," Mark ordered.

Alyse ignored him. She shook as she stood and stretched out her hand. The boats rocked hard and she almost fell into the water, her squeal of terror cutting through Kim.

Hurry. He wanted her on his boat, safe.

"You can do it," Tamara called.

Alyse lunged for the Marine Rescue boat and Tamara and Quentin both pulled her on board. Alyse collapsed to the floor, sobbing and shaking, her face pale and her body so much thinner than it used to be. Even her once vibrant red hair seemed duller.

Kim ached to hold and comfort her. "Tamara, take the wheel."

Tamara took over and Kim hurried to Alyse's side. "Throw Mark a tow rope," he said to Quentin. He couldn't leave Mark there and hope his boat sank. Quentin nodded.

Kim turned to Alyse. "Hey, Aly. Let's get you down in the cabin where it's warmer." He slid his arm around her waist, shocked at how cold she was. He'd have to watch her for hypothermia. "Come on." He hauled her to her feet, keeping a firm arm around her as she leaned against him shaking. He shuffled them into the cabin. Behind him, his crew did what was necessary to rescue Mark.

Kim towel-dried Alyse's thick red hair and then took off her shoes and socks and warmed her feet. She sat there, hugging herself, sobbing. Kim really wanted to hit something, but he kept his voice gentle. "Aly, you need to get out of those wet clothes. Do you want me to get Tamara for you?"

She clutched his arm, shook her head. "Don't leave," she whispered.

"I won't," he promised. "Can you unbutton your jeans for me? I can help you out of them so we can warm you up."

She nodded, her hands shaking as she undid her pants and let him pull them down. He ignored her beautiful white skin and the black cotton knickers she wore and focused on warming and drying her. He wrapped a blanket around her legs. "How are you feeling now?"

She still trembled. "I want to get off the boat."

"I know." He stripped off his thick, waterproof jacket. "Put this on." She took off her wet top and he took her clothes out of the cabin to squeeze out the water. Discovering her phone, he dried it and when he returned, he gave it back before wrapping his arm around her shoulder. "How'd he get you on a boat in the first place?"

"Needed my help—" She cut herself off and shook her head.

It didn't matter. It was one more reason to dislike Mark and he had plenty already. He rubbed her arm, trying to soothe her and inhaled deeply. She smelled sweet like honey, the way she always had. This was the first time he'd had her alone in years, but memories of their teenaged years at the markets flooded him—Alyse laughing at one of his lame jokes or telling him stories about her bees.

"Aly, remember old Mrs Kendrick?" he asked.

She hiccoughed, or maybe it was a laugh. "That old witch."

He mimicked the old woman. "You two should be working, not gossiping like geese." He smiled. "Remember how we'd take turns saying ridiculous things she could overhear?" Alyse had always come up with the most outlandish.

She grimaced, brushed the tears away and exhaled. "I hated going to the markets until you started to go."

The confession warmed his heart. "We had fun." He'd only accompanied his father after he'd discovered she would be there with her parents, selling honey. She'd gone to the agricultural college in Year Ten so he rarely saw her except at the markets. "I miss hanging out with you."

She stiffened slightly. "I thought you hated me."

"Never." Guilt hit him. He'd been an idiot back when she'd first dated Mark. "I'm sorry for what I said."

She raised her eyebrows. "That there was only one thing Mark wanted from me?"

"I didn't mean it. It hurt that you stopped coming to the markets."

She placed a cold hand on his arm. "Mark overwhelmed me, taking all my time..."

Did she regret it? "Maybe we could catch up next week, go shoot some hoops."

Her smile was forced. "I'm pretty busy."

Frustration filled him. "That's bullshit. You always said the bees were quiet in winter. Aly, if he's abusing you, we can go to the police."

She shook her head violently. "No, you can't." She opened her mouth as if she wanted to say something else and then closed it.

"I hate seeing you like this." She'd once been so vibrant, so full of life. He barely recognised this shell of a person. "Please let me help."

"There's nothing you can do," she repeated, her voice firm. The boat jolted as it went over a wave and she gasped, the colour leaving her face. "How much further?"

He glanced out the window, estimated how far they'd come. They couldn't go as fast while towing Mark. They should have left him behind and returned for him after Alyse was on dry land. "We're about halfway," he said. "Not far now."

She shuddered, huddled in on herself.

Kim had to keep her distracted. "How are the bees?"

"Fine."

"I hear you do candles and lotions now."

She nodded. "The lotions are still being tested, but they're nice."

"That's great. Must keep you busy when the bees aren't as active."

"Keeps me out of the house."

His heart fell. Alyse loved her house, or at least she had when they'd been teenagers. It was one of those old brick farmhouses, built at the turn of the twentieth century with high ceilings and large rooms. "How's Flossie?"

Tears pricked her eyes. "My imaginary ghost? She doesn't come around anymore."

"Flossie wasn't imaginary. You said she used to live in your house."

"She did, but she was never a ghost." Alyse smiled. "I just loved thinking about those who lived in the house before me, imagining all the secrets the walls contained."

He'd bet they could tell some secrets about Alyse's life since her parents had died.

"How's the restaurant?" Alyse asked.

Good. She was trying. "Really great. The home delivery service has been popular." Especially during winter. People didn't want to leave their house to pick up their Vietnamese food.

"Whose idea was that?"

"I got it from Mai," he said. "After her bakery burned down, she needed to continue earning money, so she baked from my parents' house and delivered it around town. It was so popular, I hired Trent to do deliveries for us."

"Does your dad still make a mean pho?" she asked.

"Absolutely. Want me to send some out to you when you get home?"

She smiled. "Yeah. That would be great."

"Done." She'd always been partial to the chicken pho and he'd throw in some dumplings as well. Maybe he'd even deliver it himself, make sure Mark hadn't hurt her.

She leaned into him, resting her head against his shoulder. That was where she belonged. His heart squeezed. He'd hoped one day she'd see him as more than the Asian kid who hung out at the Sunday markets with his father.

He'd longed for Sundays.

And while he had still been building the nerve to ask her to the Year Twelve ball, someone else had asked her. And then high school ended and Mark came along. He'd disliked Mark from the start. He'd been all Alyse could talk about on their Sundays together and then she'd stopped coming, her parents telling him she was with Mark.

The boat engine slowed, the noise diminishing, and

Kim peered through the window. They were almost at the boat ramp.

Alyse looked up, hope in her eyes.

He nodded. "Almost there."

She leapt to her feet and he stopped her. "Wait until we stop. I don't want you to fall."

She squeezed his hand, hers freezing cold, and sat.

"Are you sure we can't take you into town? You should go to the hospital, make sure you don't have hypothermia."

She shook her head before he'd even finished his first sentence. "I have to get off."

He understood her fear. "I can pick you up after we get back. Take you to the emergency department to be checked over."

"I'm fine." She reached for her wet jeans and pulled them on. "I'll have a hot shower."

There was a gentle bump as the boat pulled onto the sand next to the boat ramp. Quentin called instructions to Mark and Tamara lifted the engine so it didn't hit the ground. Kim took Alyse's hand. "Let's get you on dry land."

She nodded.

She followed him out and before he could offer her a hand, she'd vaulted over the side into the shallow water. She turned back, smiled at him and he saw a glimpse of the Aly he remembered. "Thank you."

Mark bellowed at her to grab the line and she scurried to obey him. He got out, waving away Quentin's help and strode up the boat ramp to fetch his car. Quentin said something to Alyse and she shook her head. He sighed and returned to the Marine Rescue boat. "We're good to go. They don't need our help anymore." He pushed the boat off the sand and climbed aboard.

Tamara glanced at Kim for instructions. Alyse refused to look at him as she held the dinghy, fighting with the push of the waves, her shoulders hunched as if wanting to disappear. He gritted his teeth, then nodded. "Let's go."

He had no reason to stay. Not if Alyse didn't want him there, not with the rest of his crew wanting to get out of the cold.

But as soon as they had packed up, he would personally deliver the soup to Alyse.

Now they'd reconnected, he wasn't letting Mark push him away again.

Chapter 3

Mark said nothing to Alyse as they loaded the boat onto the trailer and drove home. She'd been expecting an explosion, abuse and recriminations, but his silence was unexpected. And it chilled her more than the ocean.

She hugged Kim's jacket around her, inhaling the comfort of his scent, and then froze. If Mark realised she was still wearing Kim's jacket, he'd be furious. She'd been in too much of a hurry to get off the boat to think about giving it back. She turned the heating to full so it blasted her feet and face, warming some of the chill from her bare toes. Her jeans were damp, wetting the car seat.

The headlights illuminated her farmhouse up ahead, but the view no longer brought the sense of safety it once had when her parents had been alive. Instead it felt more like a prison. She longed to lock herself inside and keep Mark out, but it wouldn't work. The one time she'd tried, he'd threatened to burn the whole building down. She had little left of her parents as it was. She wasn't losing this as well.

Mark pulled up outside his large man cave.

"Get out," Mark ordered.

Alyse lunged for the handle and her hands shook in her

urgency. She slammed the door behind her and Mark drove into the shed. No point waiting here. He might be five minutes or five hours. Instead she jogged back to the farmhouse, the dirt hard against her bare feet. She'd have to fetch her boots from Marine Rescue in the morning. Now though, if she was quick, she could shower before Mark returned. The lock on the bathroom door did little to keep him out and she daren't put anything stronger on it. It would only infuriate him.

She hurried inside, dumping Kim's jacket on her bed.

In the distance, the ute roared to life. She grabbed her warmest jumper, some tracksuit pants and thick socks, and locked herself into the bathroom. Mark slammed through the back door of the house, calling her name, as she turned the shower on. She froze, staring at the door, expecting him to pound on it or force himself in. Steam wafted around the room and Mark's footsteps stopped outside the bathroom. The door handle jiggled. Alyse held her breath.

A lengthy, raw curse and then the footsteps faded away. Mark would have time to stew. That wasn't good.

Quickly she stripped off her clothes and stepped under the hot spray. She didn't have long. Mark might come back. The heat stung her extremities, pain tingling her feet and hands. She soaped her body, cleaning and warming her skin. Ducking her head under the spray, she heated her cold, wet hair and then squeezed out the excess. Every part of her wanted to stay under the water, soak it in, let it warm her from the outside in, but she'd be so much more vulnerable naked and wet if Mark forced his way in.

He was already mad as hell.

With shaking hands, she shut off the taps and dried herself fast, the rough fabric reminding her she would have to ask Mark for money to buy new towels soon. Skin still damp, she struggled to dress, her clothes sticking where she hadn't dried herself properly. With her jumper and pants on, she let out a breath and allowed herself a second to dry her feet and tie her hair in a towel turban. Then she slid on her warm socks and cautiously opened the door.

Wind whipped around the outside of the house, making whistling noises through decade-old gaps, but no sound came from the television, or from the kitchen or from anywhere.

Where was he?

Should she act normally, pretend she had nothing to fear, that she'd done nothing wrong? Damn it, she *had* done nothing wrong! Mark knew she was terrified of boats. She crept down the hallway towards the kitchen, making as little noise as possible. The shower had warmed her a bit, but her insides were cold. A hot drink would help. Kim had been concerned about hypothermia.

She sighed and closed her eyes. Kim.

She'd forgotten how easy it was to talk to him. She'd instantly felt safe next to him, had hoped things would be all right. Of all the people she'd pushed away when she'd first met Mark, Kim was the one she'd missed the most. Her other childhood friends had expected her to be more girly, had liked to play with makeup and hair and talk about boys. From the age of fifteen, she'd known she wanted to work on her parents' apiary. She loved working with the bees and the ag college had allowed her to specialise in beekeeping. Her friends hadn't understood why she didn't want to leave Blackbridge as soon as she was old enough.

Maybe that was why Mark had been able to separate her from them so easily. They'd been going in different directions anyway. And Mark had encouraged her passion for bees, had wanted her to stay in Blackbridge with him. He'd been the attractive, successful older man. People had talked about him playing professional football, there'd been scouts from the state league watching his games.

She walked into the empty kitchen. Moving fast, she filled the kettle and switched it on. As she retrieved a mug from the cupboard, movement in her peripheral vision made her spin around. Mark blocked the doorway, his face a thundercloud.

Her hand tightened around the mug. It was a crappy weapon, but the solid feel of it gave her some measure of comfort. She didn't speak. This quiet, cold Mark was terrifying. Mark's temper was usually quick to flare and when it did, she'd get new bruises for whatever she'd done wrong. But sometimes, when she hadn't been within easy reach, he would stew over it, let it fester and boil until she was there, and then there was no telling what he would do.

Nausea welled in her stomach and she shifted back to the kettle, flicked the button off so it stopped boiling.

She bit her bottom lip, waiting for him to speak. He didn't move from the doorway, the only exit from the room.

Her heart thumped in her chest, hard and fast, and her skin prickled. Her body flushed with fear.

She flinched as he spoke. "Make me a coffee."

She hesitated, remembering the sharp sting and the blisters when he'd flung boiling water at her before. She had little choice, so flicked on the kettle, then turned to retrieve another mug from the cupboard.

In an instant he was across the room, twisting her around, pressing himself into her, pushing her back against the kitchen bench so hard she winced. "What the fuck were you doing?" His voice was a low growl.

"Wh…what?" She kept her eyes down, watching him in her peripheral vision, preparing for the first strike.

"You contacted Marine Rescue. They don't just go out

waiting to rescue someone."

"Mark, I don't know what you're talking about."

He held up her phone. "Shall I show you the last text you sent?"

Sweat trickled down her back. Confession was her only option and hope he'd forgive her. "I'm sorry! I was so scared. The boat wouldn't start and we were stuck out there—"

His backhand snapped her head back and stole her words. Pain stung her cheek and she clenched her teeth to stop from crying out.

"We had cargo on board," he snarled. "If they'd seen it, recognised what it was…"

Tears blurred her vision. "I don't even know what it was," she said. "Just a heavy black box. You covered it with a tarp. It could have fish inside for all they knew." Her words came in a rush.

"I told you I'd fix the engine."

"Mark, I'm sorry. Please forgive me," she begged, hating herself for it. "My fear stopped me from thinking. You know I hate boats."

"So this is my fault?"

Yes. "No! Of course not. I'm weak, I'm soft. I was just so scared…"

He leaned closer, rubbed himself against her.

Bile rose in her throat.

"Are you fucking him?"

Alyse blinked, confusion filling her. "Who?"

"That guy you were all over in the Marine Rescue boat. He used to sniff around you all the time."

Kim. "No. That's the first time I've spoken to him in years."

"You don't need words to fuck."

She shook her head. "Mark, I only see Kim when I

watch you play football and you're playing his team. There's nothing between us."

"I saw him squeezing out your clothes. Did you strip for him?" He slid his hand down the side of her leg, his fingers rough.

She tried not to show her revulsion. "No. I was freezing. He wrapped me in blankets and treated me like a patient."

"I wanted to rip his hands off. No one gets to touch you but me."

And thankfully he hadn't touched her since she'd caught him having an affair. "Of course." She kept hoping Mark would leave her for Yvette—not that she would wish Mark on another woman—but the apiary was too valuable to him.

"I don't want you seeing him again. I'd hate for his family restaurant to run into trouble."

Fear for Kim and his family ran through her veins. "I won't. I don't even like him," she lied.

"You're mine." He pressed his lips against hers, thrusting his tongue into her mouth and she fought the urge to gag. His breath was stale, like he hadn't cleaned his teeth in days. She kissed him back, knowing if she didn't respond it would incense him further.

What would he do to the On family? Kim's father owned the local Vietnamese restaurant and his mother was a lawyer. He could burn their premises like Mai's bakery had been torched at the beginning of the year. Alyse couldn't let that happen. The one flicker of hope of rekindling her friendship with Kim died.

Someone pounded on the front door and Mark stepped back, breaking the kiss. He swore. "Get that. It's probably Craig."

She hurried away, waiting until she left the kitchen

before she wiped her mouth, trying to erase the taste of Mark from her lips. Was the kiss a show of dominance, or would he force her back into his bed? The last couple of months while he'd been having an affair had been bliss, even if she'd had to listen to them in the next room. Mark thought it a way of punishing her and Yvette hadn't known she was there, but Alyse was grateful it wasn't her in the master bedroom. Even during the first three years with Mark, before her parents had died, when Mark had wooed her, he had been a selfish lover.

She removed the towel from her head and ran a hand through her still damp hair, pushing it off her face, and opened the door. She gasped. Kim.

He handed her a paper bag. "Chicken pho as ordered." His smile faded as he studied her face. "How are you?"

She clutched the bag. She'd forgotten his promise to send food. It smelled incredible, the scent of herbs tickling her nose. She glanced over her shoulder. "Fine. Thank you."

"That's a new bruise."

Kim reached out to brush her cheek, and she stepped out of reach. If Mark saw, he'd be furious. "I must have bumped something on the boat."

He stared at her. "Bullshit." He searched for Mark behind her. "Come with me now," he whispered.

Her heart clenched. If only it was that simple.

"I'll keep you safe." He reached for her hand. "I'll take care of you."

She stepped back, fear striking her. Mark used to say that, used to murmur it to her while she cried over her parents. She reached for the door. "Thank you for the soup." Behind her, Mark's footsteps clomped down the hallway. Shit.

"What the fuck is he doing here?"

Alyse winced. "He brought me soup."

"Why?" Mark pushed in front of her so he was blocking the door. He was taller and broader than Kim's athletic leanness. She shifted to the side so she could see past Mark.

"Chicken soup is my father's remedy for everything." Kim smiled. "I figured after Alyse's ordeal, she could do with some." Though his tone was light, friendly even, his steely gaze didn't waver from Mark.

"What ordeal? We broke down is all."

"If that's all you think it was, you're more stupid than I thought."

Alyse held her breath. Kim was the stupid one to antagonise Mark. She brushed a hand along Mark's arm, to distract him. "Why don't we eat this before it gets cold?" She forced a smile and didn't look at Kim. "I don't want it to go to waste."

"You go. I have words to say to him."

Alyse's eyes widened and she mentally told Kim to leave, but his hands were in his pockets, feet apart, defiance in every pore. How fast could an ambulance get here? Maybe she should call it now.

"Go!" Mark shouted.

Alyse flinched. She didn't dare say anything to Kim as she returned to the kitchen. She placed the soup on the table then picked up her phone which Mark had left on the bench. She couldn't hear what Mark said, but his tone was pure threat. Her fingers squeezed around the phone as she got bowls out and strained to hear the sounds of a fight.

The door slammed and she jumped, her hands shaking as she poured the pho into two bowls.

"He shouldn't bother you again." Mark grabbed both bowls of soup and tipped their contents down the sink. He glanced at her and raised his eyebrows.

"Thank you."

He grunted. "Make me some dinner."

"Of course." Alyse opened the fridge and then she heard the sound she'd been listening for. A car engine. It meant Kim wasn't lying unconscious on the front step.

She sighed.

He was safe for the moment.

***

Kim breathed slowly as he sat in his car, trying to rein in his temper. His skin was so tight it felt like it would split and his heart pounded. He'd never wanted to hit a man until today, but violence would only make Alyse fear him. Perhaps he was foolish to antagonise Mark, but the words had come out before he could think. Would Mark take his anger out on Alyse?

He wanted to be sick.

He wanted to storm in there and drag Alyse away with him.

Mark had told him to stay away, said Alyse was mentally unstable and seeing him brought up horrific memories of her parents' death. He'd said if Kim cared for Alyse, he'd stay away, give her time to recover. Mark had said something similar three years ago after Alyse's parents had died. Kim had believed him then.

No longer. Mark wasn't chasing him away this time.

His hand still trembled with rage as he flicked on the headlights and drove out of the property. His friend Jeremy lived only two houses down. He'd be good for a vent.

After pulling up in front of the wooden, custom-designed cottage Jeremy had built, Kim sat for a moment to control his anger. Alyse was scared. Somehow Mark had her trapped. The Alyse he'd known as a teenager wouldn't have put up with the way Mark treated her. She would have kicked him out a long time ago. So why was he still there?

Jeremy appeared at the entrance to the shed he was rebuilding and lifted a hand in a wave. Kim wandered over to him. "Sorry for just dropping in."

"No problem." Jeremy moved towards the house. "What's up? I can practically see smoke coming out of your ears."

"Alyse."

"Wilson?" Jeremy glanced at him. "Has Mark hit her again?"

Kim nodded. The whole town knew about the abuse. Surely Alyse realised she'd have support if she wanted to leave Mark. "Mark took her out in his dinghy this afternoon."

Jeremy's eyes widened. "In this weather?"

"Yeah. And she's petrified of boats." He followed Jeremy into the open-plan living area and slumped onto one of the stools next to the kitchen bench. "The dinghy broke down and she contacted Marine Rescue. She was absolutely terrified when we picked her up."

Jeremy fetched two beers from the fridge. In case he didn't know the story, Kim said, "She was in a boating incident with her parents when she was twenty-one. Her parents drowned. As far as I know, this is the first time she's been out on a boat since then."

Jeremy swore. "Mark's such a prick. I hope the police can pin something on him."

Kim frowned. "What do you mean?"

"Didn't you hear? Mark was messed up in the stuff involving Morgan and the stolen cars last week. He followed Elijah a couple of times to scare him."

Hope made Kim perk up. "Can they arrest him?"

"Not until they get some kind of firm evidence."

"What do they need?" Maybe he could convince Alyse to turn Mark in. She had to know something. She'd been living with him for almost three years.

Jeremy shrugged. "We should ask Adam." He handed Kim a beer. "Is Alyse a friend of yours?"

He snorted. "She was. Kind of. In high school. Before Mark."

"And you still like her."

"She should be with someone who treats her better."

"Someone like you?" Jeremy smiled. "I'm all for it," he said. "Zamira met her and was worried. When she moves in, she's making it her mission to help Alyse, and I don't want her to get hurt. If I can help you get rid of Mark, I will."

Kim smiled for the first time since seeing Alyse. "Thanks, mate."

"We might need backup." Jeremy grabbed his phone and called someone. "Hey. Kim's here. Want to bring out some pizza and tell us what you know about Mark Patton?" A pause. "Bring Elijah and Adam." Another pause. "Great. See you when you get here." He hung up. "Jamie's on his way."

Kim sipped his beer, the tension seeping out of his muscles. One way or another, he would help Alyse.

Half an hour later Kim's other friends arrived. Adam was a police constable and Jamie and Elijah both volunteered for the State Emergency Services. They'd removed a tree branch from Alyse's roof during a storm recently and had seen Mark hit her.

Jamie carried in four pizza boxes and plonked them on the kitchen table. "Dinner is served."

Kim greeted them and moved over to the table while

Jeremy handed them each a beer.

"So what gives?" Elijah asked, hugging Kim.

"I just rescued Alyse Wilson out on the ocean," Kim said.

"In this weather?" Adam asked.

Jamie frowned. "I heard she's frightened of boats after what happened to her parents."

"She is. Mark forced her to go."

Adam sat next to him. "What were they doing out there?"

Kim shook his head. "No idea." Though there had to be a reason. He hadn't thought about it, too concerned about Alyse, but now he did… "They didn't have any fishing gear."

"They'd be stupid to fish in this weather." Jeremy handed out plates and opened the pizza boxes.

"What did they have?" Adam's tone was casual, but his body tensed. This was police-mode Adam.

Kim visualised the boat. "They had a black crate on board," he said. "Mark tossed a tarp over it as we approached. Whatever was in it was heavy because the boat sat low in the water."

"What time did Alyse call?" Adam asked.

"About four."

"Where were they?"

"Off Southpoint boat ramp."

Adam pushed back his seat. "I'll be back in a second."

Kim exchanged a glance with the others as Adam walked outside. Adam walked past the window with his phone to his ear.

"Mark has to be smuggling something," Jeremy declared. "Going out on a day like today, forcing Alyse to go with him…"

"Can the police trace the boat it came from?" Jamie

asked.

Jeremy shrugged. "My bet is Adam's calling it in in case they can."

"I hope so," Kim said. Mark behind bars was about the prettiest picture he could imagine. He grabbed two slices of pizza as Adam returned.

"Any luck?" Elijah asked.

Adam frowned. "Huh?"

"Can you figure out which boat Mark got the stuff from?" Elijah clarified.

Adam shook his head, colour tinging his cheeks. "Don't know what you're talking about."

He always refused to talk about cases. Instead Kim asked, "What can Mark be charged with? Assault?"

"Yeah, if she charges him. We've only had one call out to her place since I've been in Blackbridge and Alyse wouldn't press charges. So unless there's evidence of escalation, or she asks for help, there's not a lot we can do."

"I don't get why she stays with him."

"Fear, love, nowhere else to go to," Adam said. "There're all sorts of reasons."

"I told her I'd help her," Kim said.

"So did I," Elijah added. "If enough of us tell her, she may believe it."

"It's hard to tell her when she never goes anywhere," Jeremy said.

Kim considered the options. "We all think Mark is involved in something illegal, right?"

Everyone except for Adam nodded.

"So what if Alyse could get the police the evidence needed to arrest him? Could the police offer her protection?"

Everyone looked at Adam.

He sighed. "Maybe. I'd have to ask Lincoln."

"Do you think she'd go for it?" Jamie asked. "She's made no attempt to leave him before."

"I'll convince her," Kim said.

Chapter 4

Alyse hesitated outside the kitchen door of the football clubrooms. Inside, people chattered and pans rattled as they prepared for the annual Christmas in July fundraiser. Mark had volunteered her help after his mother had pulled out. She was grieving over her husband's death less than a fortnight ago, and Alyse was happy to take her place. It was a rare opportunity to socialise. How many people inside would she know?

Would they look at her in pity, or remind her how good life had been before her parents died?

Anxiety gripped her, but she couldn't walk away, no matter how much she wanted to. Mark would be furious.

Taking a deep breath, she pushed into the kitchen, the wave of heat from the ovens rolling over her. Her heart squeezed. Barbara stuck cloves in the ham, telling the other three women about the granny flat Jeremy was building for her mother. Alyse had barely seen Barbara since her parents died, but she'd been a constant presence in her life until then— Brown Owl leader at her Brownies group, and then coach of her basketball team. Alyse swallowed the lump in her throat. The other women, all at least ten years older than her, were strangers.

Barbara noticed her and her eyes lit up. "Alyse! I was so thrilled when Mark said you'd volunteered to help." She strode over and then realised her hands weren't clean so she held them up. "Give me a hug."

Tears welled in Alyse's eyes as she hugged the woman, pressed up against Barbara's ample but soft bosom. A hint of rose scent reminded Alyse of her mother, of all the hugs she'd had and would never have again. Barbara wrapped her forearms around Alyse, as Alyse struggled to keep back the tears.

"You're nothing but skin and bones. I'll make sure you eat plenty tonight." Barbara stepped back and studied Alyse. She frowned. "That's a nasty bruise on your cheek."

Alyse blushed and covered it with her hand. "I fell the other day."

Barbara narrowed her eyes but didn't call her out. Instead she said, "Do you know the others?" When Alyse shook her head, Barbara said, "That's Bec, stuffing the turkey. She's the college coordinator at the ag college. Chopping carrots is Dee who works at the pub, and Juanita by the drinks fridge has a gorgeous new shop in town next to the bakery. Everyone, this is Alyse. She owns the apiary just out of town."

Alyse smiled. "Hey."

The women smiled back but Dee's expression contained pity. She probably knew all about Mark and what he did.

It was easy to judge, easy to say she could just leave, but no one knew the leverage Mark held over her. Alyse straightened her spine. "What can I do to help?"

"We have a bucket-load of potatoes that need peeling." Barbara showed her to the table and handed her a vegetable peeler. "Have at it."

Pleased to have something to do, she began her task as Barbara continued her story about the granny flat as if she hadn't been interrupted. "Jeremy is a wiz," she said. "Mum's enamoured with him. If she was fifty years younger, she'd be after him, I'm sure."

Alyse smiled. Jeremy had regularly dropped around for honey when she'd sold from her shed. He'd been pleasant and told her about the house he was building, even took her on a tour of it before her parents had died.

The conversation switched to children. "Do you have any kids, Alyse?" Juanita asked.

Alyse shook her head, her gut clenching. "No." She wasn't bringing any child into a house where Mark lived.

"Don't do it," Bec said. "They might seem sweet at first, but they turn into monsters." The other women laughed.

Alyse already lived with a monster.

The kitchen door swung open and she was relieved by the distraction until Kim strolled in. Her heart lurched. He must have come straight from a shower because his short black hair was slightly damp, but the red hoodie he wore had no raindrops on it. The blue jeans and sneakers added to his casual look. He grinned at Alyse but directed his comments at Barbara. "What needs to be done?"

"Shouldn't you be playing?" she asked.

"Just finished our game. Figured you'd need some help in here."

"Then you can start on the pumpkin," Barbara said.

Kim picked up the box of pumpkins as if they weighed nothing and brought them over to the table where Alyse worked. "Hey. Fancy seeing you here."

Had he known she'd be here? No, that was wishful thinking. Mark had told Kim to stay away and Kim wouldn't cross him—not if he was sensible. Kim simply understood the work required to prepare a feast for over a hundred people. She stamped down her pleasure at seeing him. "I didn't expect to see you." At least she didn't need to worry about Mark catching them together. He was playing football and he'd never venture into the kitchen. When his game was over, he'd shower and then get himself a beer until it was time to eat.

"I like to help out. Seeing you is just a bonus." He chopped the pumpkin.

Her heart stuttered. That wasn't good. She couldn't let her heart get involved, couldn't hope. There was no escape from Mark. It would only cause Kim and his family heartache. She should move to another table, but her body refused to cooperate, and plus it would be rude. Surely an hour catching up with an old friend was allowed if Mark never found out.

"Did you enjoy the soup?" Kim asked.

"Yes. It was perfect." The lie was easy.

He grinned. "Dad made it especially for you. He remembered you like it spicy."

She ached inside. Mr On had always been so nice to her at the markets. He'd slip her free dumplings and make the pho exactly how she liked it. Her parents hadn't been as keen on spicy food as she was. "Please thank him for me."

"You can thank him yourself. He's coming tonight." Kim paused. "You're staying for the dinner, aren't you?"

She nodded. Mark expected it.

"That's great. Maybe we can get a table together."

Was he crazy? Mark would never allow it. "Maybe." She focused on the potato in front of her.

"How are you after yesterday?" Kim chopped through the pumpkin as if it was butter.

Alyse shrugged. "Fine."

"Did Mark hit you for calling us?"

Her hand halted as she reached for another potato. People didn't normally ask her outright. But she was so sick of lying, of pretending everything was OK, as if her life was perfect. This was Kim and she'd always told him the truth. She checked to make sure no one was watching and nodded.

"He shouldn't have forced you on the boat in the first place." Though he kept his tone mild, Alyse heard the undertones of anger.

She shivered. "I left my boots on the boat. Do you have them?"

Kim swore. "Yeah. Sorry, I meant to bring them when I brought the pho. I can drop them off tomorrow if you'd like."

Mark wouldn't like that at all. "It's Richard's funeral, so I won't be home. If you leave them at the restaurant, I'll pick them up."

Kim changed the subject. "How are Bessie, Beatrice and Beyoncé?"

She frowned. "Who?"

His smile shone in his eyes. "Your queen bees. Weren't they your favourites?"

Shock speared her. "You remember that?" She'd forgotten. Once upon a time, before Mark, she'd given all her queen bees names, she'd indulged in silly stories about some of her colonies and had shared them with Kim during those long mornings at the markets.

"Of course. The last I heard Bessie was planning to overthrow Beatrice. I've always wondered what happened."

Tears pricked her eyes and a lump formed in her throat. When had she last been so carefree? Her bees gave her solace and distance from Mark but she'd lost the childlike joy a long time ago. She swallowed hard. "They're all dead now."

"Oh."

She dragged the peeler over the skin of the potato, revealing its white flesh. Just like how Kim made her feel—raw—exposing parts she'd long since hidden. If only she could go back to the days before her parents died, before she met Mark, and do it all over again. She wouldn't make the same mistakes, including losing Kim as a friend. "What about you? I thought you were getting into graphic design."

Kim shrugged. "I dabble on the side. The restaurant keeps me busy."

She frowned. He used to love drawing and design, had talked about starting his own business. She'd assumed he had. "Do you work in the kitchen?"

"I help with the prep." He gestured to the pumpkins he'd finished chopping and stood. "Barbara, can I have a pan for the pumpkin?"

"Of course." She hurried over with one. "You're so fast!"

After he'd transferred the pumpkin, he picked up another vegetable peeler and took a potato from Alyse's pile. His movements were confident and fast, his fingers wrapped around the peeler with firm gentleness.

Alyse flushed. She shouldn't be admiring his fingers, even if they were long and competent. When she'd leaned into him on the boat the day before, she'd felt safe and warm. But the teenager who had been her friend was now a man. And even further from her than before. Kim had filled out with lean muscles that made her think of fitness, not danger. His black hair was no longer the shaggy mess it used to be and he'd replaced the baggy T-shirts with fitted clothes that clung to his chest. No good would come from wondering how his fingers would feel on other parts of her body.

She shifted, the tingling between her legs a sensation she hadn't felt in years. She forced her attention back to the potatoes. Mark was jealous already. If he realised she felt anything for Kim, he'd do what he could to destroy it.

"I haven't seen you at the basketball courts in a while,"

Kim said.

Why did he insist on raising all these old memories? There was no going back to those days. She'd lost them by being weak, by trusting the wrong person. Kim waited for an answer. "I don't play anymore." But she'd loved it. The fast pace, the exhilaration of getting past someone and driving to the hoop, the elation of seeing the ball drop through the net. She clenched her teeth and forced the memory away. Peel these damn potatoes so she could get out of here, away from Kim and memories best left forgotten. "You're captain of your football team?"

He nodded. "And the cricket team. I can't say no." He grabbed another potato. "Jeremy tells me you met Zamira a couple of weeks ago. She arrived back today. She's moving in with Jeremy."

Alyse's movements slowed. Zamira had come onto her property chasing Jeremy's dog. They'd only spoken briefly and Alyse had given her some honey, but it was the first time in a long time that she'd spoken to someone without Mark around. Someone her own age who didn't know Mark and was unaware of the situation. It had been nice. She'd wanted to accept Zamira's offer to go for coffee, but Mark had forbidden it. Didn't want her to make friends of her own. Easier to control her if she was isolated. But maybe with Zamira living only a couple of properties away, Alyse could walk over. Mark would never know. She could say she was checking her hives, or simply out for a walk, getting some exercise.

No. It was too dangerous. Why was she even considering it? It was Kim's fault. He gave her hope when there was none. She forced a smile. "Is she coming tonight?"

"Yeah."

She pressed her lips together. That wasn't good. If Mark saw her with Zamira, he'd forbid her from seeing her again. She'd have to be careful.

She picked up the last potato. "We've finished."

Kim nodded and called to Barbara. "What else do you need?"

"We're about done," she called back. "The food needs to cook. Thanks for your help."

Disappointment washed over Alyse as she placed the potato on the pile and stood. It was for the best. Mark's game was almost over. He'd brought clothes to change into, but she had to go home and make herself presentable for him.

Kim touched her arm and a zing went through her. "I'll see you tonight?"

She nodded, not trusting herself to speak and then strode out of the kitchen before hope overwhelmed her.

It was pointless. Mark controlled every part of her life and if he saw her in the same room as Kim he'd be mad.

Maybe she could fake being ill.

Despair washed through her. She wanted this, one evening to pretend her life was normal. This afternoon had reminded her what it was like.

Mark wasn't taking that away from her.

It was only one night.

∗∗∗

Alyse clenched the steering wheel as she drove straight home, her mind whirling. What was wrong with her? Mark had told her to stay away from Kim and now he was everywhere, saving her, smiling at her, making her feel things she didn't want to feel.

And what was wrong with Kim? She'd barely spoken to him in the past three years and he chatted to her like they'd seen each other yesterday. What did he want from her? Why was he taking an interest now?

Too many questions and no answers.

She parked in front of her farmhouse and let out a deep breath. Mark's big ugly shed loomed behind it, reminding her she had no control. Her gaze drifted to the brown tiled roof of her house. The tarp no longer covered the cracked tiles where a branch had fallen onto the roof. She'd climbed up herself to replace them because Mark had broken his leg.

She'd wished he'd broken more.

Her parents had never approved of the relationship. What was a twenty-nine-year-old man doing looking at an eighteen-year-old? He could only want one thing and Alyse's mother had given her the talk, handed her a box of condoms and told her to be careful. It had been mortifying, but she'd taken the condoms and tucked one into her purse just in case. She still had the box in her bedside drawer.

She should have listened to their warnings.

Her mother's garden was full of weeds, and dead and dying plants, the upkeep too much for Alyse. She had the apiary to run, a house to maintain, a man to obey whose whims changed with his mood. She squeezed her eyes shut, her throat closing over. Why hadn't her mother swum free of the boat? Had she been trapped as the boat went down?

Questions that would never be answered.

But a reason she'd clung onto Mark, not wanting to be completely alone. He loved her, the redheaded farm girl who liked bees.

She sighed and climbed out of the car, her attention drawn to the basketball ring mounted on the side of the shed, a deflated basketball next to it. Pathetic, like her. Her movements were slow as she pushed open the front door. Inside was no longer recognisable as the home she'd once known. Mark had moved in after her parents died and way before she was ready he'd started making changes. First the television, because how could anyone watch sport on a forty-inch screen? Then her mother's round, comfortable couches. She'd come home from a conference to find a whole new lounge suite in its place. He swore he'd spilt coffee on the old couches and had to replace them, hadn't wanted to upset her. She'd wept in his arms and he'd soothed her, but later she'd remembered him joking about how all the flowers and colour in the house sapped his masculinity.

Alyse wandered down the hallway to the master bedroom. That had been their first big argument. She'd only had a single bed in her room and Mark wanted to move into her parents' room, but the pain of losing them was still too raw, she hadn't even cleared out their drawers yet. She'd put her foot down and said no, screamed at him she wasn't ready. He'd cried, said she didn't love him, asked her if she wanted to break up with him.

How she wished she'd told him to go right then, the manipulative bastard.

But she'd been so desperate not to lose anyone else. He was all she had. Her friends had stopped coming around, unable to cope with her grief. At least that's what Mark had said. And fool that she was, she'd believed him.

So, she'd begged him to stay, agreed they could move into her parents' room.

Her phone rang. Mark. Not answering would only make him angry. "Hello?"

"Where are you? You're supposed to be at the clubrooms."

She closed her eyes and forced a smile so he wouldn't hear her annoyance. "I'm at home, getting changed."

"You should be in the kitchen."

"I was, but they didn't need me for anything else. I'll be back in half an hour."

"Make sure you are." He hung up.

Why did he even care? He had Yvette now, was even seen in town with her, though he was always careful to say she was a colleague. His father would never let scandal touch the family and had been the only person who could get Mark to do anything. Mark had always been desperate for his father's approval.

Exhaustion swamped her. She was so tired of all this. Maybe it would have been better if she'd fallen overboard yesterday and drowned. It would have ended this half-life.

She dragged herself to the shower, locking the bathroom door automatically, and washed her hair, letting the warm water run over her.

What would her life be like if her parents had survived, or if she'd kicked Mark out when he'd wanted to move into her parents' room? Who would she be? Certainly not this husk of a person, going through the motions, trying to keep her parents' business afloat. She scrubbed at her body as if she could wash the shame away. She'd lost control of her parents' house, their land, their business. Trapped with no way out.

Not one where she didn't end up dead or in jail.

It was so easy to blame Mark, but it wasn't just him. She'd let him do this, signed those papers without reading what was on them.

With a jerk, she turned off the hot water and shivered as the spray turned cold. She deserved it for being so naïve, so trusting.

She shut off the shower and dried herself. A check of the time had her hurriedly dressing in jeans and boots. Which top? A small part of her wanted to look nice, pretty even, because Kim would be there.

But looking attractive would only stir Mark's interest. Goosebumps leapt to her skin. She should get a stronger lock for her bedroom door. Her hands shook as she finished dressing.

She definitely had to keep him happy.

The photograph of her parents on the dresser filled her with shame. They would be so disappointed in her.

She blocked the thought, grabbed her purse and drove back into town.

The clubrooms were well lit and the car park almost full. Alyse hugged her jacket around her as the wind blew and she strode inside into light, warmth and laughter. So many people, some already sitting at their tables, others chatting by the bar, waiting for their drinks. Tinsel and baubles decorated the hall to celebrate the Christmas in July theme. Alyse spotted some high school friends, but they all ignored her. No matter.

Her gaze caught on Kim standing with some of his friends. He laughed at something Jeremy said, his eyes crinkling at the sides and the joy hit her in the chest. She couldn't remember the last time she had laughed.

Jeremy shifted and a small Asian woman next to him came into view. Zamira.

Alyse clenched her teeth. She'd like to say hello, but it would only cause trouble. Where was Mark? By the bar, two empty pint glasses already in front of him. She swallowed hard. Would he be too drunk to care tonight, or just drunk enough to want to show her who was in charge?

She moved towards him and a voice called, "Alyse!"

Surprise had her stopping to find Zamira crossing the room, waving at her. Her gaze darted to Mark. He spoke to the guy next to him, oblivious to her. Phew. Alyse waited for Zamira and then gave her a small smile. "Kim mentioned you arrived back today."

Zamira beamed. "Yes, they were all so welcoming. I'm glad to see you again."

Her enthusiasm warmed Alyse. When was the last time someone had been glad to see her? Her gaze found Kim. Well, aside from him. "So, you've moved to Blackbridge?"

Zamira nodded. "Got a new job at Border Force and I'm living with Jeremy." Her face flushed.

Alyse stepped back. Border Force. They'd raided her next-door neighbour's place about a month ago and Mark had been furious. She hadn't dared ask why, but he'd mentioned an 'Asian bitch' who'd ruined everything. He really wouldn't like her talking to Zamira. "That's great."

"Maybe we can get that coffee soon?" Zamira continued. "It would be nice to get to know my neighbours."

She was far too nice to be hanging around Alyse. Not with the problems Mark would cause. Still Alyse nodded. "Sure. If you'll excuse me, I'm helping with dinner."

"Of course." Zamira stepped aside so Alyse could move past.

She stopped by Mark. "I'm going into the kitchen to help."

He snaked his arm around her waist, pulled her close, his beer breath wafting over her. "Princess, I was wondering when you'd get here."

She stiffened and at his glare, forced herself to relax. She smiled at the man he was talking with. "Hey, Troy."

"Nice to see you again, Alyse. Has Mark been hiding you away again?" He laughed but Mark's scowl was sharp enough to cut glass.

"Been busy with the bees." She winced at her choice of words.

Mark lowered his voice, pulled her closer. "She's been going through a depressive stage. Her mother's birthday is coming up."

"What—"

Mark pinched her side and she shut up.

Troy's expression was sympathetic. "I'm sorry. It must be hard. I have a cousin who is bi-polar." He cleared his throat. "I'll have to get more of your honey. Where are you selling from these days?"

What lies had Mark been telling people? She swallowed. "Mostly online," she said. "But the shop next to *On the Way* bakery has some too." If she had her way, she'd have her products in multiple shops around the state, but Mark wouldn't let her. Didn't want her business to get too big, didn't want her to become too stressed… didn't want her to become financially independent more like it.

"I'll pick some up tomorrow," Troy said.

Alyse nodded and moved towards the kitchen but Mark pulled her back.

His voice low he asked, "Who were you talking to?"

"Jeremy's partner," she said. "You met her a couple of weeks ago at the apiary. She's new in town."

He grunted. "Thought I recognised her. Don't see her again." He turned back to Troy.

Alyse's skin crawled as she walked away. He dared restrict her actions, because she'd let him get away with it. To disobey him meant pain and terror. But it had been years since she'd had a tiny flare of hope, the idea she could perhaps have a friend Mark didn't know about, who he couldn't control. She pushed into the kitchen and inhaled the heat that came from the ovens roasting the turkey, ham and vegetables. It smelled like Christmas.

Her heart ached for her parents.

"Do you need a hand in here, Barbara?" Alyse asked.

"Oh, I think we're all set," she answered, bustling from the oven to the stove where a pot of gravy was simmering. "Only the meat needs carving." The doors behind Alyse opened and Kim walked in. Barbara grinned. "And here he is now. Knives are on the bench, Kim."

Kim gently placed his hands on Alyse's hips and moved her to the side. "Excuse me, Aly." His grin sent her heart racing and her body still felt the gentle press of his hands on her hips. It had been far too long since anyone had shown her any affection that her body was overreacting now. That's all it was.

She hesitated by the door. Staying here was far preferable to being out there with Mark, but she didn't want Kim to suffer from Mark's jealousy.

"Aly, why don't you grab the other knife?" Kim called. "You can cut the ham."

Her feet moved on their own accord towards him. Barbara placed the ham on the big stainless-steel table next to Kim and Alyse picked up a knife.

Mark couldn't complain. She was doing exactly as he asked. She was helping with dinner.

But she glanced towards the door to make sure he couldn't see her anyway.

Chapter 5

When Kim finished carving the first turkey, Barbara rolled up the divider which separated the kitchen from the function room. "Dinner's ready!" It would take time for everyone to serve themselves. Alyse had said nothing since she'd started cutting the ham, but he didn't mind. It was nice simply having her next to him.

"Think we'll finish this before the horde empty the plates we've done?" he asked.

"They're a bunch of locusts, so probably not." She smiled and then her gaze darted towards the opening into the main room. She shifted away from him and kept her eyes on the ham in front of her.

Kim frowned and checked the crowd. Mark waited in line, his eyes stony as he glared at Kim. Right. Mark's comments hung between them, but Kim was beyond caring. He nodded a greeting.

Kim finished carving and washed his hands. Alyse moved confidently, slicing the ham with precision, all of her attention on the meat. Watching her work reminded him of the focus she'd had talking about the apiary and the changes she wanted her parents to make.

Had she done any of them?

When Alyse finished, Barbara moved the trays of meat over to the serving area. "Thanks for your help. Make sure you both get a plate before you leave."

Kim gestured for Alyse to go first and then filled his plate. He followed her out, almost bumping into her as she paused outside the kitchen. Her gaze was on Mark's table which had no spare seats. What an asshole.

He bent close so she heard him over the din in the room. "Sit with me." Kim had asked Jeremy to save two seats in case he could convince Alyse to sit with them.

She hesitated, scanning the room, but it was the only place still free.

"All right."

Elation filled him as they moved through the crowd and placed their plates on the table, Alyse sitting next to Zamira.

"Can I get you a drink?" Kim asked.

Again she hesitated.

He smiled, trying to appear as friendly and non-threatening as possible. "Soft drink, wine, beer?"

"Lemonade, please." She fumbled in her bag. "Let me get you some money."

"My shout." He walked to the bar. Tonight would be good for Alyse. If she could see she had support, it had to help. Mark had isolated her from everything and everyone.

He ordered the drinks and then grunted as someone shoved him hard against the bar. He tried to move but was pinned to the wooden surface. Pain spread through him and he twisted to see who it was.

"Keep your hands off my woman," Mark growled, his yeasty beer breath wafting over Kim.

Kim gritted his teeth, his temper spiking. No, better he keep calm around Mark. "My hands are over here. She's only sitting with us because there was no room at your table."

Mark grunted and shoved him again before stepping back. "I saw you with her on the boat. You undressed her."

Kim breathed through the pain. "Because she was freezing to death," he said. "It's part of my job. I did the same with the women I rescued a couple of weeks back. Hypothermia's a real threat."

The barman put Kim's drinks in front of him and took his card, giving Mark a wary look. "Another beer, Mark?"

Mark nodded. He lowered his voice. "If I catch you around her again, you'll both pay."

Kim froze, his hackles raising. "What do you mean by that?"

"Alyse doesn't know what's good for her. Sometimes she needs to be shown."

The barman handed Mark his beer and Mark strode away.

Kim took a minute to steady his breathing, tension coursing through his body. If Mark had meant to scare him off, he'd done the exact opposite. Now Kim was more determined than ever to help Alyse—but he'd have to be careful. He didn't want her to suffer further.

When the tension in his stomach calmed, he returned to the table. Elijah regaled Alyse with tales from his time in Europe and Jamie watched him, the love in his eyes clear. Kim smiled as he placed Alyse's lemonade in front of her. He liked seeing his friends falling in love.

Last year half the team had sat at their table, all bachelors spending the night bullshitting each other and it had been fun. But this year with Zamira, Alyse and now Elijah, it was different. A shift. Only Adam and Guy were unaccompanied and if Will wasn't still on his honeymoon, he would have brought Fleur with him.

Kim frowned. He shouldn't think of Alyse in that way. She wasn't his. She still might see him as the dorky friend she'd hung out with at the markets because there'd been no better options.

He barely tasted the turkey he ate.

Alyse laughed at something Elijah said, a throaty, sexy sound that shot right to Kim's groin. He hadn't heard her laugh in years, he'd forgotten the sound. She slapped her hand over her mouth, eyes wide as if she hadn't meant to. Kim murmured, "You OK?"

She nodded, swallowing hard, not looking at him. Instead her gaze darted across the room to Mark. He spoke to the blonde next to him. She relaxed and turned to speak with Zamira.

Kim wanted to hear her laugh again. Wanted to be the one to make her laugh. Wanted to bring her back to life.

It didn't matter if Alyse only saw him as a friend. He would help her.

Whatever it took.

***

The night ended way before Alyse was ready. Though most of the people were practically strangers, she'd had fun listening to their stories and banter. They were all people who'd seen her at her worst; Elijah and Jamie had witnessed Mark hitting her after he'd fallen off the roof, Adam had come to her place when she'd finally built the courage to report a domestic assault, and Guy was the paramedic who'd been there when Mark had broken his leg. She'd expected judgement, but instead they'd welcomed her and included her in the conversation.

Next to her, Zamira asked about the people the men spoke about and Alyse pointed out most of them and explained where they fit into the community. She might have been isolated from the town, but she still knew who was whom.

Between the courses, the organisers sold raffle tickets

and organised games to raise more money. At the end of the night, the trophy was awarded to the football team who'd won the Chrissy Cup and people began to go home. Alyse had lost count of the number of times Mark had ordered another beer, so he would be well plastered. Hopefully he'd be so drunk he'd fall asleep in the car. If not, she'd have to move fast and lock herself into her room before he could get stuck into her for everything she'd done wrong that night.

She kept an eye on Mark as the others on her table spoke about leaving.

"Do you need a lift?" Kim asked.

She jolted as he touched her hand to get her attention. "No. I drove." She checked for Mark and saw him on his feet glaring at her. Quickly she pulled her hand out from under Kim's and stood. "I should go."

"Wait." Zamira pulled out her phone. "Let me get your number so we can go for coffee next week."

Alyse felt Mark's gaze on her as she rattled off her number. She forced herself to smile at Zamira. "I'll talk to you later." She waved at the table to say goodbye, avoiding Kim, and hurried to Mark. "Are you ready to go?"

"Yeah." He placed his arm on her shoulder, laying claim. His palm squeezed her breast and she flinched, but it only made him squeeze harder. "Let's see how he likes this." A slight slur in his words hinted he'd had way too much to drink.

She stiffened and increased her pace, hoping to get him out of the building and into the dark outside before too many people saw them. Without looking, she knew Kim was watching. Shame washed over her and her face flushed. Mark fondled her breast.

Despair and fury fought a duel in her mind, each battling to win. She gritted her teeth and finally they stepped out of the clubhouse into the cold darkness. "Let me get my keys." She stepped away and he let her go. Her hands shook as she fumbled with her bag, finding the keys, and she strode towards the car, not waiting for Mark, but he kept up with her. He held his liquor well.

Without another word, she drove home. He was silent until they left town and darkness fell around the car, no street lights to illuminate the way. She switched on high beam to give her more warning of any kangaroos crossing the road.

"He wants to fuck you."

He could only be referring to Kim, but still she asked, "Who?"

"The Asian prick. You want to fuck him too."

She swallowed hard, fear crawling over her skin. She recognised that soft conversational tone. He was furious. Would she have time to unlock the front door and get inside before he caught her? "No, I don't. I sat with him because there was nowhere else to sit. I spoke with Zamira most of the night."

"She's the bitch who ruined Henk's operation. I told you not to see her again."

Alyse clenched her jaw. It wasn't fair of him to choose her friends. But she daren't defy him. "I'm sorry. It was the only spare seat."

"I mean it, Alyse. If I see you with her…"

She could fill in the blanks. He'd beat her, or mess with her hives, or make her life more miserable than it currently was. But that wasn't far of a stretch. Her life sucked. Today was the first day in years that she'd felt like a real person. She'd laughed with Kim's friends. She thought she'd forgotten how.

"I'd hate for the bitch to have an accident again."

The threat cut through her. It was the second time he'd threatened others rather than her. Did he know his threats no longer worked? Her life was worthless. Perhaps jail would be preferable to this. But as she turned into her property and saw the farmhouse ahead, her heart squeezed. It was all she had left of her parents. The apiary had been in the family for generations. The police seized property involved in illegal operations and if Mark was involved in drug trafficking, the police could confiscate it permanently.

Her shoulders fell. Did it really matter? There was no one to leave it to.

As she parked in front of the house, Mark squeezed her hand. "You and I need to have a little chat before you go to bed."

Fear caught her breath in her throat. She nodded rather than speak. To disobey a direct order in his current mood would only be worse for her. He'd likely break down her door like he'd threatened to do before. Slowly she climbed out, her muscles tight. She waited for him and together they walked up the front path. The keys dug into her palm, as she waited for the first attack—verbal or physical—it didn't matter. As long as it started.

Her hands shook as she unlocked the front door, Mark crowding her, breathing down her neck. She squeezed her eyes closed before flicking on the hallway light. When he still stayed silent, she hurried towards the kitchen. "Would you like a cup of coffee?"

"No."

She stopped. If he wasn't having one, she couldn't either.

He slammed the door and stalked towards her. She tensed but resisted the urge to back up. There was nowhere to go.

He grabbed her arm, fingers digging into her skin and dragged her into the lounge room, pushing her towards the couch. "What the hell were you doing tonight?"

It didn't matter what she said, it would only enrage him

further, but so would silence. "I helped in the kitchen like you asked." Her gaze didn't leave his, waiting for the first hit. "When I came out, there was only one spare seat."

"So it's my fault for not saving you a seat?" he growled.

She swallowed. "No, of course not. I should have arranged it before I went into the kitchen."

"You should have." He slapped her face. The sharp sting caused tears to blur her vision. "That's for being too stupid to think of it." He brought his hand up and hit her again. She tasted blood as her lip split, the pain making her wince. "And that's for sitting next to Kim." He punched her in the stomach, knocking the air out of her. "You are not—" Punch. "seeing—" Punch. "him—" Punch. "or that Asian chick—" Punch. "again."

Alyse huddled over, protecting herself as much as she could, as her stomach convulsed in pain. She gritted her teeth to stop from crying out, tears leaking from her eyes. His last hit knocked her to the floor. She curled into a ball. The fury in his eyes made her heart stop. He was just getting started. She whimpered. She didn't want to die.

A single night of friendship had given her hope. Life could be better. She could learn to laugh again, could have friends. All she had to do was escape Mark.

"I hope this hurts you as much as you hurt me." He kicked her hard and pain flooded her. She cried out. "Good. That's better. Cry for me." He kicked her again. "You laughed with them. You don't laugh with me."

She couldn't talk through the pain. She prayed for it to be over soon. But this was calm Mark, not enraged, knee-jerk reaction Mark. He'd been simmering for hours. Which meant the abuse would keep coming. Her heart raced and she fought to stay conscious, fought to think of something that would make him stop.

His next kick bruised her ribs. She wouldn't be able to walk tomorrow and it was his father's funeral. Hope flared.

She was expected to be there.

"Why do you make me do this to you?" The hint of real pain in his voice made her look up. Tears glistened in his eyes, but so did satisfaction. He didn't care.

"Your father's funeral is tomorrow," she choked out. Her breath hitched and he stepped back, shaking his head and swore. Instantly his expression morphed to concern.

"Did I hurt you?" He crouched, brushing her hair off her face. "I'm sorry, Alyse. You shouldn't make me so mad."

She fought not to cringe away. "I'm sorry," she gasped. "Why don't you go to bed? I'll be right after a cup of tea."

"You will." His tone contained a threat. "You need to be at Dad's funeral." He caressed her cheek. "Princess, you know I love you. I'm only trying to take care of you. I'll put the kettle on." He walked out of the room and Alyse exhaled. She lay there as he clomped down the hallway to his bedroom and slammed the door.

So much for the kettle.

Gingerly she shifted, wincing at the agony coursing through her. Part of her wanted to stay on the floor, curled in a ball until the morning, but experience had taught her it hurt far worse if she did that.

Slowly she moved, using the couch next to her for support to get to her knees. She breathed shallowly, the movement painful. Were her ribs broken? It didn't matter. There was nothing that could be done. After she stood, she'd clean herself, examine the damage. Warm blood dribbled down her nose and she wiped it away. She climbed to her feet, squeezing her eyes closed. She swayed, giving herself a moment to get used to the pain and stop her head spinning before she shuffled out of the room, heading for the kitchen. They didn't have enough ice packs in the freezer for all her injuries, but she'd make do.

She dampened a tea towel and washed away the blood,

using the window above the sink as a mirror. Her cheek was swollen, her eyes darkening with bruising. Her stomach would be a lot worse, but at least it was easily hidden. Mark must have forgotten about the funeral, otherwise he would have left her face alone.

Wrapping the ice packs in tea towels, she then lowered herself onto a chair, placing a larger pack on her stomach and holding one against her cheek. Her makeup skills had improved over the years, but no amount of makeup would hide her injuries tomorrow.

But she would go to the funeral. The family expected it, and Mark's mother had been kind to her over the years. Alyse would support her and Mark's teenaged nephews, no matter how much pain she was in.

Richard's death had come as a shock to them all.

As the cold of the ice soothed some of the aches, Alyse breathed out. It hurt. Would Mark have stopped if the funeral wasn't tomorrow? She couldn't go on like this, fearing for her life. She shifted and her body throbbed. Could she risk calling an ambulance? Mark should have passed out by now, and if she asked them to come without using sirens, she could sneak out, get some scans to make sure she had no internal bleeding. But then she had no one to bring her back before he woke in the morning. She couldn't call Zamira, she barely knew the woman.

No, she'd patch herself up as she always did and hope there was nothing more serious.

When she had healed, she would explore how she could escape Mark. She'd thought losing the property was the worst thing that could happen. Now though… she knew better.

Mark had to be stopped. Her life wasn't hers, hadn't been in a long time.

The only way she'd be safe was if Mark was behind bars. Maybe, just maybe, she could prove Mark was involved in the criminal activity occurring around Blackbridge, prove he was laundering money through her apiary accounts.

She smiled and then grimaced at the pain.

As of tonight, she was fighting back.

Chapter 6

Kim shrugged his black jacket onto his shoulders and smoothed down the lapels. He sighed. He hated funerals, and he particularly didn't want to go to this one. Not when he could clearly visualise Richard's limp and battered body as they'd pulled him from the ocean. It was a part of the Marine Rescue role he hated. He shivered and pushed the thought away. This wasn't about him, he was going for Alyse. She might have been close to Richard, and he wanted to show her she wasn't alone.

Not any longer.

The memory of her laugh washed the cold from him. Last night had been fun.

Though she hadn't said a lot, she'd smiled and laughed, and having her next to him had soothed a missing part of him. It was a shame the night had ended so soon. Then Mark had laid claim on Alyse, groping her. She'd cringed away from him for a split second which had confirmed Kim's assumption she no longer had feelings for Mark.

At the knock on his door, he grabbed his phone and wallet, and answered it. His older sister, Mai stood there. "Ready to go?"

He nodded, locking the granny flat behind him and

following her through his parents' backyard to the car out front.

"I'm surprised you wanted to come today," Mai said as they got in, her fiancé Nicholas behind the wheel.

"Alyse will be there." He greeted Nicholas and settled on the back seat.

Mai frowned. "I didn't think you were friends with her anymore."

"I rescued her on Friday. We reconnected."

"How does Mark feel about it?" She glanced at him.

"I don't care."

Mai sighed. "Be careful, little brother. I don't want you to get hurt."

"I won't talk to her if Mark's around," he said. "I just want her to see me there, know she has someone to turn to."

She nodded, but her forehead remained furrowed.

When they arrived at the cemetery, a large crowd, mostly dressed in black, had already gathered. Alyse was probably with the Patton family.

He spotted Jamie and Elijah and joined them.

"Didn't think you'd be here," Jamie said.

Kim shrugged. "I thought Alyse might need some support."

Elijah glowered. "She needs more than that. Her makeup's not hiding anything."

Tension gripped him. "What do you mean?"

Elijah jerked his head over towards the hearse and Kim clenched his hands. Alyse wore a black pant suit and her red hair fell loose below her shoulders. It didn't hide her black eye, the bruises on her cheek or her split lip.

Dread filled him. Had she been punished for talking to him last night?

Fury simmered as Mark said something to Alyse and she nodded. How dare he touch her, how dare he treat her like this?

The funeral director spoke to Mrs Patton and gestured towards the hearse. The family fell in behind it and Alyse flinched as Mark took her hand. She moved slowly, in obvious pain.

Kim took half a step forward only for Mai to stop him.

"Going over there isn't going to help matters," she said. "Wait until after the ceremony when people are giving their condolences. Then you can talk to her."

Mai was right, but it hurt not to whisk Alyse away to safety.

Instead he hung back with his friends and waited until the majority of the mourners went into the building. Next to him Jamie squeezed Elijah's hand and murmured, "You all right?"

Kim had forgotten Elijah had seen Richard fall from the cliff, had tried to save him. Kim squeezed his eyes shut as the image of Richard's broken body floating in the water came to him.

Elijah nodded and let out a shaky breath. Mai touched Kim's arm, her eyes asking him the same question. He nodded.

He'd had little to do with the Patton family and while he was sad for them, his only reason for being here was Alyse.

The service dragged on. People in the community spoke about how generous Richard was and how much he'd done for the town. Photographs of family life were projected onto a screen and in the front row, Mrs Patton wept. Her three children were dry-eyed, but the Pattons didn't usually show their emotions. Mark was the exception with his temper.

Finally, the celebrant announced an end to the ceremony, and the family moved into the sheltered courtyard. Alyse struggled to stand, gasping in pain as

Mark jerked her to her feet.

Kim ground his teeth. Bastard.

Mai gripped his knee, keeping him in place. As much as he hated it, now wasn't the time or place to make a scene.

He waited, his eyes on Alyse through the windows where she stood next to Mark. She spoke to two teenaged boys, hugging them gingerly and then spoke to people who came to talk to the family. Every now and then her face screwed up as if she was fighting the pain. Kim murmured to Mai, "Do you have any painkillers in your purse?"

She handed them to him. "Drinks are on the table to the left."

He moved outside, pouring a glass of water and then hesitated. How could he get Alyse the pills without Mark seeing?

The last people spoke to the Pattons and then Mark and his siblings, Craig and Kay, encircled their mother. Alyse moved away from them, heading for a corner. Kim didn't hesitate. He strode to her and handed her the water. "Do you need any painkillers?" He showed her the two packets Mai had given him.

Her eyes widened and she checked over his shoulder for Mark and then sighed. "Please." She popped out two tablets, swallowing them quickly. "Thank you."

She didn't even deny she was in pain. "Let me help you." He sent her a text. "That's my number. Call me anytime."

"Thank you." Another look in Mark's direction. "Can you ask Mai over here? If Mark sees you talking to me alone, he won't be happy." Quickly she saved his number, putting it under the name of Beatrice's Beekeeping Supplies. Clever.

Before he could gesture to Mai, Elijah and Jamie walked over.

"How are you?" Elijah asked, kissing her cheek.

She winced. "Coping."

"Honey, we're here for you, if you need help," Elijah said.

Kim wanted to hug his friend. Maybe the more people who told her, the more she'd realise it was the truth.

Alyse opened her mouth to say something and then closed it again. Finally she nodded.

Mai and Nicholas joined them, and they gave Alyse their condolences. The whole time Alyse kept glancing to Mark. Kim hated her fear.

When Kay stepped away from her mother, Alyse interrupted Mai. "I'm sorry. I have to go." She hurried over to the Pattons before Mark looked for her.

Mai lay a hand on Kim's arm. "Maybe Lincoln has some contacts who can help her."

Kim nodded. One way or another he would ensure Alyse had a safe place to run when she needed it. "Let's go." The Pattons were holding a wake but only for invited guests.

"Is it too early for alcohol?" Elijah asked as they walked out of the crematorium.

"The pub will be open by the time we get back to Blackbridge," Jamie said.

It sounded good to Kim.

"I'll tell Adam and Jeremy to meet us there," Elijah said.

Mai nodded. "And I'll call the musketeers. Between all of us, we'll figure something out."

Kim smiled. He hadn't even had to ask.

Alyse would have more support than she knew what to do with.

***

Alyse's mind whirled as she re-joined Mark and his family. She had a whole group of people who wanted to help her, but what would Mark do to them? When Mai's bakery had burned down earlier in the year, Mark had commented that she'd got what she deserved for poking her nose into other people's business. Alyse hadn't asked what he'd meant.

Bringing others into this mess wasn't her preference. There was no guarantee they would stick with her, especially after they realised how dangerous Mark was.

Alyse closed her eyes.

She could do it on her own. She'd gone through her options last night while applying the ice packs to her bruises. Changing the locks wouldn't keep him out for long, and she'd heard too many stories about how useless the domestic violence laws were for protecting victims. The only way to be free of him was if he was behind bars. Which meant she had to gather evidence about his crimes.

Mark's eyes glistened as she moved next to him. Her heart clenched. She'd forgotten for a moment that this was his father's funeral. She might hate him but he was grieving. Losing a parent in a tragic accident threw your whole world upside-down.

Craig turned to her. "We're heading to the winery," he said. "Can you drive?"

Every movement was torture. Simply shaking someone's hand or being pulled in for a hug hurt every single bit of her body. Still she couldn't refuse. Mark had started drinking before they'd left the house. "Sure."

Craig put his hand on the small of her back and pressed her forward. "After you."

She winced and moved slowly out of the building. Behind her Craig hissed to Mark, "What the fuck did you do to her?"

Mark grunted.

In the past Craig's outrage would have given her hope, but not anymore. The Pattons might tell Mark off, but they did nothing to offer her any help, nothing to stop him. Outrage didn't stop the bruises or the beatings, and sometimes they caused the next ones.

She gritted her teeth as she slid behind the steering wheel of Mark's ute. Exhaling, she braced herself before shifting into a more comfortable position and then she followed the convoy of family cars out of the car park.

Mark was silent the whole way, staring out the window. Alyse let him be.

She hoped her injuries would stop him from hitting her again until they healed, but she was never sure.

A sign at the entrance to the Vale winery said it was closed for a private function. She used to love coming here with her parents, seeing the treehouse-like restaurant on stilts and the quirky fantasy creatures inside. She parked next to Kay's four-wheel drive and waited while Kay's sons climbed out before she opened her door. Don, Kay's oldest son, glanced at her. "Do you need a hand?"

She shook her head. "I'll be fine."

He frowned and stayed with her, offering her an arm to lean on. Love and gratitude filled her. She had a soft spot for Don. Kay wasn't the most mothering person and Alyse had watched Don grow from a sweet young boy to a surly teen who barely said a word. But he always sat next to her when they had a family dinner and occasionally told her about the ag college.

She took her time, hoping slow steps would reduce the pain. They didn't. Mark had already gone inside by the time she reached the bottom of the steps to the restaurant. Who built a damned restaurant on stilts? Right now she didn't care about the spectacular view over the vineyard, or the fact that underneath the restaurant made the perfect shady place to sit and eat on a hot summer's day. There were twenty or more steps to the top.

This was really going to hurt.

Alyse inhaled and moved one step after the other. She

didn't lift her gaze to her destination, it would only show her how much further she had to go. Instead she tried to find a way to move that wouldn't pull on her ribs.

"What happened to you?" Don asked.

Alyse hesitated.

"Were you in an accident?" The concern in his eyes touched her.

"Yeah, your uncle accidentally hit me a dozen times." The words were out before she thought about the consequences. But did it really matter? The whole town already knew Mark beat her.

Don's eyes widened and he lifted his gaze to the entrance of the restaurant. His hands clenched. "Why?"

Oh no. She placed a hand on his arm, surprised he didn't already know. "He was jealous," she said. "Don't worry. I'll heal. Tell me how you are. It's a shock to lose Grandpa like this."

They entered the warm restaurant, and she breathed a sigh of relief. The room was already full. Some people she recognised as extended family, and others as people from town, but many were strangers.

Don's hands unclenched and his shoulders slumped. "He was sick."

"Doesn't make it any easier. He was teaching you the ropes at the winery, wasn't he?"

A scowl crossed Don's face before he said, "Something like that."

She frowned. A faint memory tugged at her. When had she last heard Don's name mentioned? She couldn't remember. She poured herself a cup of tea from the urn and perched herself on a stool out of the way. Mark's mother was surrounded by people her age, presumably friends, and Kay and Craig moved around the room talking to guests. Mark was by the bar, drinking. Please let him be too sad today to beat her. She turned her attention back to Don. "If you need to chat about anything, you can call me any time." Knowing Kim and his friends were there if she needed them had lightened her soul, even if she'd never call them.

He gave her a long look. "Thanks. Can I sit with you?"

"Sure." She gestured to the stool beside her and then winced.

Don's younger brother, Tyrone joined them, sliding onto a stool with a whole plate of food.

"Got enough?" Don grumbled.

He flashed them a grin. "Just about."

Alyse smiled. The only positive of being with Mark was watching these boys grow up.

"Can I get you some food?" Don asked her.

Her heart warmed. "That would be great. Thank you."

Don returned with two plates and they chatted until the guests started thinning out. Now though, the bathroom beckoned.

Only about half a dozen people remained talking to Mark's mother and Mark and his siblings weren't in the room. Alyse shuffled past the bar towards the bathroom. Angry voices came from the kitchen. She froze. That was Mark. Should she leave so he didn't see her, didn't turn his anger on her?

"What the fuck was he even doing there in the first place?" Mark growled.

"Who knows?" Craig replied. "He wasn't in the right century some days."

"That cave had to have meant something to him," Mark insisted.

"It's where he used to smuggle things in," Kay said, fatigue in her voice. "He was mumbling something about a shipment being due when I found him, and the pulley system is still in the rocks."

Alyse's skin prickled. Smuggling? She understood Mark

was smuggling, but why would his father, a successful vineyard owner, need to smuggle anything?

Craig swore. "Maybe it's best he died."

"How can you say that?" Mark was pissed. "He was our father, our leader. He knew everything." His grief was clear.

"He was becoming a liability." Kay's matter-of-fact tone sent chills through Alyse. "The dementia made him forget to be cautious."

"It sounds like you're happy he's dead," Mark said. "Maybe you pushed him off the cliff."

"Don't be stupid," Craig snapped.

Alyse shifted away. It was far too dangerous to stay here. She winced as she moved to the other side of the hallway.

"Watch it, Mark," Kay barked. "It's bad enough Alyse shows up to Dad's funeral bruised and battered. If people hear you running your mouth off, they won't hesitate to report you."

"It's not so bad."

Kay's sound of disgust was loud. "Of course it is."

Alyse moved quickly past the open doorway, not daring to glance in and her shoulders relaxed when she pushed into the female bathroom. Safe. For the moment.

The mirror showed her the bruises had darkened since the morning. Her makeup wasn't fooling anyone.

But this was the first time she'd been allowed in public showing her injuries. Normally Mark kept her hidden.

Now the whole town had seen.

Could she use it as evidence? Probably not. She couldn't risk writing down any of the conversation she'd just heard either. Mark might find it.

She'd have to figure some other way of gathering proof of Mark's crimes, some way of getting it to the police without him finding out.

Because if she understood the conversation correctly, Mark wasn't the only Patton involved.

She shivered.

This could be more dangerous than she'd thought.

<h1 style="text-align:center">Chapter 7</h1>

It was already light when Alyse woke the next morning. Concerned, she sat up and flinched as pain flooded her. That's why she'd overslept. It had been almost impossible to find a comfortable position to lie. She'd ended up piling pillows and sitting almost upright to relieve the pain in her chest. She panted, trying for shallow breaths. If her ribs weren't broken, they were definitely bruised.

Was Mark already awake? Normally she left the house before he woke, so she didn't have to deal with him.

He'd been subdued when they'd arrived home from the wake. He'd sat in the lounge room and watched a football game but hadn't yelled at the screen as usual. She'd taken more painkillers and told him she was going to bed. He hadn't responded. Once in bed, she'd put together a mental list of where she could gather evidence. His office was the obvious starting point. He had a filing cabinet full of the business contracts and his laptop contained the login for the accounting software he used for her business.

Carefully she climbed out of bed and dressed. A button-up shirt meant the least amount of pain. Maybe she'd drive into town today and see a doctor, if only to get some decent painkillers. She unlocked her bedroom door and pulled it open. Down the hall, Mark's bedroom was also open. Mark was awake. Her footsteps made little sound on the wooden floorboards as she walked to the kitchen. Empty.

She breathed a sigh of relief and flicked on the kettle.

The cereal was on a shelf too high for her to reach with the pain she was in, so she dragged out the toaster and popped in two slices of bread.

"You're up late today."

She jumped. "I forgot to set my alarm."

Mark stood at the doorway watching her, his expression unreadable. "How are your ribs?"

Surprise swept through her. He'd never asked about the injuries he'd inflicted before. "Sore."

"I wish you didn't make me so angry all the time."

Of course it was her fault. "I don't mean to."

"Doc Eriks will give you some painkillers if you see him today."

Damn it. She didn't want to see the family doctor. She wanted to go to the emergency department where they would record her injuries, but if she didn't go to Eriks, Mark would be unhappy. "Thank you."

"I'll be at Mum's most of the day," Mark continued. "But I'll be home for dinner."

So she'd have to prepare something. "All right."

The toast behind her popped, and she retrieved the butter and Vegemite from the fridge. Mark left the room. The back door slammed and a few moments later, his ute roared to life. She peered out the kitchen window as he drove away.

Gone. She relaxed.

She leaned against the kitchen bench, eating her breakfast, too sore to sit at the table. Though Mark had said he'd be gone all day, he'd lied before. Sometimes he tried to catch her doing things she hadn't received his approval for. But if she was quick, she might achieve the first item on her freedom plan—get a copy of her accounts.

She swallowed the last bite of toast and checked outside to make sure Mark hadn't come back. Then she grabbed a pair of latex gloves from under the sink and slipped them on. It might be her house, but she wasn't allowed into Mark's office and couldn't leave any traces behind.

She crept down the hallway, checking each room in case one of Mark's associates was inside. It had happened before. When she was certain it was clear and she double-checked Mark hadn't returned, she hurried to the office, her heart thumping in her chest.

His laptop was in the centre of his desk. She switched it on, pleased when it booted immediately. Sometimes Mark's need to have the latest technology was an advantage. When the password screen appeared, she typed the password he'd used three years ago when he still told her those kinds of things. The computer logged on.

Bingo. She clicked on the desktop link to the accounting software. It logged her right in. Last night, after the painkillers had kicked in and the icepacks had grown warm, she'd searched for information about how to make a backup and now ran through the process, glancing at the doorway as the file was created. She opened her webmail—an address Mark didn't know about—in incognito mode and then attached the file and emailed herself. The sounds of an engine and tyres crunching over the dirt outside reached her.

She froze, heart pounding.

Shit.

While she waited for the email to send, she shut the accounting browser, deleted the file from the desktop and the rubbish bin, and then closed her webmail. A car door slammed. Her skin prickled and she frantically pressed the buttons to shut down the computer. She slammed the screen shut.

Someone knocked on the front door.

Not Mark. Her heart rate settled, and she took a moment to check that nothing was out of place before she closed the door softly behind her. She shoved the gloves in her jacket pocket and hurried to the door.

Her heart fluttered for an entirely different reason. Kim. He shouldn't be here.

He held her work boots in one hand and her jumper in the other. "Hey. I thought you might need these today."

She'd forgotten all about them. "Thank you." She winced as she took them from him. "I'll get your jacket." She fetched it from her bedroom and Kim waited by the front door.

He tucked the jacket under his arm. "How are those ribs?"

"Painful," she replied. "I'm going to the doctor today." She wanted to invite him in, offer him a coffee, but there was still the risk Mark might come home, might have forgotten something.

"Want me to take you?"

The offer shouldn't surprise her or make her feel so warm inside. "I'll be fine." If she accepted, word would get back to Mark that she'd been seen in Kim's car.

"Mark isn't home, is he?" Kim peered behind her.

She shook her head. "He's gone to his mother's."

"Good." Kim stepped forward, took her hand. "Aly, I meant what I said about helping you, whatever you need."

Her throat closed over and tears pricked her eyes. "Kim…" She swallowed so she could speak. "Mark is dangerous. You don't want to get involved."

His eyes were fixed on hers. "Yeah, I do. I want you safe, Aly. I want you happy."

It was too much. He was offering her more hope than

she deserved. She had to keep him safe. "He threatened you," she said. "He said if I see you again, something bad will happen to you or your family business."

Kim's expression turned to thunder. "I'd like to see him try."

"No, you wouldn't." How could she convince him? She stepped past him, heading towards his car. Could she trust him, tell him her plans? Perhaps if he knew she was doing something about her situation, he'd stop interfering. She closed her eyes, prayed she was doing the right thing. "You're right. I'm not happy, and I'm not safe." She turned to him. "Having dinner with you and your friends on Saturday night showed me I wasn't really living."

He touched her arm. "I'm glad."

"So I have a plan to escape—"

He grabbed her hand. "Let me help."

She snatched it back. "No, I can't endanger you, Kim. Not when you've shown me so much kindness."

He opened his mouth to argue but she interrupted when she realised how he could help.

"Who's your business accountant?"

He blinked, tilted his head confused. "Accountant?"

She nodded. "Mark's been managing my accounts for the past few years. I don't think he's been doing it properly." If she told him too much, he might go to the police.

"We use a friend of Fleur's and Hannah's who lives in Perth," Kim said. "I can give you her details."

"How quickly can she look at my accounts?"

"I'll call her right now." Kim pulled out his phone and dialled. After a short conversation, he hung up. "Olivia'll make time this week if you email her today."

Her chest tightened. This was it. She was really doing it. "What's her address?"

She memorised it and then smiled at Kim. "Thank you.

You've helped a lot. I need to go." She turned and then hesitated. "Maybe, when this is done, we could catch up over coffee?"

His dimple showed when he smiled. "I'd like that. And if you need *anything* in the meantime, you call me."

She nodded although she would never risk it and hurried inside to send the email.

***

Kim waited until Alyse was inside before he got into his car. Frustration bubbled in him. He should be happy she'd admitted to wanting out, but he wanted to carry her away now and save her like some white knight.

Mai would tell him he was a chauvinist.

His three younger sisters would be split between whether it was *so romantic* or just plain creepy.

So he pushed down his frustration and drove back into town, parking near Mai's bakery. Alyse was already living with a control freak, he'd only make things worse by forcing his way into her life. He had to be happy with what she gave him.

He frowned. Why had she asked him for an accountant recommendation? How would getting her accounts in order help her get rid of Mark? Unless he'd been stealing from the business… He dialled Adam.

"What's up?" Adam asked.

"How long does someone go to jail for if they're caught stealing money from a business?"

Adam grunted. "And here I thought you were calling about footy training. Give me a second." A muffled sound, then a hint of voices before Adam came back on the line. "Depends on how much they stole. They might get a fine or could be up to ten years in jail. Why? You thinking of stealing from your old man?"

Kim laughed. "No way. Alyse asked me for the name of

an accountant, said she wanted to get her accounts checked because she wasn't sure if Mark was doing them properly."

"When did she ask?" Adam demanded.

"Just now. I dropped off the boots she left on the Marine Rescue boat the other day."

"Who'd you recommend?"

"Olivia does our accounts. You met her at Fleur's wedding the other day."

Adam was silent a moment. "So does this mean Alyse is leaving Mark?"

"I think so. She's working on an escape plan but won't let me help."

Adam spoke to someone, their voices muted as if he'd placed a hand over the speaker. When he came back he said, "Will she talk to the police?"

"I don't know. I can ask."

"Do that. We can't get too close to her in case Mark sees us."

Hope filled Kim. "I'll call her now." He checked no one was in the cars around him and dialled Alyse's number. It rang and rang and then went to voice mail. He hung up. No way he could leave a message Mark might intercept.

Instead he walked across to his sister's bakery and pushed the door open, inhaling the sweet scents of baked goodness and fresh coffee. "Hi, Jodie. Is Mai in?"

"Out the back." Jodie gestured for him to go through.

Mai and Penny were still up to their elbows in flour as they prepared new treats for the customers. "Hey, Kim. What are you doing here?"

He shrugged, leaning against one of the stainless steel benches out of the way. "Thought I'd visit my older sister."

She raised her eyebrows as she expertly cut what looked

to be scones from the dough in front of her.

"Need a hand?" He didn't only drop in when he needed something. Today he wanted the comfort of family, but his younger sisters were home from uni and still in the driving-him-crazy stage.

"You can make a dozen banh mi for me," Mai said.

Pushing off the bench, he fetched the ingredients from her walk-in fridge. When he was set up, Mai said, "Penny, do you want a break?"

Penny nodded and put the items she'd finished preparing into the oven. After Penny left, Mai turned to him. "So what do you want to talk about?"

He smiled. "Nothing in particular." He sliced open the fresh bread rolls to let them cool and chopped the vegetables. "I saw Alyse this morning."

"Where?"

"Took her boots back to her."

Mai transferred the scones to a tray and rolled the remaining dough flat. "How did Mark take that?"

"He wasn't there."

Mai glanced towards the cafe and lowered her voice. "Didn't we agree you'd stay away from her for a while?"

He grimaced. Their discussions at the pub the day before hadn't been fruitful. While everyone agreed they wanted to help Alyse, no one could come up with a concrete plan. Mai and Hannah had suggested Alyse would be safer from Mark's wrath if Kim stayed away. But he couldn't. So when he'd seen Mark drive past while he'd been at the shop getting milk, he'd jumped in his car and headed out. "Does Alyse ever come in here?"

She frowned. "Yeah, but I don't know how often."

There had to be ways he could run into her, check on her, without her worrying Mark would get jealous. "If she stops by, will you call me?"

"Why?"

He focused on the coriander. Mai had been involved in some nasty business at the beginning of the year when she'd been targeted by someone wanting to hurt Nicholas. Perhaps she'd understand. "Alyse asked me to stay away, because Mark is jealous," he said. "But I figure if I bump into her in town, I can at least check on her that way."

His sister gave him a long look and sighed. "I'll ask the others to tell me if she comes in."

"Thanks, Mai."

Now he had to figure out how else to help Alyse. Would it be creepy if he hung out at the emergency department in case she arrived for those painkillers? Yeah, that was leaning into stalker territory and he didn't want to scare her.

He dialled her number again and a man's gruff voice demanded, "What?"

Mark. His heart pounded. What name had Alyse put his number under? "This is John from Beatrice's Beekeeping Supplies. I'm ringing to confirm an order with, ah…" he paused as if he was checking paperwork. "Alyse Wilson."

"She's not available."

Why not? What had Mark done? Keeping his tone light he said, "Could you ask her to call me back?"

"Yeah." Mark hung up.

Mai stared at him. "Beatrice's Beekeeping Supplies?"

"It's the name Alyse saved my number under. Mark answered the phone."

"Kim, I know you care for her, but you've got to be careful." The worry in her voice tempered his annoyance.

"I will be." He finished making the rolls and his phone rang. Alyse.

He hesitated. What if it was Mark calling back, checking the number? He cleared his throat. "Beatrice's Beekeeping Supplies, John speaking."

A grunt and then the dial tone.

He breathed out and went into Alyse's contact details and changed them so they read John, Beatrice's Beekeeping Supplies.

"Kim?" Mai asked.

"Mark called me back."

"Crap. I don't like this at all."

Neither did he. "Don't worry. I'll be fine." But he'd leave before she kept on about it. "I'll catch you later." He kissed her cheek and walked out.

Maybe Mark was slightly smarter than Kim had given him credit for.

Chapter 8

"Alyse!"

She flinched at Mark's yell and whirled around, heart pounding. He strode into her work room, taking up all the space with his large frame. So much for being at his mother's all day. Just as well she'd left further snooping until she had a response from the accountant. She swallowed. "Mark. I wasn't expecting you back so soon."

"Mum wants me to take you to the doctor."

Right. Well it was nice someone in the Patton family cared. Her phone rang and Mark took it from the table and answered.

She'd held out her hand.

"She's not available." Mark hung up.

"Who was that?" She only received business calls on her phone.

"Beatrice's Beekeeping Supplies," he said. "I don't remember ordering from them."

She gaped. Kim. Thank God he'd remembered what she'd put as his contact name. "It's a new place," she said. "They contacted me and I told them I'd trial some of their stuff."

Mark grunted.

Alyse reached for her phone, her heart pounding. "Can I have it back now?"

He didn't answer, just pressed a couple of buttons and

held it to his ear. He was calling Kim back. She held her breath, waiting for the explosion. She was so screwed.

Instead, Mark grunted again and hung up, scowling as if insulted. He tossed the phone at her. "You should ring them back."

She nodded. "I will, but I don't want to hold you up. Shall we go to the doctor now?"

Mark's phone rang and after a moment of conversation he hung up. "Something's come up. You'll have to take yourself." Without waiting for her response, he walked out.

That was close. Too close. She waited until his car started before she moved, her legs jelly at the near miss. What if Mark made her put the call on speaker next time? She had to create a code with Kim in case.

She hugged herself, trying to calm her rapid heartbeat. Her work room was too small, too confining. She hated how Mark could sneak up on her, trap her in there. Who was she kidding? She was trapped anywhere she went.

Alyse left the shed as Mark drove out of the property and then called Kim back. His perky 'Beatrice's Beekeeping Supplies,' made her smile. "I can't believe you remembered what I put you in as."

Kim sighed. "I nearly didn't. He rang back didn't he?"

"Yeah. Listen if I ever call and say, 'It's Alyse Wilson here' it means he's listening in."

"Got it." A pause. "Aly, is all this necessary? Can't you kick him out? I'll protect you."

If only it was that simple. "Please trust me." Could she even ask that of him? "I mean, I know we don't really know each other anymore, but—"

"I trust you."

At the faith in his words she stopped, closed her eyes, acknowledging the almost overwhelming relief flooding through her. "Thank you."

"The reason I was calling was I spoke to Adam. He wants to know whether you'll talk to the police."

She frowned. "What about?"

"Mark. Not just about the abuse, but about whatever illegal stuff he's doing."

Her muscles clenched. She should have known Kim would go straight to the police. "I don't know details, it's safer that way." She stopped outside her garden gate. Better not go inside while she spoke to Kim. Here no one could sneak up and listen in.

"Is he embezzling from you? Is that why you need a new accountant?"

Kim wouldn't let this go. If she told him more, would he be more or less inclined to leave her be?

"Aly, talk to me. You used to confide in me at the markets. Remember when you told me you'd let Tina cheat off you so she passed her test? I never told a soul."

This was far more important. She stared at Mark's hideous man cave, a blight on her property. She had to start trusting sometime. "Promise me you won't tell a soul."

He cleared his throat. "What about Adam?"

"Not even Adam, not yet."

She bit her lip. Maybe she was a fool to trust Kim. People changed a lot in three years. Just look at her.

"All right, Aly."

She walked away from the house, needing distance as if her parents could overhear her confession. "Mark's been laundering money through my accounts," she said. "I don't know where the money's coming from but a couple of years ago when I tried to throw him out, he told me the apiary was tied up in all of his businesses."

Kim swore and she continued.

"He said he would go to the police, blame it all on me and I'd go to jail."

"So that's why you didn't leave." Kim's understanding soothed her.

It had been more than that. Mark had broken her ribs and told her she would never be free of him, he'd chase her down if she ran. The following week he told her all the places she'd been, and who she'd talked to, to prove he could get to her wherever she was. She'd been terrified. "Yeah. But I can't keep living like this, Kim. Better I go to jail for something I didn't do, then live here with him."

"Let me talk to Adam. Even if some evidence points to you, they might be able to promise you immunity for turning Mark in."

It was too much to hope for. But even though she'd been planning to go to the police, she wasn't ready yet. "Wait until the accountant emails me back," she said. "I want to know how bad it is first." Her skin prickled. It was all happening too fast.

"What if I put it to Adam hypothetically?"

She'd had enough of being pushed around. "No, Kim. You promised." A movement by her beehives made her look up, her heart racing. Zamira and Jeremy's dog, Fetch walked towards her. She sighed. "I've got to go. Zamira's here."

"Call me as soon as you hear from the accountant," Kim ordered.

She stiffened. She wouldn't be ordered around by him. Instead of answering, she hung up.

Her body ached, so she waited for Zamira to come to her.

"Morning!" Zamira chirped. "I thought I'd stop by and see how you were. I heard you were hurt."

Alyse sighed. She wasn't hiding anymore. "Yes."

Zamira's expression was sympathetic and she gently hugged Alyse. "What can I do for you?"

All of a sudden it was all too much. Too many people

wanting to help, too much pain, too much stress wondering about where Mark was and if he'd be back soon. She didn't want this lovely woman bearing the brunt of Mark's wrath.

She stepped away, tears welling in her eyes. "You can go. You can get as far away from me as possible. It's not safe for you."

Zamira hesitated. "But you need help."

Alyse shook her head, her vision blurred. "No. Not from you. You don't even know me."

The woman reached out and touched Alyse's arm. "I'd like to get to know you."

"Why?" Alyse cried. "Why would you care about some messed up woman who allows herself to be beaten by the man who's supposed to love her?"

The compassion in Zamira's eyes made Alyse's heart clench. "Because you need help. Besides," she smiled, "we're neighbours, and I'd like to make some friends."

Sobs wrenched Alyse's chest, sending pain through her body. It was too much. She'd been alone for too long.

"Please let me help you."

She shook her head. "Mark will hurt you."

Zamira scowled. "I'm tougher than I look and I'm not alone. Jeremy supports me and his friends support him. They'll help you too."

Why would no one understand how dangerous Mark was? Or maybe she feared him because she'd been fearing him for years. Perhaps his reach wasn't as far as she believed. How she wanted to latch onto Zamira and hold on.

Zamira stepped closer, wrapped her arm around Alyse's shoulders. "You're not alone anymore."

The softly spoken words broke Alyse, and she turned into Zamira's arms and sobbed.

***

Physical pain stabbed Alyse every time she sobbed. She fought to stop, swallowing hard, breathing slowly and shallowly. Zamira rubbed her back and the comforting touch made Alyse sob harder. She stepped away, held up a hand for Zamira to give her a minute. As she regained control, embarrassment flooded her. She wiped her face with the back of her hand and sniffed. "Sorry."

"Don't be." Zamira moved closer. "You look like you're in pain. Have you seen a doctor?"

"I was going today."

"Let me take you. Jeremy's at home and I can use his ute."

She was tempted. It would be far easier if she didn't have to drive herself. "Shouldn't you both be at work?"

Zamira smiled. "I don't start until next week, so Jeremy cleared his schedule to help me settle in."

Guilt hit her. Zamira probably didn't even know her way around town. She should be spending time with her partner, not trying to help someone as pathetic as Alyse. "I'll be fine. I can drive myself."

"Don't be silly. You're in no state. I'll take Fetch home and then pick you up."

Fetch had finished exploring the overgrown garden and sat by Zamira's feet.

If Zamira left, it would give Alyse time to go. That way running into Mark or any of his friends in town wouldn't be an issue. No way was he at his mother's. The phone call had to have been business related. She nodded at Zamira and walked with her towards the main drive.

Zamira frowned. "On second thoughts, I might get Jeremy to bring the ute over. It will be quicker. You need decent painkillers." She phoned Jeremy.

Alyse's shoulders slumped. Arguing was exhausting. If Zamira wanted to help, she'd let her this once. And if they went straight to the doctor, hopefully no one would see them together.

When Zamira hung up, Alyse said, "I'll get my keys."

She didn't ask Zamira into the house. Didn't want anyone to see the masculine hell-hole it had become. She retrieved her keys and bag and by the time she returned, Jeremy was driving into her property. He waved as he got out. "Hey, Alyse. How's things?"

"Fine."

Fetch trotted to his owner and Jeremy ruffled his head. As Alyse moved towards the ute, he asked, "You still got your van?"

"Yeah."

"Might be better if you take that," he said. "A friend cracked his ribs a few years ago and he said getting into cars was far harder than into something bigger like a van or four-wheel drive."

Good idea. She'd had to use Mark's ute yesterday because he refused to be seen in something with the apiary advertising on the side. She glanced at Zamira. "You OK driving a van?"

She nodded.

Jeremy walked them to the shed. "Need me to come with you?" He towered over her, boxing her in against the van. She recoiled. He was as big as Mark. "No." She forced a smile. "Thanks for the offer." She handed Zamira the keys and slipped past him to the passenger seat. He was right. Getting in was a lot easier.

As Zamira drove, Alyse asked, "How did you and Jeremy meet?"

Zamira pursed her lips. "How much do you know about what happened at Henk's?"

"Only that he was arrested for something to do with migrants."

She nodded. "My cousin was one of those migrants," she said. "After the dormitory burned down, she called me and I came to Blackbridge to find her. I went to Jeremy's place by mistake and then I kept bumping into him. He agreed to help me find my cousin and prove what Henk was doing was illegal."

"You must have made an impression on him."

Zamira blushed. "The feeling was mutual. I was so comfortable with him and I couldn't help falling in love."

Comfortable. It wasn't a word she associated with being in love, but it made sense. Why would you want to spend a lifetime with someone who made you nervous, or where you couldn't be yourself? She'd always been comfortable with Kim.

Zamira parked at the hospital. "Is Fleur back from her honeymoon yet?"

"I don't know." She wasn't up to date with the current news in town. But she should be at Mark's doctor not here.

Screw Mark. The doctor would send her to the hospital for x-rays anyway, so she was saving herself a trip. They walked into the emergency room. "What can I help you with?" the triage nurse, Tim asked.

"I'm worried my ribs are broken."

"All right, let me get some details and I'll take you through." Tim recorded Alyse's information and then took Alyse and Zamira out the back to an examination cubicle. A child lay on one of the other beds in the room, a sling on his arm. The child's mother sat next to the bed.

Poor cherub.

Tim closed the curtain to give them some privacy and then asked, "What happened?"

Alyse's throat closed over. Now she was here, it was difficult to form the words. Would the hospital report it? Zamira squeezed her hand.

She'd come this far.

"My partner was jealous on Saturday night. He punched

me multiple times and when I fell on the ground, he kicked me." She pulled up her jacket to show the purpling bruises on her stomach and chest.

Tim hissed out a breath. "Let me get the doctor." He left the cubicle and Zamira sat next to her. "Do you have much work over the next few weeks?"

"I need to make new equipment and investigate the spring hive sites, make sure there are no issues there."

"What kind of issues?"

Her shoulders relaxed. Talking about her bees was better than anticipating the doctor's reaction. "Ants are the worst. Sometimes they take over an area, so I need to switch sites. Then I check none of the plants have grown so high that they'll affect the hives."

"How often do you move them?"

"A few times a year. They need to be near where the plants are flowering. The bees only travel about five kilometres from the hive."

Tim arrived back with the doctor. She gently prodded the area and Alyse grimaced at the pain.

"I'll get you some pain meds, but first we need to do an x-ray," the doctor said. "I can get you a wheelchair, but it might be easier for you to walk."

"I can walk."

"Tim will take you through."

Alyse followed Tim into the x-ray room where they met the radiographer. When the scans were done, they returned to the cubicle.

"I'll get the doctor." Tim walked away.

"Do you want to get a coffee after this?" Zamira asked.

Alyse's phone rang. Mark. It was as if he had a sixth sense for when she was disobeying him. Did he know where she was? She swallowed and then answered.

"Why haven't you been to the doctor yet?" he demanded. "I told him you'd be right there. He's waiting for you.”

Relief filled her. He didn't know. “Sorry,” she said. “I got distracted. I'll call and tell him I won't be long.” But she couldn't get coffee with Zamira. It would be too dangerous for them both.

“Do that. He's doing you a favour.” Mark hung up.

She returned her phone to her pocket.

“Mark?” Zamira guessed.

“Yeah. He told me to go to the family doctor to get pain medication. Can you take me there when we're done?”

“Why?”

Alyse lowered her voice. “Mark won't like that I came here.” She gestured to her stomach. “It's not worth angering him.”

Realisation crossed Zamira's face. “Of course.”

The doctor returned.

“There's some nasty bruising, but your ribs aren't cracked, and there are no internal injuries,” she said. “I'll give you some pills for the pain, but there's nothing else I can do. Do you need a doctor's certificate for work?”

“I work for myself.” She took the prescription the doctor handed her.

“I understand your partner did this to you,” the doctor said.

Alyse nodded.

“You should report it to the police.” She handed Alyse some brochures for domestic violence help centres. “Do you want me to call them?”

“No.” Not yet.

The doctor looked like she wanted to say more, but then sighed. “You're free to go.”

Alyse followed Zamira back to the van.

“Where to next?” Zamira asked.

“The doctor's surgery on the main street. You can

probably find parking at the bakery. Do you know where that is?"

Zamira nodded. "It's my favourite place."

"Why don't you get a coffee while you wait?" Alyse suggested as they arrived. "I should go in alone."

"All right."

Alyse walked the short distance to the GP, preparing an excuse for being late. The waiting room was half full of retirees and parents with children. The receptionist smiled at her. "Alyse, there you are." She handed Alyse a piece of paper. "Doctor Eriks said to give you this when you came in."

"Does he want to see me?"

"I don't think so. Let me check." The woman called the doctor. "You're fine to go."

Annoyance filled her. She should report the doctor for prescribing drugs because Mark had told him to. Did Mark have something on him? Alyse couldn't imagine Eriks would risk his licence for something this small. She went next door to the pharmacy and filled both prescriptions.

At the bakery, Zamira sat near the large glass windows. A couple of Alyse's former primary school teachers sat at one table and a blonde woman was having coffee with a friend. Yvette. She would mention to Mark that she'd seen Alyse.

Alyse ordered a coffee and bee-sting to take-away and then texted Zamira. *Can't sit with you. Will meet you at the van.*

The woman serving her handed her the pastry in a white box and then disappeared into the kitchen. A moment later she was back to make the coffee. Mai wandered out, her apron covered in flour, drying her hands on a paper towel. "Hi, Alyse. How's things?"

Alyse's heart tugged. The On family were so friendly, they made her yearn to be normal. "Fine."

Zamira stepped up to the counter and Mai grinned.

"Hey, Zamira." She glanced at Alyse. "Have you met Zamira? You're neighbours."

Alyse cringed and nodded. "Briefly." She checked how much longer her coffee would be. Her gaze took in the cafe and Yvette watching her. Damn. She had to get out of here.

"Mai, can I get this to go? I can't quite finish it." Zamira handed her plate with a half-eaten vanilla slice to Mai.

"Sure."

Zamira stood next to Alyse but didn't speak. She must have realised something was wrong.

"Here's your coffee."

Alyse took it and rushed out the door, crashing into someone. Pain ricocheted through her and she dropped the coffee, the lid falling off and splashing over the person in front of her. "I'm so sorry." She squeezed her eyes closed to breathe past the pain then lifted her gaze. Kim. Of course it was. "Are you all right?" She brushed at the coffee staining his white shirt.

He took hold of her hand, stopping her. "Yeah, I'm fine. How are your ribs?"

Agonising, but she couldn't stay here. The longer she stayed, the angrier Mark would be when Yvette reported back to him. Her shoulder blades itched and she longed to glance over her shoulder. Why had she thought she could do this? He had spies everywhere. He would know she was up to something.

Mai opened the door. "Are you two OK?" She spotted Kim's shirt. "Oh, you'd better come in and get cleaned up," she said. "You too, Alyse."

Coffee seeped through the canvas shoes she'd slipped on this morning. Kim pressed his palm to the small of her back and gestured her in front of him. It would be a bigger scene if she refused.

Inside Zamira watched with wide eyes. Alyse didn't acknowledge her as she followed Mai through to the kitchen and out of sight of the public.

"I'm sorry." Alyse gestured to Kim's shirt.

"Don't sweat it." He stripped off the T-shirt and turned to the sink to clean it.

The moisture left Alyse's mouth. Kim's torso was far more toned than she'd expected. His shoulder muscles rippled as he rinsed out the coffee. He must work out somewhere. Maybe he had a home gym.

"I'll get Jodie to make you another coffee," Mai said, dragging Alyse's attention away from Kim.

"Thank you." She retrieved the painkillers from her bag and reviewed the instructions. She could take two now and maybe they'd dull the ache in her ribs.

"Here." Kim handed her a glass of water, his chest still bare.

She avoided looking at him and swallowed the tablets. Someone walked into the bakery and a gust of cold air swept into the kitchen, cooling the room momentarily from the heat of the ovens. Alyse frowned. "Why aren't you wearing a jumper? It's cold outside."

Kim stared at her a moment as if lost for words. He turned to squeeze out his shirt. "Oh, I ah, was doing prep at the restaurant and needed coffee. Didn't realise how cold it was until I was halfway here."

Something in his body language was off. He was lying. Alyse stepped closer to the door. "I'll see you later."

"Aly, wait."

She shook her head. "I'm busy and Mark's mistress is likely taking notes of how long I'm in here."

Kim's eyes widened. "Shit. I was hoping we could have coffee together."

What didn't he understand about Mark's threat? "No. It's too dangerous."

Mai walked in with another coffee. "Here you go. You two have time to chat?"

What was she talking about? Out of the corner of her eye she saw Kim shaking his head. All at once everything clicked. The T-shirt, Kim slightly breathless when she'd crashed into him. "You told him I was here," she said to Mai.

Guilt crossed her face, and she glanced at Kim.

Betrayal ripped through Alyse. Mark wasn't the only one spying on her.

"I asked her to," Kim said. "Mark will get suspicious if Beatrice's Beekeeping Supplies keeps calling you."

"Then don't," she snapped. "I've told you to stay out of this." Anger and relief battled in her stomach. The thought of someone watching out for her shouldn't give her so much hope.

Kim sighed. "Don't be mad. I want to keep you safe."

Fear pierced her. That was always Mark's excuse back when he was kind and charming. Back when she loved him and thought he cared. She whirled on Kim, grimacing as her ribs protested. "Of course I'm mad," she hissed, keeping her voice down so no one outside could hear. "How many spies do you have around town? Adam, or one of your shopkeeper friends?" She'd thought Kim was different, but she wouldn't be fooled by those excuses again. She didn't need anyone to keep her safe. She could do it herself.

"No, it's not like that—"

"It's exactly that." Without another word, she walked out, her heart as sore as her ribs.

Chapter 9

Kim swore as the door shut behind Alyse. He'd royally stuffed that up.

"You didn't mention Mark spies on her when you asked me to do the same." Mai glared at him.

Great. He'd pissed off his sister as well. "I didn't think of it that way."

"Honestly, I would have thought growing up with four sisters would have made you smarter than this."

He hung his damp shirt close to one oven, guilt filling him. She was right. He should have known better. "Do you think she'll forgive me?"

"I don't know."

"I should go after her." He took two steps towards the door, but Mai blocked it.

"No, you shouldn't, especially not half naked. It would only set tongues wagging."

Frustration filled him. "Then what do I do?"

"Give her time. Let her calm down and then ring and apologise. Don't ask her for anything, wait for her to come to you."

"She needs my help."

Mai raised an eyebrow. "She's probably had enough of

men thinking they know what's best for her."

Her words hit him right in the chest and he took a step back. "That's not what I meant."

"I know, little brother, but remember you're dealing with someone who has been traumatised for years." Her smile was sympathetic. "Think of how we have to tiptoe around Eden when she's in a bad mood," she continued. "And then add real trauma to the equation. Stay friendly and supportive. Ask her what she needs, don't tell her."

Kim nodded. He treated his youngest sister Eden like a ticking bomb when she was upset. "I need to placate her?"

"You need to be gentle with her," Mai corrected. She cleared her throat. "I know someone who was sexually assaulted six years ago and she's only now becoming comfortable being alone with men."

Kim frowned. "Who?" He knew all of Mai's friends.

"None of your business. The point I'm making is Alyse needs to be treated carefully, especially if you want to be more than friends with her."

He wanted it, but Alyse wouldn't rush into another relationship. He'd make her understand he'd asked Mai to call him because he cared. He winced. Nope. That sounded creepy too, like he was justifying his inappropriate actions. He sighed. "I'll do better."

"Good. Now put your shirt back on and get out of my kitchen." She waved him towards the door.

"Yes, ma'am." His shirt was still damp, but warm from the ovens. He'd deal. Slipping it on, he ordered a coffee from Jodie. When he stepped outside, the wind turned his shirt into an air-conditioner. Hunching his shoulders and cupping the coffee close to his chest, he strode back to the restaurant.

Alyse was right.

It was freezing today.

***

Alyse stormed to the van where Zamira was waiting and slid into the passenger seat, her heart pounding, fear stiffening her skin. "Are all men controlling jerks?"

Zamira glanced at her. "No." She started the engine. "What happened?"

"Kim happened." She struggled with the seat belt, her hand jerking it too fast and it caught, her chest aching. Letting out a breath, she forced herself to slow down and finally strapped herself in.

"What did he do?"

"He asked Mai to spy on me. He was at the bakery because she called him to tell him I was there."

"Huh. How far away was he?"

Alyse frowned. Odd question. "At the restaurant. It's at the other end of the main street."

"He must have run to get there."

She was right. Did that make it better or worse? "So now I have to worry about two men watching me." Would she ever find someone who didn't want to control her?

"What do you mean?"

"The reason I couldn't sit with you is because Mark's mistress was in the cafe. She'll tell Mark I was there and Mark will be mad."

"Which one was she?"

"The blonde who looked as if she'd stepped out of the pages of a glossy fashion magazine." Although she didn't love Mark anymore, it still stung. She would never be that glamorous. She was comfortable in her white bee suit or jeans.

"I'll keep an eye out for her." Zamira drove out of town. "For what it's worth, I don't think Kim is like Mark."

Alyse glanced at her. "Why?"

Zamira blushed. "Well, the thing is… I know we've just met, so I don't know how you'll take this. Just know it comes from a place of concern and caring."

Alyse's stomach churned. "What does?"

"When we met a month ago, I figured Mark abused you. I wanted to help you then, but I was dealing with saving my cousin, Henk and all of that." She waved her hand. "When Jeremy asked me to move in with him, I hoped we could be friends."

"Because you pitied me?" Alyse stared out the window at the bush rushing past.

"No! Because you were friendly and nice until Mark turned up."

It had felt defiant to invite Zamira into her shed, to give her some honey, to have her there without Mark knowing.

"So, anyway after the Christmas in July dinner, I told Jeremy I would invite you for coffee, and he told me about Kim rescuing you."

A shudder ran through her at the memory.

Zamira took a deep breath. "Then he told me Kim had gone to his house after he'd taken the soup to your place and the guys—Jeremy, Adam, Kim, Elijah and Jamie—had discussed how they could help you and stop Mark, maybe get him arrested."

Alyse closed her eyes. How should she take that? Suddenly these men wanted to help her and they never had before. She shook her head. That wasn't fair. She hadn't been open to help, and still wasn't ready for anyone to face Mark's wrath.

"So my guess is, if Kim has Mai watching for you, it's only because he wants to see you."

She wanted to trust, that's all it was, but it was so close to how Mark behaved when he first showed interest in her, turning up to watch her play basketball, stopping by the markets to buy honey, finding ways to bump into her. "That's a lot of guessing. You don't know Kim."

"No, I don't. But you do. You went to school with him,

didn't you?"

"People change. I'm not the person I was back then." It was too much of a risk to think Kim might care for her. Far easier to stay angry and keep him away. Far safer for him.

"And I'm not the person I was a couple of months ago. But when Jeremy gets demanding, it's because he loves me."

Alyse recoiled. "Kim doesn't love me."

Zamira shrugged. "Maybe not. But from what Jeremy told me, it sounds like Kim remembers your friendship fondly."

Her heart squeezed. It would be too easy to be lulled into thinking she could have friends, convince herself that getting rid of Mark would be easy if she had so much support. But she knew Mark better than that. "Mark isn't someone you should mess with. He'll take it out on you and Kim, as well as me."

"The police are monitoring him now. He won't get away with things easily, particularly if you help them."

"Maybe."

Zamira pulled into Alyse's property. Mark's ute was still gone. Thank God. Alyse winced as she climbed out.

Zamira held her boxed vanilla slice. Alyse hesitated. Could she risk inviting Zamira in? With no car here to tip Mark off if he arrived, there'd be time to hide Zamira or sneak her out the front while Mark came in the back. "Do you want to come in and finish your slice? I can make you a cuppa."

"Sure."

Her muscles tightened as she walked down the hallway, evidence of Mark in every room she passed. When she got rid of him, she was throwing out all of his furniture even if she had to sit on the floor until she could afford her own. She paused as she entered the kitchen. She'd thought when not if. Fear and excitement mixed in equal parts. It was happening. Alyse switched on the kettle. "Can you get the mugs for me?" She gestured to the wall cupboard. After she'd washed the mugs, she'd leave them on the bench top so she could reach them.

Zamira retrieved them and then picked up the handout from Richard's funeral. "He looks familiar. Who is he?"

"Mark's father, Richard Patton."

She frowned. "Why do I know that name?"

"He owned the Vale winery."

Zamira's eyes widened, and she dropped the paper on the table. "He almost drove me off the lookout."

Alyse froze. "That was you?" Mark had mentioned Kay had made her father turn in his driver's licence after an incident almost a month ago.

She nodded, still looking at the photo. "I didn't actually see him though, so I'm not sure why I recognise him. Maybe it was at the Vale."

An uneasy sensation swirled in Alyse's stomach as she recalled what the Patton siblings had said yesterday. Was Zamira's incident not an accident? She'd been investigating Henk's operation, and Henk had run to Mark when the police had raided. The Pattons protected their own.

She placed the tea on the table in front of Zamira.

"So what do you do for fun?" Zamira asked. "Are you part of the vintage motocross club?"

"No." When was the last time she did anything for fun? "My bees keep me busy."

"You must enjoy it."

"Yeah, I do. I used to love hanging out with Dad at the hives and letting the bees crawl over my hands. They're beautiful." Her heart clenched. She tried not to think of those days.

"It sounds amazing."

"I'll show you around when my bruises have healed."

The frames of honey would be too heavy for her to lift at the moment.

"Thanks. I'm looking forward to getting to know Blackbridge. I've never lived in the country before. I can't wait for summer when I can go swimming every day."

"Green's Pool is a nice spot. It's sheltered from the waves." Not too deep and not too rough. It was all she could handle since the accident.

"Jeremy tells me you get a lot of whales around here too. I'd love to go whale-watching."

"They're amazing creatures." They used to see them when they were on the boat. She sipped her tea. She missed those carefree days. Her mother would pack a thermos of tea or coffee, some soft drinks and freshly made sandwiches for lunch. And there was always some kind of home-made biscuit or slice.

The ocean used to give her such joy. If she hadn't grown up on the apiary, she might have become a marine biologist.

Zamira's hand covered hers. "Are you all right?"

Alyse gave her a small smile. "Just remembering going on the boat with my parents."

"You can't go out anymore?"

Alyse figured Jeremy had told her what had happened. "No. I can't. It terrifies me."

"Have you ever seen a therapist?"

"No." Mark hadn't believed in them and she'd been too traumatised to insist.

"Do you want to go out on the ocean?" Zamira shrugged. "You seem like you miss it."

"Maybe." One thing at a time. She had to get rid of Mark first. She caught sight of the time. Damn. Mark might be home soon. She collected the empty mugs.

"Can I help you with anything?" Zamira asked. "Anything else you need me to get down for you?"

Alyse thought about it. "No, I'll be fine. I need to get to work."

"Of course."

Alyse walked her out. "Thank you for taking me to the doctor." She hesitated. "And for caring."

She smiled. "You're welcome. We're all here to help. Don't let your fear stop you from reaching out."

Alyse waved. Was Zamira right? Could Mark actually target all the people who helped her? No, he'd focus on the ones he was aware of—Kim and Zamira. Caution was required. Zamira walked past the hives to the firebreak at the back of the property. Alyse glanced at the house. Should she risk going back into Mark's office now?

Her skin prickled. No. He could turn up at any time and she'd have to explain what she was doing in the house rather than working in the shed. He was already suspicious.

Tomorrow was soon enough.

Chapter 10

As Alyse strode back to the house in the evening, she scanned her property. No ute. She hadn't heard a car, so it probably meant Mark wasn't back. Still, after she'd walked inside she called, "Mark?" She went through the house, room by room, in case he hadn't heard.

Empty.

In the kitchen she swallowed two of her painkillers. The rough ground in the national park hadn't been easy on her bruised ribs, but at least the site didn't need any work. She'd be able to move her hives there in another couple of weeks.

All afternoon her mind had played through Zamira's words. She had support, and the police were watching Mark. Though she was still scared, the idea of people willing to stand up for her and protect her from Mark comforted her. Then there was something she hadn't considered in years, something Mark might actually approve of, something she could do with his blessing. Maybe she could overcome her fear of boats. A therapist was out of the question, but there were other options.

The memory of those happy days had been so strong, had awakened such a longing in her. It wouldn't be easy, but she wanted to try, to give the joy and freedom of the ocean back to herself.

But first she had to make dinner before Mark returned.

She assembled the makings for cottage pie. Warm and filling—comfort food was what she needed today. She reached for a potato and remembered Kim. Had she overreacted at the bakery?

He had said he wanted to help her. Perhaps his good intentions were a little off. Should she call him?

She set the potatoes on to boil and then worked on the filling. Her mother had taught her this very recipe, which had been her grandmother's. Strange that her parents were on her mind so much lately. They would be pleased she was finally doing something about Mark.

She mashed the potatoes and finished assembling the pie, placing it in the oven for the top to crisp. Then she fetched her laptop from her room. Time to research her fear.

About half an hour later, her phone rang. She tensed. Beatrice's Beekeeping Supplies. What should she say to him? "Hey."

"I'm sorry about today," Kim blurted. "I was way out of line. I didn't see it from your perspective, I only wanted to catch up with you. I didn't mean to be like Mark. I *never* want to be like him."

The heartfelt apology warmed her heart, but, "It freaked me out."

"I get that now." He huffed. "Mai pointed it out to me. She wasn't impressed."

Alyse smiled. It had been clear when they were teenagers that Kim was close to his sisters, even if he complained about them. She'd envied him, had always wanted to have siblings. "She agreed to call you."

"Yeah, but she didn't realise Mark spied on you."

"Few people do." She wandered through the house, peering out the windows to ensure she hadn't missed Mark coming home. The wind was noisy.

"Will you forgive me?" The hope in his voice cut through her.

She wanted to. She wanted to trust him and believe they could be friends again. "As long as you're upfront with me in future," she said. "I can't deal with you doing things behind my back."

He was silent a moment. "OK. I should tell you about the session I had with my friends the other day. They all agreed they'd keep an eye on you."

Pleasure filled her that he was admitting to what Zamira had told her. "Which friends?"

"Jeremy, Adam, Jamie and Elijah. Elijah was still angry about the way Mark hit you after he fell off the roof."

Although Elijah had been kind, they were all still men. On one hand it was comforting because they had the physical strength to challenge Mark, but that same strength could be a threat to her. "What about Zamira?"

"Yeah, she's in too. So are the musketeers." He paused, cleared his throat. "We kind of met after the funeral to talk about how we could help you. Mai and her friends, and their partners want to help too."

"Did you warn them about Mark? They need to understand the danger."

"They do. But you can call any of them if you need help."

She would call the police before she'd put his friends in danger. She returned to the kitchen, and the laptop caught her eye. Perhaps Kim could help her in one area of her life—if they could keep it secret. Her stomach swirled and her throat closed over, but she said, "There is something you can help me with."

"Sure. Anything."

She closed her eyes. He was so willing, so eager. "Do you know how to kayak?"

"Yeah. We used to hire the kayaks down on the river on the holidays. Why?"

She breathed out. "I've been reading about my fear of boats. They suggest finding sheltered, shallow water and starting small. I thought if you're free one day, we could hire one of those kayaks, test it out." A chill ran through her body at the suggestion. No. She could do this. If they went to a stretch of the river out of town, Mark would never know.

"Absolutely. Tell me when and I'll be there."

His immediate agreement gave her confidence. "It depends on Mark."

An annoyed grunt. "We could turn the tables on Mark," Kim said. "Get people in town to monitor him and tell you where he is."

The idea had merit. It would give her freedom to go through his office without worrying he would catch her. "Who? Mark's involved with lots of people and the town is loyal to his family. Could we trust anyone?"

"All the guys plus my sisters and Mai's friends. Between them, we'd get a good coverage."

"All right. Thank you." The front door slammed. Her heart leapt. "Mark's home. I'll talk later." She hung up, tucked her phone into her pocket just before Mark strode into the kitchen. He had wet hair, mud smeared all over his clothes and he traipsed mud over her floorboards. She didn't say a word.

"You made dinner?"

She nodded. "It's in the oven. I've already eaten."

He dished up some pie and sat at the table across from her. "What are you doing?"

No reason to keep it a secret. "Searching for ways to conquer my fear of boats. Friday was a nightmare and I don't want to disappoint you again."

He grunted. "Good. About time you got over it."

She bit her tongue to stop snapping at him. Instead she asked, "How's your mother?"

"Grieving. She doesn't want to get rid of Dad's stuff yet."

Of course not. He'd been dead for less than a fortnight. "Some people need time to process. He hasn't been gone long."

"They're things. They're not bringing him back." His voice was rough.

"No, but they remind her of him." She'd tried to explain it when her parents had died but he hadn't comprehended. She clicked on the next website link.

"What did you do today?"

Surprised, she looked up. He never asked about her day unless he wanted to catch her out. Yvette. "I went to the doctor, got some painkillers for my ribs."

"They broken?"

She opened her mouth to tell him no, then remembered Doctor Eriks hadn't seen her. "I don't know. I picked up the prescription from the receptionist."

"Then what did you do?"

Yep. Definitely testing her. "I stopped for coffee." She told him about running into Kim. "Then I checked the spring hive locations."

Mark said nothing.

She scanned the next article, most of her focus on waiting for Mark's response.

"It's tax time," he said. "I'm going to the accountant in Albany on Friday."

She tensed. Had he discovered she'd downloaded a copy of the file? Forcing a smile, she said, "All right. What time?"

"Three. You should come with me."

Alyse leaned back. "Why?"

He stared at her, anger tinging his tone. "So you can see the mess the business is in."

"Of course." No point arguing if her finances were a mess, it was his fault. "I'll add it to my calendar."

He grunted and pushed back his chair. "I'm going to watch TV." He left the room, leaving his dirty plate on the table.

Her fear screamed at her to run, that Mark knew what she'd done and would make her pay. Taking slow breaths, she pushed the thoughts away. Don't panic. He couldn't know.

But perhaps in the morning she'd call Olivia and explain the urgency.

No, Mark might check her phone. She had to be patient. She could ask Kim to contact Olivia the next time she spoke to him.

And hope it wasn't too late.

***

Kim sliced through the raw chicken to go into the pho, his thoughts on Alyse's request. Overcoming her fear wouldn't be easy. He'd read about it last night and there was no single solution. It would be trial and error.

"Why are you so deep in thought?"

At his father's voice, Kim jumped and looked up from the table. "What?"

Anh chuckled. "You've been staring at the meat for the past five minutes. It won't chop itself."

"Sorry." He started slicing again. It was just the two of them in the restaurant's kitchen, preparing for lunch hour.

"You thinking about your design business?"

"No. I don't have any work at the moment."

His father sighed. "Then you should give it more attention," he said. "I enjoy your company here, but you're wasting your talent."

Kim smiled. "Thanks, Dad, but that's not what I'm thinking about."

"What then?"

His dad might have some advice. He had spent time with Alyse at the markets. "Do you remember Alyse Wilson?"

He frowned. "Of course. Tragic what happened to her family. She was a sweet girl. You had a crush on her, didn't you?"

He nodded, not surprised his father knew, although Kim had never said anything to him.

"What about her?"

"I caught up with her the other day—rescued her when their boat engine failed."

"How is she? Wasn't she with one of the Pattons?"

"Yeah, Mark. He hits her."

His father stopped making dumplings and gave Kim his attention. "What?"

"He's an asshole."

"You look like you're planning on doing something about it."

"She needs help, even if she doesn't want it."

His father pursed his lips. "Does she say she doesn't want help?"

"Yeah. She's scared of what Mark might do to anyone who helps her."

"He sounds like a bully."

And neither of his parents liked bullies. They'd immigrated to Australia in the eighties to escape that kind of treatment. "He is. I told her I'd call her if he came into the restaurant." He wrote Alyse's phone number on the white board on the wall. "And tell her when he left. Will you keep an eye out for him?"

"You might need to remind me what he looks like."

Kim transferred the sliced chicken back into the fridge. His phone rang and he washed his hands before answering. Alyse. "Beatrice's Beekeeping Supplies."

Her laugh made him smile. "Mark's gone to his mother's. Do you have time to hire a kayak for an hour?"

Kim checked the time. Another hour before the restaurant opened. He might be a little late, but one of his sisters would cover for him. "Sure. Do you want to meet me down there, or should I hire it and meet you somewhere along the river?"

She paused. "How about by the SES depot?"

"Sounds good. I'll see you soon." He hung up and dialled his sister, Eden. "Edie, I need a solid favour."

Her annoyed hiss made him roll his eyes. "What is it?"

"I need you to come to the restaurant and help Dad for an hour."

"Now?" she whined.

"Right now." He turned to face his father who was waiting for an explanation.

"What's in it for me?"

He took a second to control his temper before answering. His youngest sister was also the most spoilt. "You'll make me happy."

"You're always happy."

Annoyance prickled his skin. "I have a friend who needs my help, so get off your lazy ass and get here now."

She gasped. "All right. I'll be there soon."

He hung up. "Alyse wants to work on her fear of boats and asked me to kayak with her. But she can only do it when Mark's away."

"Why?"

"Because he's jealous of me."

Anh glanced at him. "Does he have a reason to be?"

"She's a friend."

"But you'd prefer she was more than that?"

No putting anything past his father. "Yeah, but Alyse doesn't need that now."

"I'm glad you realise." He gestured for the door. "You'd better not wait for Eden to arrive or you'll be late. I'll call her to hurry up if I need to."

"Thanks, Dad." He hugged him, then grabbed his jacket and dashed out the door.

It took very little time to hire the kayak and paddle upstream close to the SES depot. Eucalypts covered the sloped banks, but there was a small sandbar Alyse could use to get into the kayak. Kim checked the time. She should be here by now. Had something gone wrong?

The grumble of a car made him glance towards the street. A few moments later, Alyse walked through the bush towards him.

He'd never known anyone to look as comfortable and yet stylish in jeans and work boots. Her beautiful rich red hair was tied back in a low ponytail and she wore a black jacket with her apiary's logo on it. Her smile was a little unsure as she reached the edge of the bank.

"Hey, Aly." He handed her a life jacket.

She examined it before slipping it on and tightening the straps. "Thank you."

"Are you ready for this?" She looked like she would bolt at any minute.

Alyse shook her head, her hands clenched.

He wasn't certain how to help her. "Tell me what you fear, is it the boat or the water?"

"The boat." She lifted her eyes from staring at the kayak to look at him. "The river's not deep enough to worry me."

"What about the boat scares you—that it'll sink?"

She was quiet for a long moment. "That it will trap me."

Hell. Her father had been caught on something in the boat which prevented him from getting free. Kim examined the plastic kayak. "Well everything here is open," he said. "If we tip, it's light enough for us to lift. We can stand on the bottom of the river and only be chest deep." He glanced at the tea coloured water below him. "Do you want me to demonstrate?" He should have left his shoes back at the car.

"No." Alyse swallowed hard. "Logically I understand everything you're telling me, but the fear grips me right here." She wrapped her arms around her chest and winced.

He pulled the kayak further onto the sand bank. "Why don't you sit in it while it's out of the water—get used to it?"

Her steps were small as she shuffled onto the sandbank. She ran her hand along the bow, but every other muscle in her body was tense. Kim said nothing, waiting for her to be ready to take the next step. Fear filled her eyes. He wanted to wrap her in his arms and soothe her.

Not going to happen. He climbed into the stern of the kayak.

She lowered herself into the bow like it was a chair, wincing a little, her breath fast.

"I'm right here, Aly. I've got the skills and experience to rescue you if needed."

Slowly she slid towards him and settled on the seat in front. The boat rocked a little and she gasped, her hands gripping the sides.

Kim placed a hand on her back. "It's all right. Stay still, let it settle." When the rocking stopped he asked, "Shall we sit here a little longer?"

"Yeah."

"OK. Tell me when you're ready." He rubbed circles on her back, hoping it would help. She should have addressed her fear years ago, but he would almost guarantee Mark had told her to get over it.

A kookaburra laughed in the tree next to them.

"It's not funny," Alyse said.

Kim chuckled, pleased at the annoyance in her tone.

Finally, she said, "Can you push off?"

"Yep. You tell me what you need me to do." He pushed the paddle into the bank and pushed off the sand bar. The kayak glided into the centre of the river. He stroked through the water, the paddles dipping under the calm surface. Alyse's white knuckles clung to the sides of the boat.

Maybe something on the shore would distract her. "There's another kookaburra in the tree on your left." He pointed with his paddle and her chin lifted.

A splash in front of them and her gaze moved to the river. The water was clear down to the bottom where a few twigs and leaves lay. "Do you still go fishing?"

She shook her head. "Boats, remember?"

"What about in the river or off the shore? I've heard there are some nice sized trout along here."

"It never occurred to me." Her voice had lost some shakiness.

"We could go together."

She turned her head to the side and her fingers relaxed a little on the edges. "You never liked fishing."

A rush of pleasure swept through him that she remembered. "I can go with you. It might help to be around water more."

Her lips quirked up. "Thank you."

The river curved up ahead and the paperbarks overhung its edges. He inhaled deeply. It had been a long time since he'd hired a kayak. He'd forgotten how peaceful it was. "It's so quiet." No man-made noises around them, just a soft hum of some insects and the occasional chirp of a bird. They were out of town now and on one side of the shore were open fields with cows grazing.

"Oh, look, a blue wren!" Alyse pointed.

Kim grinned. She was so enchanted by the bird, she didn't seem to realise she no longer held onto the kayak. "Their colours are brilliant at this time of year."

"Yeah, I saw a few yesterday when I was checking my spring hive locations."

"By yourself?"

She glanced at him. "Of course."

"But you're injured. Shouldn't someone be helping you?"

"Who, Mark?" She laughed. "Not a chance. Besides I was simply examining the sites, seeing if there were any issues which had to be fixed before I move the hives."

"I'll help you if you need it." With Eden and Sarah on winter break from university, he had a little more flexibility around work.

"I'm fine. I do it on my own all the time." A brief touch of sadness crossed her face before she turned back around.

Maybe she hadn't even realised she'd moved. Good. "I'm going to head back down river."

Her body stiffened and then relaxed. "OK. Should I paddle?"

"If you want."

She picked up the extra paddle and set it across her lap. As Kim started to turn them, she joined in, stroking into the water in time with him. With her help, they returned to the little sand bar. "Do you want to continue?"

"I don't want to go further into town." She steered them towards the sand bar and the kayak rubbed against the shore. She huffed and carefully climbed out.

Kim wasn't ready for her to go. "How was it?"

A slight wobble to her smile. "Lovely. Better than I'd expected. Thank you."

"We can go again tomorrow, or try a dinghy along the

river."

She stepped back, hugged her arms around herself. "Sorry. Too fast?"

"A little. Plus I don't know what Mark will be doing."

He smiled, keeping his annoyance at Mark off his face. "Call me when you're ready."

"All right." She climbed the bank, then turned back to him, clasping and unclasping her hands. "Kim, I don't know how to thank you. This means a lot to me."

"You don't have to thank me. I want you to conquer your fear as much as you do."

She hesitated and then said, "It's not just this. It's everything."

"You're my friend, Aly. That's what friends do."

Her eyes widened and then she gave a small nod. "I'll see you later."

Kim watched until she was out of sight. He let out a breath. She was beginning to trust him. He could be happy with that.

He pushed off the bank again and headed back to town.

Chapter 11

Alyse drove out of town, heading for one of her hive sites, her spirit lighter than it had been in ages. She'd done it! She'd stepped onto a boat and not had a panic attack. The urge to sing in celebration was strong. It hadn't been easy moving past her initial fear, but with Kim there, and the river so tranquil, she'd enjoyed it.

Switching on the radio, she turned the volume up loud, singing along to a popular song.

This was what freedom felt like.

Kim had been so patient with her, so understanding. He'd not mocked or yelled at her.

He wasn't Mark.

No, he was a far better man than Mark. His continued defence of her and then his offer to help her again... it boggled her mind. They'd chatted as easily as they had sitting side-by-side at the markets all those years ago.

She drove into Kit Zanetti's property. Kit had allowed Alyse's parents to set up some hives on her land, and in return Alyse supplied her with honey throughout the year. She drove past the dairy as Elijah walked out of the machinery shed. In the past she'd wave and keep driving, but today she pulled up and wound down her window. "Hey. Can you tell Kit I'm checking the hives?" She'd emailed Kit last week to tell her.

"Sure. Do you need a hand?"

The easy offer surprised her. "No. I'm right."

"How are the ribs?"

"Still sore, but I've got good painkillers."

"Good." He tilted his head. "You look different today. Have you done something with your hair?"

She shook her head. "I can't lift my arms far enough to do more than tie it in a low ponytail."

"Maybe it's not that." Elijah shrugged. "You look happier."

The words struck her hard in the chest. "I am."

His grin was wide. "I'm glad. Listen, if you want help, call me." When she took out her phone, he gave her his number. "I'll be fixing fences, so any interruption is welcome."

She laughed. "Will do." She waved and drove off.

Elijah was being so nice to her, despite how rude she'd been to him the night of the storm. She'd been embarrassed the whole SES team had seen Mark hit her, figured they were all talking about her, asking why she didn't leave him, not understanding it wasn't so easy.

She frowned. Should she have saved Elijah's number? If Mark questioned it, she'd tell him Kit asked her to call Elijah about anything related to her hives. It was a decent excuse.

The van bumped over the dirt track and her hives came into sight. A couple hadn't done so well over the summer so it might be time to get them a new queen bee if the worker bees didn't kick her out themselves. One thing she loved about the insects was everyone pulled their weight. If you didn't perform, you were out, and it didn't matter if you were the queen. It was a society where everyone understood their role and its success relied on the many not the few. Unlike her, the bees had a community. It was a reason she'd been so powerless for such a long time. She'd been alone, isolated by a hostile man, but now she was building a hive of her own. Not that she was queen bee, but she had people around her, wanting to do their part. It strengthened her.

She parked and checked the hives for anything amiss. It was easy work and the cooler weather meant most of the bees were inside staying warm. Nearby some grevillea still flowered, so she donned her beekeeping suit, and then retrieved the smoker from the back of the van. She was running low on pine needles, so she'd stop on her way home and fill her bucket from the nearby pine plantation. It took very little time to add the needles to the smoker and light it, puffing air until white smoke appeared. She inhaled the soothing pine scent and smiled.

A couple of puffs at the entrance to the hive and then she lifted the lid and puffed some more smoke inside. The gentle buzzing was music to her ears. She placed the lid on the ground and examined the hive. The frames were full of honey. Using her hive tool, she tried to lift one frame and her ribs pulled. Nope. She wouldn't be able to do this herself and she couldn't leave the frames full. She hesitated for a second and then called Elijah.

"Please tell me you need my help," Elijah said as he answered.

Alyse laughed. "Yes, please. The frames are full and I can't lift them with my ribs hurting."

"I'll be right there."

Alyse took her suit off so Elijah could wear it when he arrived. The rest of the things she needed were in her van, but she'd get him to get them out.

A couple of bees buzzed around her, curious but not attacking. They had a home to guard, a queen to protect, but she wasn't a threat to them. What would it be like to live in a home with no threats, where she didn't have to consider how every word could be misconstrued? She'd taken her life, her safety, her home for granted before her parents had died.

She wouldn't take them for granted ever again.

It was mid-afternoon by the time she returned home. Mark's ute wasn't there. By the time she'd filtered the honey she and Elijah had extracted from the hives and filled her jars, evening had fallen. She walked to the house. Mark still wasn't back. She could see whether Olivia had emailed her and there was plenty of leftover cottage pie for dinner.

After locking the door, she switched on her laptop and put some pie in the microwave to heat.

The evening was quiet, so she should hear Mark returning home. Still, her skin prickled as she logged into her webmail, holding her breath for an answer.

There it was. An email from Olivia. She clicked and waited for it to load.

The email was short, to the point. *Please call me about your accounts. There are some things we need to discuss.*

Using her mobile was out of the question because Mark regularly checked it and Alyse hadn't had a land line in years. There wasn't a pay phone in Blackbridge. She'd have to borrow a phone.

Frustration itched at her. She didn't want to wait. Olivia had given her mobile number, so even if she'd gone home, she still might answer.

The growl of an engine made her dash to the window. Mark. Damn it. She shut the webmail, got her dinner out of the microwave and retrieved her e-reader from the bench. By the time Mark stomped in, she was engrossed in the romantic suspense she was reading. Still she looked up. "How's your Mum?"

"She's fine. I'm going out tonight."

It was always a guess whether he wanted her to ask for details. "All right."

"Don't you want to know where?"

Not really. "If you'd like to tell me."

"I'm going out with Yvette."

Good. "Have fun."

He growled. "Don't you care that I'm fucking someone else?"

Not if it meant he wasn't forcing himself on her. "No, because you'll do what you want no matter what I say."

His eyes widened, and she bit her lip. Usually she was pliant and agreeable. But after her success on the kayak today, she was tired of being weak.

"What's got into you?"

Standing up for herself would only make him suspicious. She sighed. "Sorry, I've had a bad day. Some of the hives have an ant problem," she lied.

"Want me to look at them tomorrow?"

Her mouth dropped open. What? He never offered to help. "No, I fixed it."

"Fine. I'm going to shower."

Alyse stared after him. Why the concern all of a sudden? It was reminiscent of what he'd been like when they'd first started dating. Her skin crawled. This was a new level of unpredictability. Would he want to sleep with her again? Please, God, no. She had to act normally, watch her words and call the accountant as soon as possible.

She had to get him out of her house.

***

Half an hour later Mark had showered and left the house smelling like expensive, but overly strong aftershave. Alyse stood at the window, watching his taillights disappear. She longed to get into her van and drive somewhere to call Olivia, but Mark might be faking. Instead she showered, dressed in warm clothing and then checked the house again to ensure Mark hadn't returned while she'd been in the shower.

Clear.

Now was a good time to go through his office for evidence. She'd love to take a copy of the data on his laptop but it was above her skill level. Her phone rang. Kim. She smiled. "Hi."

"Hey. Mark just arrived at the restaurant. He's having dinner."

Her heart jumped. "Is Yvette with him?"

"Yeah."

"Great." He'd be at least an hour. This was her chance. "Is Zamira home? I need to call the accountant but I can't use this phone."

"I'll phone Jeremy. If you don't hear from me, it means they're waiting for you. I don't want to call you too many times."

Sensible. "All right. Can you tell me when Mark leaves?"

"Yeah."

She smiled. "Thanks, Kim."

"My pleasure." He hung up.

Alyse grabbed her laptop and keys and hurried out the door. No time to waste. She'd walk over via the fire break just in case Mark arrived back before she did. She could pretend she was working in the shed.

Heart beating fast, she hurried across the back of her property and onto the grey sandy fire break which ran behind all of their properties. When she arrived at Jeremy's, the back floodlight lit her way, and Zamira and Jeremy sat on the back verandah waiting for her. Jeremy's beautiful wooden cabin had the feel of a home.

Relief filled her and her chest tightened. "Thank you," she called as she trotted up the steps.

"You're welcome." Zamira wrapped an arm around her shoulder and handed her a phone. "Come in, it's cold out here."

Alyse smiled at Jeremy. "Can I connect to your internet?"

"I'll get the password," he replied.

While he fetched it, Alyse called the accountant.

"Hello?"

"Olivia. this is Alyse Wilson. I'm sorry for calling so late, but you asked me to ring."

"Yes. Hang on a moment." Muffled voices and then she came back on the line. "There are a lot of inconsistencies in your accounts, Alyse. Large sums of money have been transferred and the companies don't appear to be legitimate."

She grinned. "Can they be traced?"

"I'm sure someone with more skills in the area could," she said. "Whoever has been doing your accounts has been stealing from the business. Your profit margins should be a lot bigger than they are."

Though she suspected it, it galled her to think Mark was also stealing from her. Didn't he make enough from whatever he was doing illegally? "Is there enough evidence to go to the police?"

"More than enough."

"If I give you an email address, could you send all the details you have to it as well?"

"Sure."

Alyse covered the phone with her hand and said to Zamira, "Can I have your email?"

Zamira told her and she repeated it to Olivia.

"I'll send it right now."

"Thank you so much."

"You're welcome. Let me know how you get on."

She hung up.

"What did she say?" Zamira asked as she switched on her laptop.

"My accounts are a mess and Mark's been stealing from me." She hugged herself. "Olivia's emailing us both the information."

"Why?" Jeremy asked.

"Mark monitors my laptop," she said. "I'll have to keep the documents in my webmail account, but if Zamira has it too, she can send it to the police for me." She winced. "I hope it's all right."

"It's fine." Zamira turned her laptop around for Alyse. "Take a seat and go through it. Would you like some tea?"

Her stomach was in too many knots. "Maybe a glass of water?"

Jeremy went to get it and Zamira sat next to her at the table. Alyse skipped the accounts file and clicked on the report Olivia had written. It was comprehensive, pointing out several inconsistencies and errors. Mark swore he went to his own accountant each year, but perhaps he paid him to fudge the numbers.

This was it. She'd been determined to hand the file to the police when she had some proof, not caring if she went to jail, but the loss would be so much greater now she'd made connections with people in town. If only she knew how incriminating the documents were.

Jeremy placed the water in front of her. "So what's next?"

Alyse was silent for a long moment. No, she was far safer with Mark completely out of her life.

"Can the police arrest him?" Zamira asked.

"I hope so." They deserved the truth. "But I might be arrested too."

"What?"

"Right after my parents died, Mark had me sign a few things. I didn't bother reading them, because I trusted him." She clenched her hands. "When I first tried to leave him, he told me I'd go to jail if I ever turned him in, because he'd tied me up in what he was doing."

Zamira scowled. "What were the documents?"

"Some kind of contracts and Mark keeps them locked in his office." She sighed. "Kim thinks the police might give me immunity, but I'm not sure." Stupidity wasn't a good defence.

"You should ask," Jeremy said. "Lincoln's a good guy. I can call him."

She hesitated. It had to be done at some stage. "Please."

Jeremy made the call and Alyse sipped her water, her hand shaking. Zamira squeezed her other hand. "Things will work out."

She hoped so.

Jeremy hung up. "He's making some calls."

So she had to wait. Her breath was shaky as she exhaled. "Thank you."

Jeremy's phone rang. Concern crossed his face, and he glanced at her. "I'll tell her." He hung up.

"What is it?"

"That was Kim. Mark left the restaurant while Kim was serving a customer."

Her heart leapt as she pushed back her chair. "I have to go." It was a ten-minute drive from town.

"Why don't you stay here?" Zamira asked. "If you've got the proof, there's no need to go back to him."

"If he suspects anything, he'll get rid of evidence and it will be my word against his." All of a sudden the conversation with Troy at the Christmas fundraiser made sense. "He's been telling people I'm bi-polar." What other lies had he told to make her seem unreliable?

"It's not safe for you there," Zamira said.

"I'll be fine. I'm not abandoning my home to him." She grabbed her laptop off the table.

"Do you want me to drive you back?" Jeremy asked.

She shook her head. If Mark caught her getting out of

Jeremy's car it would be far worse. "I'll walk. Thank you for your help."

"I'll let you know what Lincoln says," Jeremy told her.

She nodded and dashed out of the house, ignoring the pain in her chest as she ran across the floodlit grass and then was forced to slow as she entered the darker bush. Her phone torch lit the way and she crashed through the low grasses. When she reached the fire break, she switched off the torch and ran again, her breath huffing and puffing. Her ears strained for sounds of a motor, but the night was silent except for her gasps. At her property she slowed so she didn't trip on the bushes. She daren't use her torch in case Mark saw it bobbing. She was halfway across her field of hives when she heard the rumble. Lights moved along the road and turned into her drive.

Crap.

She ducked down behind one of her hives. When the ute disappeared behind her shed, she ran, sprinting towards it, her muscles aching. The engine switched off and a car door slammed. Not far now. Mark might go into his man cave or the house. Either way, it gave her time to reach her shed and duck inside. She slowed in case her footsteps were loud and hurried, the shed coming closer and closer, but blocking her view of Mark and his car.

A second door slammed. Had Mark brought his mistress home again?

She crept along the side of the shed and peered around the corner. The ute was parked outside the man cave. She waited, watching for movement. Light shone from the cracks around the door. He was probably inside, but she waited another minute before ducking into her processing shed. She moved through the dark and switched on the light in her work room. Pulling a chair up to the table, she brushed leaves off her jumper, but grey fire break sand covered her boots.

Grabbing the broom from the corner she brushed them off and then threw the sand into the bin. Quickly she turned her laptop on, opened her stock inventory software and sat. Her heart still raced, so she took a few calming breaths before she read the information before her. She'd work for fifteen minutes, which would give her enough time to settle. Then if she ran into Mark on her way back to the house, she could tell the truth about working.

She closed her eyes. She was not cut out for this spy stuff.

Chapter 12

The sun hadn't risen when Kim's alarm blared the next day. Kim groaned and turned it off, before dressing in his jogging gear. He should switch to jogging in the evenings until the days grew longer. He slipped his backpack on and headed outside. Lights glowed through the kitchen window of his parents' place, but he didn't go inside, instead heading for the side gate and out onto the street. This morning he wanted to be alone. He stretched, shivering in the crisp, cold air, and rubbed his arms, then jogged down the hill, heading towards the beach in the distance.

Had Alyse made it home safely last night?

He didn't dare call to find out. When he'd discovered Mark had gone, he'd almost had a heart attack. The customer he'd been dealing with had been a pain, wanting to know about every single dish on the menu and he'd been with them for a good five minutes or more before they'd completed their order. So he didn't have a good idea of when Mark left.

Later that night, after the restaurant had grown quiet, he'd called Jeremy to find out what Olivia had said. His conscience twinged. Did it count as spying on Alyse?

Hopefully not. He would have called her if he wasn't worried about Mark intercepting it.

His breathing steadied as he found his stride, jogging past houses with smoke curling into the sky from their chimneys. The sun shone just above the horizon now and the light was soft, calming.

Would the police be in contact with Alyse today? Could they protect her from whatever Mark had tied her up in?

His mother's lawyer voice sounded in his head. How do you know Alyse isn't involved? You only have her word.

There was a possibility Alyse was lying to him and she was more involved than she claimed, but the idea didn't sit right with him. She was clearly afraid of Mark.

So what was the next step? He had to respect her boundaries and not call her every day. Mark would definitely get suspicious. And he couldn't drop around for the same reason. He was forced to wait.

It grated on him. He'd enjoyed yesterday on the kayak. He loved helping her conquer her fear, wanted to go kayaking again, or organise a boat to take her out in the calmer inlet. Nicholas's parents had a boat he could borrow, and there were a couple of secluded boat ramps out of town. If they could go out on a day like yesterday, the water would be calm. But it all depended on Mark.

He hated the man.

It had galled him to be pleasant last night when Mark had come into the restaurant with his mistress. Though there had been a certain level of satisfaction knowing while Mark was there, Alyse was working towards putting him behind bars.

He jogged past Mai's bakery, which was already full of people at this early hour. He'd stop there on the way back, pick up some fresh bread and get a coffee. Mai had got him into jogging. She'd moved home after her apartment had burned down earlier in the year and she'd dragged him jogging with her in the afternoons before he went to work.

It had been nice seeing her every day, but it had been the summer holidays which meant all of his sisters were back home. And it was too much to bear. When his parents had built the granny flat to prepare for Grandma coming for an extended visit at the end of the year, he'd jumped at the chance to move in.

He jogged along the river and reached the inlet halfway point. The water was still, but the forecast was for strong winds this afternoon. Hopefully no one would need rescuing. He didn't have time for a call out. It was tax time, so he had to prepare the accounts for Olivia, plus he had to schedule a bunch of orders. Nothing challenging, just stuff that had to be done.

Maybe his father was right, and he should focus on his design business. It had been easy to push it aside, call it a hobby, not have to worry about making a success of it. He didn't want to fail.

Kim was breathing hard when he stopped outside Mai's bakery. He took a minute to stretch before he headed inside, the heat inside a little uncomfortable.

"Morning, Kim," Jodie said. "The usual?"

"Yes, please." He handed her his reusable coffee cup and scanned the patrons but spotted no redheads. Not that Alyse would be in town this early. She had her own business to run. "I'll have a loaf of sourdough too." He glanced into the kitchen. Mai kneaded something on one of her tables. She looked up, and he waved. He knew better than to enter her kitchen while he was a sweaty mess.

She held up a hand for him to wait and wiped her hands on a tea towel before coming out. "Good jog?"

He nodded. "Cleared the head."

"Mum called and asked for you to bring a multi-grain loaf home. They've run out of bread."

"Sure." He paid and slid the bread into his backpack, taking out his jacket. "Have you made any plans for your birthday yet?" It was next week, and he still hadn't bought her anything.

"Not yet. I thought we might do dinner at the restaurant, invite all the usuals, so you and Dad can be there."

"Sounds great." The bell above the door chimed as someone walked into the bakery. He turned, ready to smile, but it was Mark.

Mark glared at him and said to Jodie, "Black coffee."

If Mark was here, then Alyse was alone. "Can I use your sink?" He didn't wait for his sister to answer, but brushed by her, ignoring her squawk of complaint.

"Kim, you're not allowed back here like that," she said as she followed him in.

He moved out of sight of the front counter and lowered his voice. "I need to borrow your phone."

She handed it to him, a frown on her face. "What are you up to now?"

"Hang on." He dialled Alyse's number.

"Hello?"

"It's Kim," he said. "Mark's in Mai's bakery." He shifted to see what Jodie was making. "He's getting take-away coffee."

"Thanks. Have you spoken to Jeremy?"

"Yeah, he filled me in." He held his breath waiting for her reaction.

"Good. I'll call you when I hear about the police." She hung up.

He reined in his frustration. She didn't have time to chat to him.

"Thanks, Mai." He handed her back her phone and went to give her a hug, but she stepped away.

"I'm not hugging you when you're sweaty. Go home,

have a shower."

He grinned. "Yes, sis."

He ignored Mark as he left, inhaling his coffee's rich steam and walked quickly to chase off the chill in the air. Crossing the main street, he trudged up the hill to his parents' place. He probably should jog, but he enjoyed his morning ritual of stopping at the bakery, seeing his sister, and taking his time drinking his coffee in peace.

An engine roared behind him, splitting the calm stillness. A black ute barrelled towards him, Mark behind the wheel.

Shit.

Kim leapt off the road, coffee sloshing out of his cup and burning his hands. He ducked behind a jacaranda on the curb. Mark gave him the finger as he shot past, way too close for comfort.

Kim swore as he shook the hot coffee off his hands, his heart racing. That was close.

"Are you all right?" Tamara trotted down the steps of her front porch towards him.

"Yeah."

She scowled, looking at the ute driving away. "Did you see who it was?"

"Mark Patton."

She grunted. "Figures. You should call the police."

He nodded. Would Mark have hit him if he hadn't leapt out of the way? "I will."

"Tell them I saw everything if they need a second witness."

"Thanks." He smiled. It was time to make Mark's life uncomfortable.

***

Alyse's heart raced like a greyhound on speed as she strode into Mark's office, snapping on her rubber gloves. She didn't have a lot of time. Mark could be back in ten minutes, or he might be gone all day. First the four-drawer metal filing cabinet. The drawers didn't budge. Locked. She scrawled the model and the number under the keyhole onto a piece of paper and shoved it in her pocket. Glancing towards the door, she pulled open the top drawer of Mark's large wooden desk. Pens and stationery. The second one had reams of printing paper.

What next?

She daren't move the papers covering the desk in case Mark had some system in place, but she read the top document. A contract for the purchase of her honey.

Frowning, she picked it up. The customer wasn't familiar and she wrote down the name. She checked the terms and her mouth dropped open. She couldn't produce that much honey in a year. What was Mark thinking? She longed to photograph it or confront him and demand to know what he was up to.

Carefully she placed the paper back on the table and checked the rest of the room. Only his laptop on the table. She pressed the power button.

The back door slammed and she jumped. Fear clutched her heart as she slammed the laptop lid closed and raced out of the office, closing the door quietly behind herself. She tore off the gloves, shoving them in her pocket and took a moment to calm herself before she walked towards the sound. "Mark, is that you?"

A tall, broad shouldered man walked into the hallway and it took her a second to process it was Mark's brother, Craig. She sucked in a breath. Why was he here?

"Hi, Alyse. I thought you'd be at work. Is Mark here?"

"No. He headed into town." She moved towards him, gestured for him to follow her to the kitchen, her muscles tight.

"Damn. He said he'd lend me some tools. Mind if I go

into his man cave?"

Alyse hesitated. No one was allowed into the man cave without Mark. He'd made it very clear when it was built. "I don't have a key."

"You don't?" Surprise tinged his tone, but his eyes studied her.

"No. I don't go near it." She forced a smile. "I have my own shed."

"I guess you do."

She filled the kettle. "Let me call Mark and ask him if he has a spare one."

"Nah, don't worry about it. I'll catch him later." He smiled. "Nice seeing you."

After he walked out, she let out a breath, unease slipping over her skin. Strange. Craig knew how Mark felt about his man cave. She glanced out the window and watched him drive away.

It wasn't her problem.

Too wired to further search Mark's office, she checked his laptop had shut down and then made herself a cup of tea. Perhaps she could find information on the company Mark was planning to sell her honey to. A quick google resulted in little information about them, only an ABN, but no website. This might be one of the companies Mark was using to launder money.

She turned off her computer and put it back in her bedroom. She needed to get to work. When she went into Albany, she'd stop by the locksmith to get a key for the filing cabinet. Winter was always slow, but it gave her plenty of opportunity to clean her tools, paint hive boxes and make new frames.

As she reached the big roller door, Mark pulled into the property and parked next to her shed. "Where are you off to?"

"I need to get some supplies in Albany so I can make

some new frames before spring. I'll be a couple of hours."

"I'll come with you."

No. That wouldn't work. She smiled. "I'm sure you have better things to do."

"What kind of man would I be if I didn't help my partner?"

A crappy one, but it had never stopped him before. She needed a distraction. "Craig dropped by. Said you were going to lend him some tools."

Mark scowled. "When?"

"He left about ten minutes ago. He wanted to get them himself, but I told him no."

His eyes widened. "He wanted to go into my shed?"

She nodded.

His whole expression darkened and Alyse stepped back, ready for the explosion, her muscles tense.

"Did he say he was coming back?"

She shook her head, edged further away. "He said he'd catch you later."

Mark stalked after her as she moved into the shed. He muttered to himself and she kept her distance, taking a notepad from her table and recording the measurements and supplies she needed, constantly checking where he was as he fumed.

With her list complete, she asked, "Are you coming?"

He shook his head. "No. Better stay here in case Craig comes back. You were right to refuse him entry. That's my space."

Relief filled her. "Of course. I'll see you when I get back."

Climbing into her van, she breathed deeply. Getting caught in an argument between the two brothers would be dangerous.

The breathing didn't help the tension in her shoulders.

Too many odd things were occurring; Mark offering to

help her and Craig turning up unannounced. Time was running out.

Chapter 13

Alyse drove out of Albany, the new filing cabinet key burning a hole in her pocket. If Mark found it, she'd never be able to explain it. Would it be better if she put it on her keyring—hide it in plain sight—or keep it in her pocket and hope Mark didn't go through her clothes? She should have bought her own filing cabinet, then she'd have a reason for a key—but he'd likely confiscate the keys anyway. She groaned, anxiety causing her heart to beat faster. The sooner this was over the better. Maybe she should call Jeremy, find out if he'd heard from the police.

Her phone rang making her jump. Think of the devil. She answered and then clenched the steering wheel. "What did they say?"

"Lincoln wants to talk to you in person," Jeremy said.

"Can he protect me?"

"He needs more information."

She bit her lip. "All I have are my accounts." No, that wasn't all. "And the name Salvatore Incorporated. I found a sales contract in Mark's office, but the quantities are far more than I can provide. Lincoln might be able trace it, find out if it's of any value."

"I'll tell him."

"Oh, and I bought a key for Mark's filing cabinet too. Hopefully I'll open it this afternoon."

"OK. I'll call you back."

"Thanks, Jeremy."

"Any time." He hung up.

Her hands shook. Would she ever have enough evidence to put Mark away for good? If the filing cabinet didn't amount to anything, she'd get into his man cave somehow.

If Mark caught her though… he was acting strangely as it was. She swallowed hard. Would he be mad enough to kill her? Should she carry some kind of weapon, like a Swiss army knife? No, Mark would overpower her and then he'd use it against her.

Her chest ached. One way or another, Mark's terrorism would end—hopefully with her still alive.

She pulled into her property half an hour later and parked in the shed. Mark's ute was by the house so he was around somewhere. She'd have to wait to get back into his office. In the meantime, she'd offload her supplies and build some new frames for the hives and paint some new supers.

The normal task of measuring wood helped to reduce the tension in her shoulders. She enjoyed this time of year. It was quieter, with only the Flat Top Yate flowering, so it meant she had time to take stock, thoroughly clean and repair all of her equipment and prepare for the rush of spring. She whistled as she measured the pieces she needed.

"Why are you so happy?"

She spun to find Mark right behind her. "Oh, you startled me." She placed a hand to her chest, to calm her pulse.

"If you weren't whistling, you'd hear me."

She nodded.

"You didn't answer my question."

"Ah, well I'm working on new frames for spring. I enjoy making them."

He scowled. "I called Craig."

Something in his tone made her stiffen. "Did you get it sorted?"

"He said he didn't drop by."

She frowned, stepping away from him. "What do you mean?"

"What, are you deaf now? You lied about him coming over so I wouldn't go with you." He moved closer, looming over her. "Who did you meet?"

Alyse shook her head, fear prickling her skin. "No one. I did what I told you—picked up supplies in Albany."

"So if I check your mileage it'll show only those kilometres?"

"Yes. I bought a coffee and pastry for morning tea after I went to the hardware store. The take-away cup's still in the cup holder." The key felt heavy and she resisted the urge to place her hand over it.

He stared at her for a long moment and then checked the van.

Why would Craig lie? Had he not expected her to be at home? It didn't matter. Her immediate concern was Mark's reaction. He was primed, ready for a fight, but leaving the shed would only antagonise him further.

Mark returned, scowling. "You're not going anywhere without me," he said. "Tell me where you are at all times."

Mark was worried. She tried for her most sympathetic tone. "Of course. Is anything wrong?"

"Something's going on and until I figure it out, I'm not leaving you alone. It's for your own safety."

All of her plans crumbled around her, her opportunity of getting into his office, disappearing in the dust. "Well it might get boring for you." She forced a smile. "I have a lot of work in here over the next couple of weeks."

He scanned the shed. "It can wait. You can go to Mum's when I have to go out."

He had to be kidding. "It can't wait. I have a bunch of new frames to build and supers to paint."

"Just do what I say." He stalked off.

She wrapped her arms around herself as nausea crashed into her stomach. She closed her eyes and breathed. Never had it felt so dangerous, not even when he'd been beating her. If she did the slightest thing wrong, she would pay for it. Standing up to him now would be deadly. She rubbed at the goosebumps on her skin.

Could she risk calling the police?

Her phone rang. An unknown number. Mark wasn't in sight. "Hello?"

"Alyse Wilson?" The male voice was familiar, but she couldn't quite place it.

"Yes."

"This is Sergeant Lincoln Zanetti."

Hope and fear filled her. She lowered her voice. "Jeremy spoke to you?" She strode to the entrance of the shed. Mark was by his man cave, getting something out of his car.

"Yes. The best we can do is ask the presiding magistrate to mitigate your circumstances."

"But no guarantee?"

"No, I'm sorry. We don't have immunity in WA."

Cold dread filled her. It was a gamble, but her whole life was a game of Russian roulette with Mark anyway. "OK, I'll tell you what I know, but we have to be fast. Mark's getting paranoid. He says he won't let me go anywhere alone or leave me out here by myself."

Lincoln swore. "Is Mark there now?"

"Yes." The man cave was open and the silver dinghy was inside. Mark was checking the motor—fixing it. Alyse eased back from the entrance so Mark wouldn't see her.

"Give me a minute." Lincoln put the phone on hold for a moment. "Adam says Mark's team has football training tonight?"

"Yeah. At six-thirty." A rare night when she knew he'd be away for at least ninety minutes.

"Will you go with him?"

"If he makes me. He usually doesn't because he goes to the pub afterwards, but after today I'm not sure."

"OK. Here's the plan. If he makes you go, we'll arrange for someone to meet you at the oval. If he doesn't, we'll come to you."

She shook her head. "He'll flip if he sees me talking to the police."

"Can you go to the library, or a cafe?"

No way would he let her out of his sight. "I can ask." Though asking would make him mad.

Lincoln sighed. "I don't want to put you in any danger."

"I'm already in danger." At least this way she might end it. "Ask Zamira to forward the information she has to you." A scuff of a shoe was the only warning she had of Mark's approach. She whirled towards her work room, hanging up and stuffing the phone in her pocket. As she reached the door, Mark bellowed, "Alyse."

She turned, her heart racing, praying Lincoln wouldn't call her back.

"We're going for a drive," Mark announced.

He hadn't seen her on the phone. Her breath shook. "Can you give me ten minutes? I've just about finished this batch of frames."

"No."

Frustration and fear bubbled inside her. "I'll get my purse."

He stepped closer, right into her personal space and

glared down at her. "No need. Get in the ute."

Her gasp came more as a whimper. Be agreeable. Do what he wants. "Of course. Where are we going?"

"Stop questioning me!" The force of the backhand knocked her back a couple of steps. He stalked towards her, fury in his eyes. Every hair stood on end. She suddenly understood the meaning of murderous intent. She backed away, heart thumping. This was it. He would kill her.

Her phone rang, and she dug it out of her back pocket and ran. Her finger shook, stabbing at the answer button. Mark grabbed her and yanked her back, pain ricocheting through her arm socket. The phone flew out of her hand.

He punched her in the face.

Agony as her eyes watered and her head spun. She screamed, "Help! Call the police."

"Shut up!" He hit her again, and she staggered, falling against the wall of the shed, using its support to stay on her feet. Move. If the caller hadn't heard her, she was on her own. Time to fight. As she stumbled outside, she blinked to clear her vision, and he hit her again.

"Stupid bitch. Don't defy me. I own you. You're mine."

She coughed, blood flying out of her mouth and he stepped back. Acting on instinct she brought her knee up, right between his legs and he bent over, bellowing in rage.

Run.

She tripped as her feet tangled together, catching herself before she hit the ground. If she stayed still, she was dead. There was no reasoning with him now.

"Don't run away from me." The fury in his voice turned her cold. Seconds later he grabbed her shoulder, yanking her back around.

Nothing nearby she could use as a weapon. Her mouth was full of blood and she spat at him, the blood landing on his cheek. She wasn't giving up. "Are you going to kill me?" she yelled. "Have I outlived my usefulness?" The swelling in her eye made it difficult to see, but his eyes widened and he let go. "Your father would be horrified," she snarled. "His son unable to control his emotions. You're pathetic. I hate you." She stumbled backwards, towards her house. She'd never make it, but she'd try. In the distance sirens wailed. Too far away to help.

He reached out, and she leapt back.

"Don't you dare touch me!"

Mark lifted his head towards the sharp pitch of the sirens and suddenly switched. "I'm sorry," he whispered. "I didn't mean to hurt you. You just make me so mad sometimes."

Relief filled her. If he was trying to talk his way out of it, she was safe. She said nothing, not willing to risk him flipping again, but continued moving away from him.

"Let me help you," Mark said. "I'll get some ice."

The sirens were louder now. She changed directions, heading for the driveway, her eyes never leaving Mark.

"I'm sorry, Princess. Forgive me."

The slight panic in his voice as he glanced over her shoulder was sweetly satisfying. The police car pulled up next to her and Lincoln and Adam jumped out. She stumbled towards Adam, tears blurring her vision. Safe.

"We need an ambulance," Adam called into his radio as he placed his arm around her shoulder.

Lincoln's voice. "Mark, you're under arrest for assault."

Alyse leaned into Adam, as Lincoln handcuffed Mark and then read him his rights. She let out a shaky breath. How long could the police hold him? "I'd like to file a restraining order."

"No you don't," Mark growled, the threat clear.

She ignored him and the spike of fear. Adam led her towards the house, but they both kept their eyes on Mark. He was compliant now, but he was a big man, much more muscled than Lincoln. Even handcuffed he could do damage.

"Get in the car." Lincoln opened the back seat, restrained Mark inside and then walked over to Adam and Alyse with a first aid kit. "Are you all right?"

She wiped the blood from her face, her eyes stinging. "I will be."

"You need a doctor." Adam opened the first aid kit, put on gloves and took some gauze to clean up the blood.

"We'll issue a police order," Lincoln added. "It will give you protection until you can get a restraining order. Do you want us to call anyone for you now?"

Her head spun as panic threatened to take hold. She stood on the precipice. A step forward would send her hurtling into the unknown where death or a real life could be waiting for her.

Or she could step backwards into the familiar fear and terror of Mark.

She swallowed the lump in her throat. "Not yet." Every breath hurt, but she was moving forwards. "I'll tell you everything I know about Mark, give you access to his office and shed."

Lincoln nodded. "When the ambulance arrives, we'll take Mark to the station and process him. Two Albany detectives would like to talk to you. They're heading the investigation into Mark."

"I'd rather talk to Adam." She knew him, Kim trusted him.

"He can be there with you."

Adam smiled at her. "Do you want me to call Kim now?"

She frowned and hissed at the pain. "Kim?"

"He called us, told us you were in danger. We told him to stay away until we assessed the situation. He's at Jeremy's."

It had been Kim on the phone not Lincoln. He had saved her again.

The ambulance pulled into the driveway. "Yes, please. Tell him to come when you leave with Mark."

"Will do."

The two paramedics hurried over. "What have we got?" Cynthia asked.

"We're worried about concussion," Lincoln said.

She smiled at Alyse. "We'll examine you in the ambulance."

Alyse walked between the two paramedics, past the police car and caught the hate in Mark's stare. Her blood froze, but she would do this. He had no power over her anymore.

Cynthia examined her while Guy spoke with Lincoln and Adam. "There are places you can go, people you can call about Mark hitting you."

"I know. I'm charging him this time."

"Good. That's courageous. I'll give you some phone numbers."

Courage and stupidity were different sides of the same coin. She wasn't naïve enough to think a simple restraining order would keep Mark away. His family would bail him out as soon as he called. She had to prepare.

"We're taking Mark in," Lincoln said. "The detectives are on their way."

"All right." She glanced at Adam.

"I'll call Kim now."

"Thank you."

Cynthia finished bandaging the cut above Alyse's eye. "It will probably need stitches."

It would be another battle scar to add to her collection.

But it would be the last one.

***

Kim paced outside Jeremy's house, waiting for his phone to ring. What was taking Adam so long? Was Alyse all right? Had Mark hurt her? Alyse's scream over the phone had chilled him to the bone. The only reason he wasn't with her right now was Adam had convinced him he would make things worse on Alyse if he showed up. But then the ambulance had driven past, sirens not on which had given him a little comfort, and Jeremy holding him back to stop him jumping in his car had also helped.

His stomach twisted, and he turned towards her property as if that would make any difference. He couldn't see or hear anything from here. He hated this. He wanted to be by her side, supporting her, holding her in his arms, soothing her, protecting her. "What's taking so long?" he demanded.

"They need to make sure Alyse is fine before they can take Mark away," Zamira said.

Good.

His phone beeped. Message from Adam. *Taking Mark now. Wait until we leave.*

Finally. "I can go." He strode to his car.

"Can I come too?" Zamira asked. "Alyse might prefer a female."

Her words made him stop. She was right. He had to stop thinking about what he wanted and start thinking what was best for Alyse. "Of course."

Both Zamira and Jeremy got into his car and after the police drove past, he headed for Alyse's place. The ambulance was parked outside the house, its back doors open and Alyse was inside on the stretcher. Her whole face was bruised, her eye swelling and dried blood still on her face and over her jumper. His heart thumped in his chest as he controlled his anger and resisted the urge to run over and pull her into his arms. Instead he said, "You OK?"

She nodded.

"We're taking her to the hospital to get stitches and a scan," Cynthia said. "She has a concussion."

Zamira climbed into the ambulance and spoke quietly to Alyse.

Jeremy tugged him back. "Give them a minute."

Stepping away hurt.

"Mate, she'll be all right."

"Not if Mark stays around," Kim said. "This is the second time he's beaten her in a week."

"I'm filing for a restraining order." Alyse's voice rang out.

Hope sparked.

She sat up in the ambulance. "I'm talking to the police. Mark won't be coming back here." The concern in her expression belied her set tone.

His chest filled with elation and trepidation. "Great." He'd researched domestic abuse. The perpetrator rarely gave in without a fight, and Mark certainly wouldn't.

"We need to take Alyse to hospital," Cynthia said. "Do you want someone to come with you?" She directed the last question to Alyse.

Alyse glanced at him and then Zamira. Before he could offer, Zamira said, "I'll go if you want."

"Yes, please."

Disappointment swept through him. He had to get over himself. Of course she'd prefer a female. "We'll meet you there," Kim said. "Give you both a lift home."

"Thank you. Could you lock the house?" She threw her keys to him.

"Maybe get her a change of clothes too." Zamira glanced at Alyse for confirmation.

"Please."

"Will do." He stood back with Jeremy while Cynthia and Guy closed the ambulance and drove off.

"Do you think she'll get the restraining order?" Jeremy

asked.

"I hope so." He'd encourage it.

They walked through the garden gate, though garden wasn't an apt description. The area inside the fence line was more weeds than plants, with only the hardiest plants still alive. There were hints of how the garden used to be, with trellises and gables, roses and grevilleas, paths trailing in different directions. Alyse's mother had been a keen gardener, bringing plants to sell at the markets as well as the honey.

Inside the house, the interior was remarkably masculine. "You can tell Mark lives here," Jeremy said.

Yeah, but where were Alyse's touches?

He found two bedrooms. The master bedroom was messy and masculine and the other room had a single bed. This room was much more the Aly he remembered. The bedspread was a vibrant rainbow of flowers and the feature wall was a rich forest green. Her bedside table had an e-reader on it and over on the chest of drawers was a photo of Alyse and her parents on her graduation day, a jewellery box, a beeswax candle and a stick of deodorant. Tidy, no fuss, but colourful. He smiled.

"You take that room." Jeremy gestured to the single room.

Slightly uncomfortable going through her drawers without her there, he opened a couple, found a spare shirt, a pair of tracksuit pants and a jumper, and tucked them under his arm. "Got it." Did Alyse not sleep with Mark?

Kim locked the doors and as they left the garden, he spotted the shed door wide open. "Better shut it as well."

He paused at the entrance, his gaze caught on the open door of the van. As he moved to shut it, he spotted flecks of red on the ground. Blood.

He clenched his hands and growled.

"He's behind bars now," Jeremy said.

"Yeah, but for how long?" He'd have to ask Adam how much time they had to gather evidence.

"Come on. Let's get into town. Show Alyse she has plenty of support."

Kim shut the van door and closed the shed. "I'm worried what Mark might do when he gets out."

Jeremy nodded. "He's unlikely to pay any attention to a restraining order."

Would Alyse be willing to go to a women's refuge? Were there even any in the area? "We can set up a watch in case he comes back."

"Yeah. I'm sure Elijah and Jamie will help."

"Thanks, mate." He spotted Alyse's mobile lying in the dirt and picked it up, brushing it off and tucking it in his pocket.

Kim drove to town and parked at the hospital. Nerves rattled in his stomach as he walked into the emergency department. Alyse might prefer to avoid all men. Maybe he should drop off her clothes and leave her with Zamira.

Tim greeted them and showed them through to the back where Alyse sat on one bed, her red hair tied back and a doctor stitching the cut above her eye. Kim stayed back until the doctor finished.

"Keep the cut dry for a week," the doctor said. "I'll give you some waterproof dressings to take home. Do you have someone who can stay with you tonight?"

"I can." Kim stepped forward. He'd call his father and tell him he couldn't work. Eden could cover for him.

Alyse hesitated.

He winced. He was butting in again. "Or we can find someone else if you'd prefer."

"Maybe we all can." Zamira smiled at him. "We'll get some take-away, watch a movie if Alyse is feeling up to it."

"That would be nice," Alyse said.

"All right. I'll sort out your discharge."

When the doctor left, Kim took her place beside Alyse's bed. "How are you?"

"Sore." Her eye was still partially closed. "Thank you for calling the police."

"You're welcome." He wanted to hold her hand, but it might frighten her. "Want me to call Dad and put in an order for pho?"

"Not yet. I still need to talk to the police."

"I can call Adam and ask him what they need."

She smiled. "Please."

Kim moved away from the bed and dialled his friend's number.

"How is she?" Adam asked.

"Banged up, but OK. Zamira, Jeremy and I are staying with her tonight."

"You heading out there now?"

"Yeah, we're just waiting for the discharge papers."

"Ask Alyse if I can come out with the detectives. We have questions."

Alyse needed rest but the quicker they found more to charge Mark with, the better. Alyse nodded her assent when he asked. "Go for it. We'll be there in half an hour." He hung up and as he returned to Alyse, her stomach rumbled. "Hungry?"

She blushed. "A little."

"What do you want?"

She sighed. "I could really go one of Mai's chocolate brownies and a banh mi."

He grinned. "Leave it with me." He dialled the bakery. It was too late for Mai to be there, but Jodie answered. He placed his order, sweet-talking her to pack it up for him and by the time he was done, the nurse was there to discharge Alyse.

Alyse's movements were slow and stiff as she shuffled out of the hospital, Zamira by her side. Kim clenched his hands. Give her space.

When they arrived at Alyse's place after stopping by the bakery, a four-wheel drive was parked over by Mark's man cave.

"Who's that?" Kim asked.

Alyse peered ahead. "It looks like Craig's car. He shouldn't be there."

Kim checked the time. Adam would already be on his way with the detectives. He handed Alyse her house keys. "Why don't you and Zamira go inside and we'll find out what he wants?"

She hesitated and then agreed, getting out of the car. Kim drove the remaining distance to the shed and parked. Both he and Jeremy climbed out. A thick chain and padlock locked the shed door, and the car was empty.

"You go that way." Jeremy pointed.

Kim jogged around the back of the shed as Craig lifted a hammer to the window. "I wouldn't do that if I were you."

Craig whirled around, eyes wide. "Who are you?"

"A friend of Alyse's. She tells me you shouldn't be here."

Craig's eyes darted around. "Mark asked me to fetch something from his shed but forgot to give me the key."

Bullshit. "Alyse might have one." He walked closer, noting the window was covered with black plastic. Jeremy walked around the other side of the shed.

"Hey, Craig."

Craig lowered the hammer. "Jeremy. What are you doing here?"

"Visiting Alyse. Your brother beat her up again. Did you hear he's been arrested?"

Craig paused. "No, I didn't. Is Alyse all right?"

"She's badly injured."

The older man swore, still looking at the window. "I'm sorry about that. I'd better call our lawyer."

Kim gestured for Craig to precede him. Craig took one last look at the window before walking back to his car.

"Do you want to talk to Alyse?" Kim asked.

"No, it doesn't matter. I'll come back later." He drove off.

"That was dodgy," Jeremy commented.

"Yeah. He definitely wants to get inside. The question is why?"

"I thought I heard something moving around in there," Jeremy said.

That was odd. "Maybe it's a possum." They got into Kim's car and drove to the house. Two cars were already parked outside and when they went into the kitchen, Adam was sitting at the table with two people Kim assumed were the detectives. Alyse had spread the brownies and rolls on a plate and Zamira was making drinks.

"This is Detective Bosch and Detective Khan," Adam said, gesturing to the blonde female and then the Middle-Eastern man. "Jeremy Mendelson and Kim On."

"Was it Craig?" Alyse asked.

"Yeah. He was about to smash a window. Said Mark asked him to retrieve something, then pretended he didn't know his brother had been arrested."

"What's this?" Bosch asked, alert.

Kim explained what had happened.

"It's the second time today," Alyse said. "He came inside without knocking this morning. When I told Mark he'd been around, he was furious, said I was right to turn him away. But when Mark called Craig about it, Craig denied being here."

Khan scribbled notes as Zamira placed mugs of tea and coffee on the table.

"All right. We should start from the beginning. What

do you know about Mark's criminal activities?"

Before Alyse could respond, Kim asked, "Shouldn't you ask about Mark beating her first?"

"Lincoln and I will talk to her about it afterwards," Adam said. "We need to act on this while Mark is behind bars. Then maybe we can keep him there for longer."

Kim was all for that. It was about time.

Chapter 14

Alyse tensed. Now she sat in front of the detectives, terror gripped her. The next few hours would change her whole life. She exhaled. One day she'd live without fear, and this was the beginning of the process.

"The rest of you need to leave while Alyse speaks to us," Detective Bosch told them.

"I'll leave if Alyse wants me to," Kim said.

"We appreciate your concern for her." Khan clasped his hands together in front of him. "But from our point of view, we don't know who's working with Mark."

She gasped. It had never occurred to her. Foolish. Mark was working with someone.

"I'd never work with that bastard," Kim said.

Adam pressed his lips together. It wouldn't look good for him to speak in defence of his friends.

She could do this. "We'll be a couple of hours," Alyse said. "You could bring dinner when you come back."

Zamira squeezed her shoulder. "Absolutely. What would you like?"

"Pho." This time she'd have a chance to eat it.

Zamira moved towards the door and Jeremy and Kim followed. Alyse longed to call them back. No, she would be fine on her own. Adam was here and the detectives would help her put Mark away for good.

Kim turned. "Call me if you need anything."

She nodded. When the back door closed, she asked, "What do you want to know?"

"Tell us when you first realised Mark was doing something illegal," Bosch said.

She closed her eyes, thought back. This would take a while.

Two hours later, Alyse was flagging. Her face throbbed and her body ached with a deep heaviness. "Can we take a break?"

Bosch nodded. "Can I get you a drink?"

"Water, please."

Adam pushed the last piece of brownie towards her and she ate it, taking small bites to avoid the cut in her mouth, hoping for some energy.

"Can you email us the documents from the accountant?" Khan asked.

"Sure." She pulled her laptop towards her. No need to worry about stealth now. Craig had seen Adam and the detectives. Whether he realised she was telling them about Mark's crimes or whether he thought it was to do with the assault didn't matter. Mark would be furious. She should change the locks. It wouldn't stop him, but it might slow him down enough so she could escape. After she emailed the documents, she asked, "Can I call a locksmith? I want to change the locks before Mark comes back."

"That's fine."

She looked up the number and arranged for him to come as soon as possible.

Bosch placed the water on the table. "You believe Mark might have evidence in his office?"

"Yeah. I was planning to go through his filing cabinet

the next time he went out." She reached into her pocket. "I bought a key from the locksmith this morning."

"Would you be happy for us to be in the room when you open it?"

"Of course. Do you want to look now?" At Bosch's nod, Alyse showed them into the office. Nothing had been moved since this morning. "The contract with Salvatore is here." She handed it to them and then unlocked the filing cabinet. In the top drawer, files hung in neat rows, each labelled with a different name in her mother's precise handwriting.

Tears sprang to her eyes. She'd never imagined Mark would keep them. Swallowing hard, she checked the next drawer, and it was messier, the labels scrawled on by Mark, and the next drawer was the same. The bottom drawer was full of ammunition, all different calibre, some of the bullets were huge. She stepped back, fear coursing through her veins. What the hell?

Khan photographed the drawer and asked, "Where are the guns?"

"I don't know." If he had access to guns, he was far more dangerous than she'd imagined. Her stomach churned. Alyse stepped back so they could investigate, wishing she could run away from this whole mess. But she wasn't hiding any longer. At the end of this, Mark would be out of her life.

"I need to make some calls." Bosch left the room.

"What's in Mark's man cave?" Adam asked.

Khan glanced at him. "Man cave?"

"The shed by the fence line is Mark's," Alyse explained. "Only he's allowed in. I've never been in there."

"Do you have a key?"

"No. It's padlocked shut. Maybe the locksmith can get into it."

"Anything else only he has access to?" Khan asked.

Alyse shrugged. "His ute. I only drive it if we're going somewhere and he wants to drink. Then there's the master bedroom. That's his domain." She saw both men's surprise, and she pushed down her embarrassment.

Bosch came back into the room. "Bail has been set, but Mark isn't out yet," she said. "Sergeant Zanetti has placed a police order on him so he can't come near you, but we don't expect he'll abide by it. We can look into witness protection for you."

"What does that entail?"

"Sending you interstate."

Alyse shook her head. She wasn't leaving.

"I've requested a forensics team to go over the office," Bosch continued. "And a warrant to search the whole property."

Someone banged on the front door and Alyse jumped. Adam accompanied her to the front door where an older man with a middle-aged spread stood. Behind him was a van with a locksmith logo on it.

"G'day. Had a break in have you?" he asked. "What needs changing?"

"All the locks," Alyse said.

His eyes widened, and he glanced at the house. "Might be tricky to get locks for a house this age."

He examined the front door, muttering to himself and then walked around the house checking the other doors. Adam accompanied them while Bosch and Khan went back inside. When the locksmith had finished, he said, "The front and back doors aren't a problem, but the side door is tricky. I'll call a couple of suppliers."

The side door consisted of two double doors; the inside ones were solid wood with an old chunky key, and the outside ones had flyscreen in them. Alyse opened them only in summer to let the breeze in and she wasn't certain Mark had a key. Still, the idea of him getting in through there gave her chills. "Please do."

The man got to work.

Adam said, "Jeremy might be able to board it up in the meantime."

Good idea. "I'll call him."

She made the phone call and Jeremy said he'd look when they brought dinner back. As they returned to the detectives, she hesitated. "Can you give me a minute?" she asked Adam. "I need to fetch money for the locksmith."

"Sure."

She strode over to the shed and grabbed her smoker, lighting it. The smoke soothed her. Then she headed for the hives at the back of her property. Adam followed her. "I thought you were getting money."

"I am." She counted the hives and went to one in the middle. The bees were docile in this one, but she puffed smoke as she took off the lid. "Stand back." She rested the lid against the hive and reached into the space missing a frame. The bees buzzed around her hand, touching her softly with their wings or as they landed on her skin. Her fingers closed around the sticky plastic and she withdrew the package, wiping it on the ground to get some of the honey off it. Then she closed the hive again.

Adam whistled. "That's a lot of money."

She hadn't thought this through. Would the police confiscate it? She sighed. Hopefully they'd understand. "I found it on Mark's desk the night a tree branch fell on the roof," she said. "Elijah came inside to set up buckets to catch the rain and went into the office before I could stop him. When I saw the money, I took it." She'd blamed the theft on the SES and Mark hadn't reported it to the police, but he had punished her for it. It had been worth the comfort of knowing she had it.

"Don't you have any money?" Adam asked.

"No. Mark controls all the bank accounts." She hadn't

dared open her own account. Instead she'd hidden the money in the one place he wouldn't look.

She withdrew a couple of hundred dollars from the stash and tucked the rest into her hoodie pocket. She'd have to split it up, hide it in different places, or maybe now she could open a bank account.

After the locksmith left, the forensics team arrived and Kim, Zamira and Jeremy returned. The bags of Vietnamese food smelled delicious and her stomach grumbled. "Do you need anything else from me?" she asked Bosch.

"We're waiting for the warrant to come through before we open Mark's shed."

"Why don't we open it now? I want to see what he's been doing on my property."

"That's not a good idea. Too many people inside might contaminate any evidence."

Alyse didn't want that, but she wanted to know what he'd been doing. "Can I go in afterwards?"

"Not until we're done."

Frustration filled her, but she sighed. "All right. Shall we examine the lock while we wait?"

Bosch nodded.

She didn't want to do this alone. Kim smiled at her. She always felt safe with him. "Will you come with me?"

"OK."

Bosch looked as if she wanted to disagree and then sighed. "Let's go."

"I'll look at the side door while you're gone," Jeremy said. "Come up with something."

"Thanks." Alyse led the way across to the shed, every step agony. Her movements were so slow she felt ancient. This was the last time she'd ever be this beaten up. Her steps slowed as she approached Mark's shed. What was inside? Would it be like opening Pandora's Box? Kim stayed by her side, supporting her when she stumbled and his presence gave her courage. At the shed, she stopped, pointed to the thick chain. "All the windows are covered too."

Khan examined the lock without touching it. "Let's see what fingerprints we can get off the entry points."

Adam nodded.

"You'll need bolt cutters." Unless one of the officers could pick the lock. Alyse circled the shed with Kim and the police and she rubbed at the goosebumps on her skin.

"Are you all right?" Kim asked.

"It's kind of scary being so close," she said. "Mark wouldn't let me near it."

From inside came a muffled shout.

She froze. "Did you hear that?"

Someone banged on the glass window and shouted in a language Alyse didn't understand. Then the woman yelled, "Help!"

Bosch swore. "Did you know someone was inside?"

Dumbfounded, Alyse said, "No."

She ran after Bosch and Khan to the entrance of the shed. Khan was already on the phone and a forensics officer ran up with a pair of bolt cutters. He cut the chain and Bosch held up her hand. "Let's step back."

"The entrance is clear," Alyse said as she complied. "Mark often drives his ute inside."

The big door slid open to reveal the silver dinghy. It was getting dark, so Alyse flicked on the lights which were in the same position as the lights in her own shed. She stepped inside, cringing at the sight of the boat which had started all of this. Perhaps she should be thankful because it had brought Kim back into her life.

A large wall with a single door separated the rest of the shed. Bosch placed a hand on Alyse's arm. "Stay here."

She nodded. The police team moved forward working

together as they checked the shed. Kim stood next to her, his body angled as if he was ready to step in front of her at the first sign of danger. She wrapped her arms around her stomach, waiting for the all clear.

Voices raised at the far end, shouts and Alyse heard fear in them. She glanced at Kim. Who was it?

"We should wait outside," Kim said, taking her hand.

She shook her head but kept her hand in his. Whatever it was, she needed to know.

Khan came back, his expression blank. "Can you call Zamira?"

"Why?"

The detective hesitated and then said, "We found two Asian women in one room. I think they're speaking Malay."

Shock pierced her and her mouth dropped open. "What?"

Kim was already on his phone.

Alyse had to see this. She'd suspected Mark was involved with Henk but had never imagined he would use her property to hold women against their will. Nausea swirled in her stomach. The shed was sectioned into rooms and as she passed each one, she looked in. Greasy car parts lined shelves in one room, barrels of chemicals were stacked in another. The third room made her stop and stare. Black crates like the one she'd helped him lift onto the dinghy, and one was open with large, lethal-looking guns inside.

Who was this man?

Finally, she reached the last room. Sitting on the two single beds, facing Detective Bosch were two Asian women in their early twenties. The room was filthy and the women's hair was a tangle of knots. They glanced at her, fear in their eyes. One woman's nails were ragged and dirty as if she'd been clawing at the walls.

"Oh my God." Alyse placed a hand over her mouth. How long had they been here? Guilt pummelled her like Mark's fists. She'd turned a blind eye for too long, she'd enabled Mark to do this, given him the means to carry out his illegal activities and these women were his victims. She stepped back, bumping into Kim. He held her steady.

"This isn't your fault," he murmured.

She wanted to believe him, but she couldn't.

Zamira and Khan hurried down the corridor towards them. Alyse stepped aside so Zamira could enter the room. She spoke gently in Malay to the women. One woman burst into tears as the other answered.

"Ask them how long they've been here," Bosch said.

Zamira did so. "They think about a week."

Nausea rose in Alyse's stomach and she swallowed hard to keep it down.

Khan gestured to Bosch and they went down the corridor to speak but Khan's words carried. "Mark made bail. Lincoln released him just before I called."

Alyse froze. Mark would likely come straight here, see the police, see his shed was open. He'd know they were on to him.

Did he have another stash of guns somewhere? Would he come after her?

She began to shake, and Kim turned her towards him, drawing her into his arms. "It's all right. I won't let him near you."

Kim couldn't stop him. No one could, but she drew comfort from his arms.

"Alyse, can we have a word?" Bosch gestured for her to follow.

She held onto Kim's hand as she walked down the corridor and out to the dinghy.

"We've had word Mark's made bail," Bosch said without preamble. "The team will watch the entrance of your property in case he comes back."

"It won't help," Alyse said. "The fire break runs along the back and he can access the property from there, or from Henk's place." She gestured towards her neighbour.

Bosch frowned. "It might be best if we find you somewhere safe to spend a few nights."

"No." Mark wouldn't scare her away from her home. "I'll stay here. The police will have a lot of work recording all of this, won't they?"

The detective nodded.

"Then it's the safest place I can be. I've changed the locks and Jeremy will board up the side door."

"I can't spare any people to protect you."

"I'll stay with her," Kim said.

Her heart expanded, but she didn't want him in danger. "Don't you have work?"

"Dad gave me some time off. Eden is covering my shifts."

She didn't want to be alone, and Zamira would be busy with the women they'd found. "All right. Thank you."

Khan accompanied them back to the house. Jeremy had found a tape measure and was measuring the side door. He glanced up as they walked in.

"Bad?"

"Yes. They found two Asian women inside."

Jeremy swore. "Zamira's with them?"

"Yeah."

He let out a slow breath. "Right. I have a bit of wood at home which should fit the door. I can board it until we can get the locks changed."

"Thank you." It was something.

"Mark made bail," Kim told him. "Watch your back when you get it."

Jeremy scowled. "Will do. Back in a jiffy."

They walked back into the kitchen where the table was

still set, and the dinner Kim had brought was going cold.

"We should both eat something," Kim said. "Take a seat and I'll heat it."

She wasn't hungry, but she needed food in her stomach before she could take more pain medication. Kim seemed right at home in her kitchen, pouring her a glass of water and heating the food.

In no time at all, he placed a steaming bowl of pho in front of her and settled with his own plate of stir fry next to her.

"How are you coping?" he asked.

Where did she start? "I knew Mark was involved in something dodgy, thought he might have worked with Henk, but to discover those poor women in there…" She shook her head. "I'm furious. Not only that he kidnapped them, but also because he used my land, my parents' land, for something so despicable." She closed her eyes, let the soup soothe her.

"You've put a stop to it now."

"He'll be back," she said. "He won't accept it's over." Mark never admitted defeat.

"The police will catch him soon."

Naïve thinking. Henk's partner had remained hidden for a month before he'd been caught. She had traded uncertainty and fear at home for uncertainty and fear everywhere she went. She had little money and a business to run. Her dangerous ex was out there.

And he still held all the control.

***

Kim tossed and turned, trying to find a comfortable position. The wall clock mocked him with its rhythmic tick tock and the darkness brought him no sleep. It would be easy to blame the hard sofa, or the too-soft pillow, but in truth he was too concerned about Alyse to close his eyes.

It wasn't until he'd seen those two kidnapped women in Mark's shed that he'd truly understood the breadth of Mark's sadism. He was no small-town thug. The cache of guns revealed how dangerous he could be. Kim couldn't protect Alyse against that kind of arsenal. Mark might have lost access to his shed, but he would have contacts who could provide him with the weapons he needed.

The police had taped off the shed and posted a guard before leaving around midnight.

Jeremy and Zamira had left far earlier with the two kidnapped women—Zamira unwilling to leave them until another interpreter arrived, and Jeremy unwilling to leave Zamira's side. The whole mess would have brought back bad memories for the both of them.

Kim sat, throwing off the quilt and running a hand through his hair. Where would Mark run?

The police had checked the Vale winery, but Mark was smarter than that.

And it appeared Mark had his fingers in multiple pies. The car parts could have come from Morgan and the stolen car racket the police had busted last week.

Kim walked to the window, peering out at the darkness. It was still tonight, clouds hiding the moon, and the trees that ran along the road were dark shadows. The silence was loud and his ears strained to catch any snippet of noise. Mark could be out there now, watching, waiting.

He rubbed his arms.

Alyse seemed certain he would be back, and she knew Mark best.

Somewhere in the house a door opened. He turned, picked up the rolling pin he'd taken from the kitchen drawer earlier. Treading lightly, he moved to the lounge room door and peered down the corridor as a person slipped into the kitchen. He followed. At the kitchen entrance he shifted slightly so he could peer inside.

Alyse stood at the sink pouring a glass of water. He lowered the rolling pin and stepped inside. "Couldn't sleep?"

She shrieked and spun around.

"It's Kim," he blurted, holding up his hands.

"You scared the crap out of me," she said. "What are you carrying?"

His face flushed and he was glad of the dark. "A rolling pin."

Her laugh was breathless. "It won't be much help against a gun."

"It's better than nothing." He placed it on the table and moved to stand next to Alyse, glancing out the kitchen window at the backyard.

"It's awful to think he's out there somewhere," Alyse said, her voice low.

"Yeah." He hesitated. "I can stay with you until he's caught," he said. "Eden and Sarah are on holiday for another couple of weeks so they can work at the restaurant and I can help you here with the bees, with anything you need."

"I can't ask you to, Kim."

"You're not asking, I'm offering. I'd like to help."

"And what if he isn't caught in the next couple of weeks?" Alyse asked. "You can't put your life on hold for me."

Frustration and guilt swirled together. "I won't desert you again, Aly."

She turned to him and he could feel her frown. "Again?"

"After your parents died, I came around to visit and to apologise for those things I said. I believed Mark when he told me you didn't want me around." Shame filled him.

She touched his hand. "We were both young," she said. "I believed him when he said none of my friends cared."

He shook his head. "I should have known better. I should have helped you. Then none of this would have happened."

"So you're here now as penance?"

"No!" He held her hand. "I've missed you, Aly. Missed those days at the markets, missed your smile and your sense of humour. I thought about calling you so many times, but I was too ashamed of what I'd done and then it felt like it was too late."

"You have nothing to be ashamed of." She led him away from the window and out of the kitchen. She hesitated in the hallway. "Let's talk in my room. It's warmer and I don't like the lounge room."

Kim followed her into the single bedroom. "This is your room?"

"Yes. I moved out of the main bedroom when I caught Mark in bed with Yvette."

Anger simmered in Kim's stomach. How could Mark treat her so callously? How could he look at another woman when he had Aly? He said nothing as Alyse slid under the covers and flicked on the bedside lamp.

"Sit down."

He hesitated. It was either sit on the edge of the bed or the floor. The bed looked inviting with Aly in it, but she'd freak. Though the cold seeped into his skin, he sat on the floor.

She looked at him for a long moment, before saying, "This won't work. We always sat side by side when we talked." Her eyes showed her uncertainty, but she patted the bed next to her.

"Are you sure?"

She nodded and handed him the throw rug at the base of her bed. "Wrap yourself in that. It's cold."

Kim moved onto the hard mattress slowly, not wanting to scare her, being mindful to give her space on the small bed.

Alyse flicked the lamp off and dark settled on the room. "It will be easier to talk in the dark."

He understood. Night was the time for confessions and secrets. "Why did you stay with him?"

She stiffened and then sighed. "It's hard to explain, hard for others to understand when they haven't been in the same situation."

He waited, letting her get her thoughts in order.

"At first it was good. He was kind, attentive and it was seductive—the older man interested in me, a red-headed farm girl who was obsessed with bees." She sounded amazed.

"I loved your obsession with bees."

"Really?"

"Yeah. You used to light up when you talked about Bessie and the gang. They felt real to me. I couldn't wait to hear the next instalment each week." Everything she'd done had been fascinating to him.

She chuckled. "I always figured you were a captive audience and were being polite."

He sucked in a breath. "Never. Seeing you at the markets was my favourite time of the week."

"If only I'd known," she said. "I had a massive crush on you."

He closed his eyes. If only he'd been a more confident teenager. He'd never suspected she'd been interested in him. "The feeling was mutual," he confessed. And had never faded.

She sighed. "Hindsight's a bitch."

It was. "So when did Mark change?"

"I started seeing it after Mum and Dad died. He took control, told me not to worry, he'd deal with everything, and I was so full of grief I let him."

The sadness in her voice made Kim reach out, slide his

hand into hers. She flinched and then relaxed, her fingers curling around his. His heart expanded. "I wish I'd been there for you."

"I don't think I would have noticed if you had been," she said. "Grief clouded my every day for months afterwards. By the time it lifted a little, Mark had control of the business and I was relieved to have one less thing to worry about."

"You were young. It was a lot for anyone to cope with."

She nodded. "The first time he hit me was when we went out on his boat after the accident. I didn't want to go out very far and when he ignored me, I became hysterical."

Kim clenched the hand not holding hers.

"I figured I deserved to be hit, to shock me out of that state. The next time he was violent was when I refused to move into the master bedroom with him. He shook me and cried, told me I didn't love him if I wouldn't let him create a home and I was so desperate not to be alone, I begged him to stay."

Nausea swirled in his stomach. He wanted to stop her talking, didn't want to hear all the horrific emotional and physical abuse she'd gone through and yet he wanted to know it all so he could help her heal.

"It became a pattern. He isolated me from my friends, from you, he controlled the finances, the business accounts. He gave me an allowance and after he was badly stung, he allowed me free range with the hives. It was only when I stood up to him, or did something he saw as defiant that he hit me. But those attacks grew more frequent." Her hand shook in his and he rubbed his thumb over her soft skin. "About eighteen months ago I finally recognised the pattern, and realised he didn't love me. I tried to kick him out, and that's when he told me he'd been using my accounts to money-launder." Her voice hitched. "He showed me a fake contract I'd signed and I didn't want to go to jail, didn't want to lose my property, the last connection I had to my parents."

The manipulative bastard.

"We'll make sure that doesn't happen." If he had to buy the property himself, he would.

"It doesn't matter anymore. I have to be free of Mark."

A loud creak made them both sit upright. "Was that a door or a window?" Kim whispered.

She shook her head. "I don't know."

Slowly he climbed off the bed and peered out the window. No movement. His heart thumped as he moved to the doorway. The rolling pin was still on the kitchen table where he'd left it. He glanced down the empty hallway, ears straining for any other noise.

"I'm going to text the police," Alyse whispered.

The guard at the shed could help them.

Kim didn't know his way around the house, especially in the dark. To his right were the main family areas, but to his left was unknown. He stayed still, waiting for another sound. Alyse came up behind him, pressed her mouth close to his ear. "Should we search the house?"

He didn't want her anywhere near the danger. "Let's wait for the police." He eased back into the bedroom and closed the door, locking it.

Time crawled as they waited for the police to contact them. Kim strained to hear any noise and finally he heard footsteps coming down the hallway. He tensed.

Someone pounded on the door and Alyse shrieked.

"It's Senior Constable Travis," a voice called.

Kim didn't know either of the police guards from Albany station. "Do you recognise the voice?" he murmured.

"No, but it's not Mark."

The door had no peep hole. "How did you get in?"

Kim called.

"The back door was unlocked."

It shouldn't have been. "Why did you come to the house?"

"Because Ms Wilson contacted us."

He glanced at her and she nodded. Kim opened the door, ready to push it shut again. He recognised the man and the tension in his shoulders released. "You didn't find anyone?"

The senior constable shook his head. "The master bedroom window has been pried open. Looks like the intruder entered that way and walked out the back door."

"It was locked when I checked it before going to bed," Alyse told him. She hugged herself, and Kim put his arm around her shoulder. She leaned into him.

"I've called it in," Travis continued. "We'll get a team out to check for fingerprints. I'll stay with you until they arrive."

"Thank you," Alyse said and moved to the kitchen where she put the kettle on. Kim was way too wired to sleep, but Alyse was pale and looked as if she'd fall over at any moment. He moved closer to her. "Why don't you go lie down?" he said. "I can stay awake until the police get here."

She shook her head before he finished speaking. "I can't sleep knowing someone was in my house."

He understood. "At least let me make you a tea. You can go back to your room, relax and I'll handle the police."

"No, Kim." She was firm. "I appreciate your concern, but I can cope." She placed tea bags into the mugs, offering one to the constable who'd followed them in. "I'm never letting someone else handle things for me again. That's how I got into this mess."

It gutted him to be put into the same category as Mark. "How can I help you then?"

"You being here is a help." Her smile was sad. "But I have to deal with this myself."

He sat at the table while she made them all cups of tea, clenching his hands together to stop reaching out to help her. He had to give her the space and autonomy she wanted.

Had to be patient.

Chapter 15

By the time the police had taken fingerprints, Alyse was shattered. Her whole body ached, and the table top lured her. It looked like a comfortable place for a nap. She desperately wanted to accept Kim's offer to take care of everything so she could sleep, but she couldn't. Not anymore.

"You should buy some security cameras," the officer said as he walked out.

"I will." She shut the back door and then double-checked she'd locked it. No, it wasn't enough. She fetched a chair from the kitchen and placed it under the doorknob like she'd seen people do in the movies. She had no idea if it worked, but even if it didn't stop someone entering, it would make a noise to warn them. Then she checked all the windows and doors again, even though the police had already done so. Her steps slowed as she made it back to the kitchen where Kim waited.

Ever patient.

"Are you ready for bed?" he asked.

She nodded, though she didn't want to be alone. Had it been Mark sneaking in? She couldn't imagine it was because he would have gone crazy the second he realised Kim was there.

But who else—someone Mark worked with? And what were they after?

Would Kim become a target? "Maybe you should go home."

He raised his eyebrows. "I don't want to leave you alone, but if you'd prefer me to go, I will."

No, she preferred him here. She shook her head. "Do you want to sleep in my room?" Nerves twisted inside her. "We could drag the other mattress in there, put it on the floor…"

"I will if you're comfortable with that."

He was so accommodating, and while part of her was relieved, a small part remembered how accommodating Mark had been in the beginning. Kim *wasn't* Mark. "Please. I'd feel better with you there."

He gestured for her to lead the way.

She left the lights on throughout the house. She wouldn't make it easy for anyone to come back. Her skin crawled as she walked into the master bedroom. It smelled like Mark and held so many bad memories. "I'll get fresh sheets." She went to strip the bed and Kim stopped her.

"I'll do it. You get the sheets."

She hurried out. By the time she returned, the mattress was bare and Kim had moved it to the floor in her room.

"That OK?" he asked.

"Yeah." Together they made the bed and then she locked the bedroom door. Locking herself in a room with a man should frighten her but it didn't. Not with Kim.

"Do you want the mattress or the bed?" Kim stood against the wall, giving her plenty of space to move around. Her heart warmed at his understanding.

"The bed." She was tossing out the mattress at the first opportunity. She climbed into bed and switched on the lamp, before shuffling to the edge of the bed to look down at him on the mattress. "Thank you for everything."

His smile was beautiful. "I wish it hadn't come to this, but I'm here for you now, Aly. All you need to do is ask."

She switched off the light, an unfamiliar, uncomfortable sensation swirling in her stomach.

Ask. If only it was that simple. Mark had programmed her not to ask for anything. It was too dangerous, his reaction too unpredictable.

"Night, Aly. Sweet dreams."

Her stomach settled and she smiled. Kim's voice reminded her of happier times.

Closing her eyes, she fell asleep.

Magpies warbling outside Alyse's window woke her the next morning. She lay there listening to the sweet sound heralding a new day, a new beginning. Sunlight streamed through the gaps in her blinds signifying it was later than she usually slept. She squinted and pain throbbed in her face. It would only get better from here. As she sat, she spotted Kim lying sound asleep on the mattress, the quilt pulled up under his chin. His face was unlined, his mouth turned up at the corners in a small smile as if he didn't have a worry in the world. She couldn't remember when she'd felt that much at peace.

Not wanting to disturb him, she crawled to the end of her bed and stepped onto the thin gap of carpet between the mattress and the wall. She moved to the door and twisted the lock.

"Morning."

She whirled around, heart racing. "Sorry, I didn't mean to wake you." She waited for his scowl, for him to tell her off and complain about her being too noisy.

He sat, the quilt falling to his waist exposing his well-toned arms and chest. "No problem. What time is it?"

Her heart rate slowed. He wasn't Mark. She glanced at her phone. "Eight." The police would be back soon. "Do you want some breakfast?" She opened the door.

"Yeah, and coffee, lots of coffee." He ran a hand

through his hair. "I can make it." He pulled on his jumper and followed her out of the room.

Alyse hesitated. "You go ahead. I'll check the house."

"I'll come—" He stopped himself and gave a wry smile. "Want me to come with you?"

He'd remembered what she'd told him last night. She smiled. "No. I'll be fine. You put the kettle on." The daylight gave her confidence.

She went from room to room checking windows and doors again and switching off the lights. Everything was how she'd left it. In the kitchen, Kim had placed flour, eggs and milk on the table and was searching through the cupboards. As she walked in, he said, "I thought I'd make pancakes, if you're interested."

A man who cooked. "I'd love some. There's a mixing bowl in the cupboard over there." She pointed, and in no time he was whipping up the batter. Alyse got out some bananas and her bees' honey to have with them, and then grabbed the maple syrup in case Kim preferred it.

"What's your plan for today?" Kim asked as he cooked the first batch.

"I'll see what the police have to say." She wanted to redecorate, remove every piece of evidence that Mark had ever been here, like he'd done with her parents years earlier. But there might be something which would add years to his jail time.

"Do you have any work to do?"

She hadn't finished building her frames, but she'd thought of something more important. "I'd like to go to the bank, change the access on the business accounts."

"Sure. We could go to lunch while we're in Albany."

She turned away from him. The idea was appealing, but if Mark saw them, if he was following them, he would be furious. She closed her eyes. It didn't matter. He probably already knew Kim had stayed the night, probably even knew he'd slept in her room. He had a way of knowing exactly what she'd done at every point of her day. She pulled back her shoulders. "I haven't been to Dylan's in years. Mum and Dad would take me there on Sunday afternoons and we'd have ice cream sundaes."

"It's a date." Kim grinned.

Shock speared her. A date? No, it couldn't be. Dates led to dating which led to manipulation and being trapped.

"Hey, are you all right? You've gone pale." Kim brushed her arm, and she flinched away from him.

"It's not a date." She rubbed her arms, shaking her head. "It's lunch."

Kim nodded slowly. "Yeah, just lunch. It was a figure of speech."

"Good." Her hands shook as she opened the fridge, staring inside for something she could retrieve. Butter, that would do. When she turned back, Kim was sliding a pancake onto a plate.

"You can have the first one." His tone was light, but his movements were stiff as if he was waiting for her to freak out again.

She slid into the chair and focused on her breathing. "Kim, I…" How could she explain?

"You don't have to say anything, Aly."

"I do. You must think I'm crazy."

He stayed over by the stove. "No, I think you've been traumatised by an abusive man. It will leave you with scars."

She nodded. "In the beginning I didn't want to date Mark."

He raised his eyebrows. "Really?"

"I turned him down multiple times before I said yes."

"Why?"

Because she'd still been hoping Kim would ask her out. She sipped her coffee. "Even then I knew it was odd that someone eleven years older was interested in me. I wasn't attractive or popular and spent my weekends helping my parents with the bees."

Kim shook his head. "Aly, you were the most beautiful girl in our year."

Her mouth dropped open. "No, I wasn't."

He laughed. "Yes, you were." He placed another pancake on her plate and retreated to the stove. "My sisters envied your pale skin and your gorgeous red hair." He poured more batter into the pan. "The first time I saw you, I thought you were a fairy-tale princess."

Heat flooded her cheeks. "Not with all these freckles."

He nodded. "My first day of school in Blackbridge was mid-year because Dad had had a nervous breakdown and refused to stay in the city. I was determined to hate everything about this place because I missed my friends and Grandma and didn't want to move."

Alyse frowned, trying to remember. "What year was it?"

"Grade five. Mrs Perrier's class. The only spare seat was next to you and I was so overwhelmed by you I tripped over my feet in front of the whole class."

The memory popped into her head and she laughed. "I remember. I felt sorry for you."

Kim slid a pancake onto another plate and sat next to her. "After I picked myself up, you introduced yourself and said 'Welcome to Blackbridge'. Then at recess you introduced me to the others in the class and told the boys to be nice to me." He drizzled honey over his pancakes.

"I can't believe you remember."

"It was a pivotal moment in my life, Aly."

And she'd been a part of it. It was so sweet.

"So even if you didn't realise it, Mark would have been attracted by your looks."

Her mood soured. That's what they'd been talking about. She shrugged. "It doesn't matter. He wooed me with gifts and compliments, and I felt special." She ate some pancake but couldn't taste it. "I knew nothing about relationships and thought since he was doing all these nice things for me, I should do everything he wanted me to do." She shook away the memories. "It doesn't matter now."

He stood. "Another pancake?"

"No, thanks." She watched as he made himself one. "Why are you doing this, Kim?"

He glanced at her. "Making pancakes?"

"No, helping me."

He gave her his full attention. "Because you're my friend."

It couldn't be that simple. They'd barely seen each other in six years. "What do you want from me? What do you get out of this?"

Kim switched off the stove. "I want you safe. I want to spend time with you again, chat about bees and silly dreams and life." He closed his eyes briefly, exhaled. "OK. Full disclosure." His eyes met hers. "I've missed you, Aly. You've always held a special place in my heart. You were my first love, even if you never knew it."

Her breath caught and her heart pounded. She had no words.

He sat next to her, a self-deprecating smile on his face. "You mean a lot to me."

She shook her head, a flutter of panic in her stomach. "I can't, Kim. I can't be someone's focus again. I can't offer you anything in return. I can't do anything until Mark's out of my life for good."

"I'm not asking for anything but friendship, Aly."

Her disappointment surprised her. She didn't need complications, and she didn't want to rush back into a relationship. "OK."

The rumble of a car engine brought goosebumps to her

skin. She jumped up, peered out of the kitchen window and relaxed when a police car drove into view. "The police are back." She walked out of the house and over to Lincoln and Adam. A plain white sedan pulled in behind them and detectives Bosch and Khan climbed out.

"No further disturbances last night?" Lincoln asked, studying her.

"No."

Kim joined them as Bosch said, "The forensics team should be here within the hour. They'll go through Mark's office and the shed."

"What about the rest of the house? Do you need to examine Mark's bedroom or the other rooms?"

"Did he do any work in there?"

Alyse shrugged. "No. He kept all his work in the office, and I wasn't allowed inside."

"We'll get the team to look."

"Have you had any word on Mark?" Kim asked.

Lincoln shook his head. "Even though Craig posted bail, the family hasn't seen him since he took off in one of the winery utes. We've put out an alert, and Ryan and Sue are going around to local businesses and friends this morning to ask them to call us if he shows up."

"Hopefully he'll turn up soon," Adam said.

Alyse wasn't holding her breath. Mark was an avid camper so he could be in the bush somewhere. Her gaze caught movement by her fence line. She frowned, focusing on it.

Crack.

Dirt sprayed up at her feet and she jumped. What the—?

"Gunshot!" Lincoln yanked her towards him, pulling her around the police car, putting it between her and the gunman.

Another shot, the sound echoing through the morning as Kim and Adam dived next to them. Adam yelled into his radio, his gun already drawn.

"Stay here," Lincoln said. "Keep your head down."

Every muscle froze except her heart which pumped so hard it felt as if it would explode.

Kim pulled her close, sheltering her body with his.

No. He was in as much danger as she was. She shifted as Lincoln yelled, "Anyone got eyes on him?"

"He's on the fence line," Alyse said. "Between the two tall gums on the border to Henk's."

Lincoln shot her a look.

"I saw movement just before the shot went off."

Adam repeated the information into the radio as Lincoln changed position to get a better view. Crouched beside the sedan, Bosch and Khan were also trying to see the shooter.

Kim caressed her back. "It will be OK." His voice shook.

What had she involved him in? It was too late now. If the shooter was Mark, he would make Kim pay.

"I can't see him," Khan yelled.

"He's on the move towards the back boundary," Adam shouted.

A motorcycle roared to life and everyone turned towards the fire break.

"He's running," Lincoln called.

Adam turned to them. "Let's get you inside." He grabbed Alyse's arm, and she ran with him and Kim back to the house. The detectives jumped in their car and tore out of the property, but Alyse knew they wouldn't catch the shooter. The firebreak sand was too soft for the police car and Mark had created multiple tracks through the bush for his own recreation. He could come out anywhere.

She entered her kitchen, her body shaky. Had Mark been trying to scare her or kill her?

"What do we do now?" Kim asked as Adam pulled the

curtains closed on the kitchen window.

"Stay here," he said. "Stay away from the windows, just until we check the area. I need to talk to the others." He walked out.

Alyse ran a hand through her hair and exhaled slowly. Kim pulled her into his arms. She stiffened and Kim said, "Please, just give me a second." His arms shook.

Understanding flooded her, and she hugged him back, running her hands over his back to soothe him. "It's all right. We're both fine."

He shook his head. "The man's psychotic."

She nodded. "Yes, he is."

He pulled back. "I'll protect you, Alyse. I don't know how, but I will."

Like it or not, they were in this together. Mark wouldn't leave either of them alone until he was caught.

Part of her wished she'd pushed Kim away at the start.

And the other part was so very glad he was here.

***

Alyse made them drinks, her unsteady hand the only sign she was shaken by what had happened. Either she was one cool cucumber, or she was used to these kinds of things. Kim suspected it was the latter.

What kind of tension had she been living with for the past few years? He couldn't comprehend it. He wanted to pull her away from the windows and keep down until they had caught Mark. Because who else would have shot at them?

He paced the kitchen.

"Sit down," Alyse told him, placing the mugs of coffee on the table.

"I can't," Kim said. "I can't believe he shot at you. Did he mean to miss? What if you'd been a step closer? He would have hit you."

She stood in front of him, stopping him. "All that matters is he missed. I'm fine, Kim, really."

He shook his head. "Why aren't you more upset?"

She shrugged, her smile sad. "He's gone for now. It was always worse waiting for the explosion, never certain how bad it would be." She sighed. "Mark'll regroup and either he'll stew and get really mad, or he'll be over it."

"That wasn't him being really mad?"

"He ran, which means he's thinking relatively clearly. If he was really mad, he'd still be shooting at us."

Chills ran down his arms and he rubbed them. This was serious. "We should get you out of here."

"And go where, Kim?" she demanded.

"A refuge or a safe house. There has to be somewhere you can hide."

She shook her head. "For how long? I've already spent too much time letting Mark dictate my life. I want to get back to *my* life—the bees, the honey, finding some friends. Mark won't drive me away from here. It's why I stayed so long."

Kim wanted to argue, but she'd already made up her mind. He huffed. "Then we need some kind of plan."

Alyse nodded. "We'll talk to the police when they come back."

It was another half an hour before Lincoln and Adam came inside with the detectives, Lincoln's expression a thundercloud.

"He got away?" Kim asked.

Lincoln nodded. "We found some bullet casings over by the fence line and some tyre tracks on the fire break. They'll go into evidence."

"So what's next?"

"We've set up roadblocks and put out a bulletin in all nearby towns. Everyone is on the lookout for him," Adam told her.

Bosch nodded. "While they search, we'll continue to go through the office and the shed gathering evidence. Forensics are due here soon."

"And what about Alyse's safety?" Kim demanded.

Bosch's expression was sympathetic. "She should be safe here, while we're on the premises."

"When do you have to go to work, Kim?" Adam asked.

"I don't. I took a few days off to help Alyse."

"Are you staying here?"

Kim glanced at Alyse.

She hesitated. "I'd like him to."

It suited Kim fine. "I'll get Sarah to pack me some clothes."

Lincoln frowned. "Get her to take them to the police station. I don't want additional people on the property. I'll get Ryan to bring them."

"I'll call her now." Kim went into the lounge room. Sticking close to the wall, he hurried across to the open window to shut the curtains. Then he called his sister.

"Do you know how early it is, Kim?" Sarah complained.

He winced. "Sorry. It's important."

"Are you OK?"

"No, not really." He told her about the past twenty-four hours. "Could you pack some clothes for me, and my laptop? Lincoln says to drop them at the police station and Ryan will bring them out."

"Is it safe for you out there?"

"I don't think it's safe for me anywhere." And wasn't that a real kicker?

"I don't like the sounds of this, Kim."

"I'll be fine."

She sighed. "OK. I'll do it now."

Kim returned to the kitchen as more officers arrived. At least Alyse would be safe with all the cops around.

And that was the most important thing.

Chapter 16

Detective Bosch introduced the lead forensic investigator to Alyse. "District Forensic Investigation Officer Humphries will be in charge of gathering any forensic evidence."

"Will you need to go through the whole house?" Alyse asked.

"Not necessarily. We'll start with the shed."

Alyse hesitated. "Can I clear out Mark's things from the master bedroom and lounge room?" She didn't want a single reason for Mark to come back. If she could get rid of his things, get Craig to pick them up, then Mark couldn't claim the need to return. She sighed. Not that he would with the police after him, but she itched to remove his presence from the house. It still felt like he was here, surrounding her, watching her.

Kim placed a hand on her shoulder, giving her support.

"Give me some time to review the property," Humphries said.

"Thank you." There was one other thing she had to do. "Do you need me for anything else?"

Detective Bosch shook her head.

"Then I'd like to go into Albany to the bank."

Bosch frowned. "Is Mark likely to approach you in town?"

"No." Not while the police were on high alert. Besides she couldn't hide here forever waiting for Mark to be caught. It might take days, weeks, or even months. So eventually she'd have to venture out. And the longer she left it, the higher the risk Mark would clear out her accounts. "I can't afford for him to withdraw all the money from my business accounts."

Bosch stared at her and then nodded. "All right. The less money he has access to, the better. Call triple zero if you see him."

Alyse turned to Kim. "I'll see you when I get back."

The concern was clear in his eyes, and he shook his head. "No, I'm going with you. You need someone to watch your back."

Her heart squeezed. "You'll be safer here."

"You just said Mark won't approach you." He took her hand. "Please, Aly, let me help."

She couldn't say no. Not with the earnest expression on his face and the worry coursing through her body. "OK. Let me get my things."

She went into the bathroom to brush her teeth and her bruised face stared back at her. The colour around her eyes had faded from purple to a faint blue with yellow around the edges. This was the last time she would look like this. The last time she'd try and fail at hiding the evidence. She applied makeup and then fetched the documents she needed. After a quick check over her shoulder to make sure no one was around, she retrieved the beehive cash she'd stuck under her clothing drawer and put it in her jacket pocket, then zipped it up. Kim waited for her by the front door and together they walked across to her van. Her shoulder blades itched as she climbed inside. "While we're in town I want to buy a new bed." The torture device on her bedroom floor was going out today.

"Good idea."

As she drove out of her property, she scanned the surrounding bush and Kim did the same. Mark would be stupid to hang around, but there was always a possibility. When she pulled onto the main highway without seeing any cars behind her, she let out a breath.

"No one's following?" Kim asked.

"No." She accelerated and it wasn't long before they reached Albany town limits. Her shoulders relaxed. She would be safe here, with people around. She parked in front of her bank.

Kim asked, "Want me to come with you?"

An arts and craft store and a cafe were either side of the bank. Far more interesting for him. She smiled. "No need. Why don't you get a coffee and amuse yourself?"

He nodded. "Call me when you're finished."

Alyse walked into the bank, the clean lines and bright colours doing nothing to soothe the tension which sprang to her shoulders. What if she couldn't access the accounts, what if Mark had taken her off them—was that possible— what if he'd already withdrawn all the money?

"How can we help you today?" The cheerful voice made Alyse jump.

She focused on the woman wearing a black pencil skirt and white blouse, with her hair tied back in a perfect bun. "I need to change the access permissions on my business account and open a savings account."

The woman blinked and frowned before forcing a smile. "Right this way."

Her reaction told Alyse she hadn't done a great job at hiding her injuries. She followed the woman into a small side room containing a desk and a computer. The woman gestured for Alyse to sit. "Terry will be with you shortly."

Alyse's hand shook as she retrieved the paperwork

from her bag. She hadn't been into the bank since her parents died and she'd done the necessary changes according to the wills. Then Mark had been by her side, encouraging and sympathetic, but making sure his name was added to the account as an authorised user.

Terry walked in, a tall, slim man with an easy smile. "How can I help you today?"

Alyse explained what she wanted and after he'd checked her identification, he logged into her account. "Which Patton did you want removed from the account?"

Alyse blinked. "What do you mean?"

He swivelled the screen to face her. "There's a Mark and a Craig here."

Her mouth dropped open. "How long has Craig been on there?"

He clicked some buttons. "About three years."

"Take them both off. Is there anyone else aside from me authorised on the account?"

"No, just you and the two Pattons."

Good. Now why the hell did Craig have access to her apiary account? "Can you print a list of transactions Craig has carried out on the account?"

Terry nodded. "I can do it for both of them if you like."

"Please."

A few minutes later, Terry said, "It's done. The only authorised user on the account is yourself. Is there anything else I can help you with?"

"I'd like a savings account." She pushed across the money she'd taken from the hive. This was the start of her independence.

"Sure." The man typed a few things and said, "You should get a card within the next fortnight."

Now she needed to figure out why Craig had had access. "Could I have those print outs?"

He handed them to her, and she stood. "Thank you for your help." She shook his hand and walked outside into the cool morning. She'd done it. She'd taken back control and taken away some of Mark's power. She almost wished she could see his reaction when he realised he couldn't access her money. Her skin prickled. On second thoughts, she didn't want to be anywhere near him. She scanned the car park for people. It was empty.

Before tucking the transaction report in her bag, she read through it. Craig had made withdrawals over the years, all in the five-figure range. She gritted her teeth. He'd been stealing from her as well. She'd hand the report over to Bosch as soon as she returned home.

Her stomach rumbled, and she pushed aside her anger. They could get some morning tea when she found Kim. She peered into the cafe window but he wasn't there, so she rang his number.

"Hi, Aly. Are you done?"

"Yeah. Where are you?"

"In the arts store. I'll be right out."

She found him purchasing pencils and a sketch book. After he paid, he turned to her a little sheepish. "I couldn't resist. It's been ages since I've done any drawing." His eyes shone with excitement as he held the door open for her.

The gesture tugged at her heart. "I'm glad."

"Do we have time to eat?" Kim asked.

"Sure." Maybe they should stay here. She gestured to the cafe. "We could eat there?"

"You choose. Didn't you want to go to Dylan's?"

"It's on the other side of town."

"I can wait if you can." He grinned.

The impulse to do what she thought Kim wanted was strong, but she blocked it. He was happy for her to choose. Standing up for herself and putting her desires forward would take practice. She unlocked the car. "It will only take a few minutes."

As she drove, she kept checking her rear-view mirror, but the streets were empty. She found a parking spot right outside the cafe which looked down on Princess Royal Harbour, its water glassy smooth this morning. They sat at a booth at the back, which had a single yellow lily in a vase on the table.

Kim grinned. "Your favourite flower."

She gaped at him. "How did you know?"

"You mentioned it once."

She'd told Mark as well, but he always insisted on buying her red roses and it seemed ungrateful to complain. Shaking off her surprise, she inhaled the rich coffee scents tickling her nose. Definitely a large mug of coffee, and the sticky date pudding being carried to a nearby table looked good. They ordered and then Kim leaned back. "Where are we going for the bed?"

Alyse bit her lip. "There's a place not far from here." She didn't want to spend a lot.

The waitress brought over the coffee and Alyse picked up her mug in both hands, inhaling the steam and letting the warmth flow through her. Then she sipped the rich, full flavour and sighed. Just what she needed.

"That good, huh?" Kim laughed.

She placed the mug down. "It was a rough night."

His hand covered hers, light, just touching, and it provided comfort and a shock of attraction all at once. "It'll get better."

"I know." She refused to think otherwise. Outside the large windows, the harbour was still, a body of calm blue ocean. Longing twinged inside of her.

"What's wrong?" Kim asked.

She blinked. "Huh?"

"Your face changed. You're sad about something."

How could he know her so well? It had been years

since they'd last spent any real time together. "I used to love days like this," she said. "When the ocean was glassy, I'd beg Mum and Dad to take me out on the boat. I loved speeding across the surface of the water, sitting on the bow, wind in my hair, feet dangling in the water and sometimes dolphins would dance underneath me." Now she'd thrown Mark out, she would continue her attempt to overcome her fear.

"Why don't we go out today?" Kim said.

She frowned. "We don't have a boat."

"I have a friend who lives in Albany. We might be able to borrow his. I can call him."

Fear gripped her heart, and she exhaled, counting to ten. There was no reason not to. She could spare an hour and Mark couldn't follow them onto the water. It wasn't like she could do much at home until forensics were finished. There wouldn't be many days when the ocean was this calm. "Can you call him?"

"Sure."

Alyse's pulse fluttered as Kim made the call. She could do this.

A couple of minutes later, Kim hung up. "He'll meet us at the boat ramp in an hour."

She tapped her foot under the table. "That's great."

"You can change your mind, Aly. We'll go with whatever you're comfortable with."

Kim was an experienced skipper. They would be fine together.

The waitress brought their food and though nerves still swirled in her stomach, she forced herself to eat. To distract herself, she said, "Tell me about your graphic design business."

"There's not much to tell," Kim said. "Mai showed me how to put together a website and it's just been word of mouth. I haven't done any advertising."

"Why not?"

He shrugged. "I don't know. I guess it felt like I was being arrogant." He glanced at his plate. "Who says I have the skills to do this?"

The uncertainty was a new side of Kim. "I do," she said. "Your drawings were always amazing, and Mai's logo is elegant. You definitely have the skills. People would be lucky to hire you."

Kim fidgeted. "Thanks Aly."

She wanted to give him the confidence he inspired in her. "What kinds of design work do you like?"

"Logos and banners, so I'd offer branding packages and website designs." He perked up, excitement shining from him. "I need to do more research."

"Sounds fantastic. Will your dad mind?"

"No. He knows about it. It'll take a while before I can quit my job anyway." He paused. "Maybe you could help me develop a business plan."

Her eyes widened. "Me?"

"Yeah. I remember the business proposal you wrote for your parents while you were at high school. You had lots of ideas you wanted to try."

Pleasure filled her. She'd forgotten about that. Every year she wrote a business plan, but Mark hadn't always let her achieve everything on it. Perhaps this was a way she could repay Kim's kindness. "OK. How about we go through it this evening?"

"That would be great."

Warmth flooded her at being useful to someone, having value in her own right.

It felt incredible, powerful, amazing.

***

An hour later, all those floaty, happy feelings had fled. Alyse stood at the edge of the harbour, water lapping at her toes, barely able to breathe. Her chest was strangling her. This was the worst idea she'd had so far. So much for the happy memories wiping out her debilitating fear.

Next to her, Kim chatted to his friend.

This wasn't a movie. Her fear wouldn't magically disappear because she was doing something about it.

"I threw in the tackle box in case you want to go fishing," Kim's friend said.

"Thanks, mate." Kim waved as his friend returned to his car and then said to Alyse, "How do you want to do this?"

Not at all. She clenched her teeth. The fibreglass boat was bigger than Mark's dinghy, but about the same size as the boat her parents had owned. It had a glass windscreen and two swivel chairs at the front where the steering wheel was. Seats were in the rear corners and a railing ran the whole way around the edge. Her first step was to get in.

The gentle shush of the water against the boat ramp was soothing. She closed her eyes, listened to the sound, let it calm her. She always loved the sound of the ocean.

"Do you have your skipper's ticket?"

She nodded.

"Then you might feel better if you're the skipper," Kim said. "You can go where and as fast as you want."

The idea of being in control soothed her. "Yes, please."

Bracing herself, she climbed into the boat. Memories of her parents' boat flooded her, the damp, salty smell of the marine carpet, the slight whiff of fish and the smell of boat fuel. Tears pricked her eyes as she heard her father call, "Cast us off," and her mother say, "Aye, aye, captain." They thought it was funny every time and she'd rolled her eyes at them, but she loved it, had even bought her father a captain's hat for Christmas one year. So many good times. So long ago.

She blinked and ran her hands over the black steering

wheel, familiarising herself with its smooth surface. A key switched on the engine and the throttle pushed forward or backwards depending on the direction she wanted to go. Finally she glanced up. Kim stood knee deep in water, his jeans rolled up, holding the boat, waiting for her.

Her heart squeezed. She could never explain how much his understanding and patience meant to her. She swallowed hard. "Cast us off."

He pushed the boat further out and jumped on the bow. The boat rocked, and Alyse adjusted her footing for better balance. As Kim joined her, she started the engine.

The throaty purr was like a favourite song she hadn't heard in ages, a song she'd forgotten she loved. With that song, her parents were with her, standing next to her, surrounding her with love. She shifted the throttle and let the boat reverse until they were in deep enough water for her to turn. Her hands shook a little as she steered the boat parallel with the shore, only ten metres away.

Kim sat in the chair next to her, quiet, comforting. A friend.

His smile made her breath catch. If she was honest, she wanted more than friendship from him. She wanted to hug him, kiss him, discover what a real, healthy relationship was like.

The idea filled her with almost as much apprehension as the boat did.

"How do you feel?" Kim asked.

Heat rushed to her cheeks. She rotated the wheel so they moved further into the harbour. It was so flat the boat didn't even bob. "It's not too bad." Adjusting the direction, she turned to run along the shore, a little further out, a little deeper. She was tempted to turn on the fish finder to see how deep it was, but it might freak her out. Better she focus on her distance from the shore.

A few people walked along the beach, but it was mostly

deserted.

No one to rescue them if they got into trouble.

She squeezed her eyes shut. Don't think like that. They weren't getting into trouble. The ocean was flat, the engine still purring, the drain bung was in.

She froze. "Your friend remembered to put in the drain bung, didn't he?"

He stood. "Yeah, but I'll check for you." He bent over the back, his jeans pulling over his butt, distracting Alyse for a moment. When he turned to her, her heart raced for a completely different reason.

"It's all good," he said.

"What about the fuel?"

"Should be full." He moved next to her and pointed to a gauge next to the steering wheel. "Yep. Looks good."

Her shoulders relaxed. No need to worry. There weren't any other boats in the vicinity and the harbour didn't contain any underwater obstacles for them to hit. Few risks to being on the water. A couple of thin clouds hovered in the sky, but nothing held any rain. No wind, no storms.

Determined, she headed into the centre of the harbour. Nothing would sink the boat. There was nothing to fear.

The water was a dark blue, fathomless, deep. Chills raced through her and she lifted her gaze to the horizon, gripping the wheel tighter. *There's nothing to fear. There's nothing to fear.*

Breathing quickly, she stared at the point across the bay. She could get there. The shore was visible, the water calm, no clouds in the sky, no sudden storm would blow up, and if it did, the harbour would be protected from any huge waves.

Sweat trickled down her back.

No. She couldn't do it.

With a gasp, she spun the wheel, causing Kim to

stumble and crash into the side of the boat. Her breath hitched as she decelerated, praying he wouldn't fall overboard.

Kim righted himself and stepped closer to her. "You OK?"

Panic gripped her. What was she thinking? She could have hurt Kim. She shook her head and accelerated again, heading for the shore.

Kim's eyes widened. "Aly, look, dolphins!" He pointed across her, breaking her focus, and then his words sank in. She spotted the small pod of dolphins swimming only about fifty metres away.

Some of her fear receded as joy shoved it out of the way and she slowed the boat, turning the wheel towards them, but keeping a safe distance. As a child she'd always begged her parents to let her swim with the dolphins. Sometimes she'd been allowed to jump in with them and she'd realised how big they were. She'd felt insignificant. The dolphins had often ignored her, but once they had swum around her and played, as curious about her as she was about them. They'd turned on their sides to look at her and the sun had glistened off their wet skin. It had been one of the best days of her life.

Kim stepped closer, placing one hand on the steering wheel to adjust the course and his chest pressed reassuringly against her back. "Feeling better?" he murmured, his warm breath tickling her ear.

She nodded. It was difficult to fear with Kim so close to her, his body protecting her, and with the calming presence of the dolphins nearby.

Kim reached around and put the boat into neutral so they floated next to the pod. "They're so sleek."

Alyse's attention was no longer on the dolphins. Every nerve in her body focused on the fact Kim was hugging her from behind. She closed her eyes. She wanted this. The affection, the security, even the lust simmering low in her belly.

But was she ready?

His hand rested only centimetres from hers. Her fingers twitched and then moved almost of their own accord and covered his hand.

He stiffened and then brought his other hand to rest lightly on her hip. Her nerves sizzled in anticipation.

The gentle rock of the boat soothed her and the dolphins circled around them as if checking them out. Kim rested his head on Alyse's shoulder. "This is nice."

She hummed in agreement. This was what being at peace was like. She was safe, content, warm.

They stood together until the dolphins swam away. Elation bubbled through Alyse, making her feel light. She spun around and flung her arms around Kim. "Thank you!"

It wasn't until Kim's arms slid around her waist that she realised what she'd done. She was pressed against Kim's body, his arms around her. What must he think? She shifted back and while Kim's arms loosened, they didn't completely let go.

Tilting her head, she stared into his eyes. "Sorry, I—"

"Aly, you never need to apologise for hugging me." He paused. "I like having you in my arms."

She enjoyed being there. His gaze dropped to her lips, and she licked them. Did he want to kiss her? She wanted his lips on hers. Ever so slowly, keeping her eyes on his, she raised to her toes. The desire in his eyes was clear. Her lips hovered over his for a second before she pressed them against him. The kiss was short, sweet and filled her heart with warmth. She shifted back. No, it wasn't enough.

This time when their lips met Kim pulled her closer. He tasted like coffee and below that, he was all Kim. She wanted more, so much more, but caution stuck its unwanted head into her thoughts. She pulled back, her heart racing. What did she say now? "I…"

He brushed back the hair that had fallen across her face and her words disappeared at his gentle touch. She swallowed. "Kim, I don't know what to do about you."

He tilted his head. "Do you need to do anything?"

"Yes. I'm a mess and I don't like not knowing what this is." She gestured between them. "It scares me."

"I understand, Aly. You've a lot to work through, but I want to be by your side, supporting you, for as long as you want me." He brought her hand to his lips and kissed the back of it. "If it's just as friends, that's fine. If you want to be friends with benefits,"—his lips quirked—"I'm good with that too."

Could he be more perfect? Worry niggled at her. Mark had said the right things at the beginning too. She hated she had to even consider it. "I don't want to hurt you."

"I'm a big boy. I can handle it." He brushed a soft kiss against her lips. "Where to now?"

The change in subject reminded her they were still on a boat in the harbour. Goosebumps leapt to her skin, and she rubbed her arms. "Back to the ramp." She'd done enough for one day.

"OK. I'll get my friend to meet us there."

Alyse slowly accelerated, directing the boat back to the shore.

Could her relationship with Kim be so simple? Would he really let her call all the shots and decide how far and how fast it progressed?

Was that fair to him?

Chapter 17

Not long after midday, Alyse and Kim returned home. Police still moved in and out of Mark's shed and around Alyse's house. Her muscles tightened. How were the Malay women today? She would call Zamira later and find out. The thought of those poor women, trapped in the shed for so long… Her throat closed over. Had Mark abused them as well? She almost didn't want to know. She parked in the shed and Adam walked over. "How'd you go?"

She pushed her thoughts of the women aside. "Achieved everything I wanted to." She had a new bed in the back of her van, ready to replace Mark's. "Any news here?"

Adam nodded. "Bosch wants to talk to you." He gestured for her to go inside and then spoke into his radio.

Dread filled her. She entered the kitchen, Kim by her side. He put the kettle on as she hugged herself. What had happened?

Bosch walked in, her expression sympathetic and Humphries followed her.

Alyse's skin prickled. "What is it?"

"Were you aware there are surveillance cameras in the house?" she asked.

It took a second for her words to register and then Alyse's head spun. She swayed and Kim steadied her. "No. Where?"

"You'd better come and look."

Her gut was ice as she followed Bosch into the master bedroom. She wanted to be sick. "Where is it?"

Humphries showed her the alarm clock on the bedside table. "There's a camera in there, and one in the light in the bathroom. We've found almost a dozen more around the house."

Alyse clenched her hands. The alarm clock had been there for years. Mark had been watching her while she slept. "How long does the footage get saved?" Maybe it had caught him assaulting her. It would be something else to add to his long list of crimes.

"Depends on the model," Humphries replied. "Bosch requested a warrant for the footage. It's probably uploaded to the cloud."

"He'll have a link on his computer." She strode down the hallway, her stomach a swirling sea of nausea, and turned on the laptop. She scanned the desktop and then clicked on Mark's internet history.

Humphries peered over her shoulder. "That one."

She clicked on the link and it logged her into the website. A dozen cameras showed every corner of her house including her bedroom and the processing shed. She was always being watched. No wonder he'd always known when she lied. She pushed down the surge of anger and fear. "How do we save this?"

"Start by changing the login and password," Humphries said and showed her how. "If he has the app on his phone it won't work anymore."

He could have been watching her all of this time. Could have seen Kim with her. Could have seen her go into his office and get the information off his computer... She scanned the camera footage but there wasn't one in the office or the hallway. He didn't need to monitor himself.

"Alyse, can we examine your phone and laptop?" Humphries asked. "There's software which is nearly undetectable but can monitor everything you do on the device and where you are."

She grabbed her phone out of her pocket and thrust it at him. "Take it off. I'll get my laptop." She pushed past Bosch and Kim and ran into her bedroom. God, she wanted to scream. Mark had been tracking her every move. She hadn't thought of checking her devices. Hadn't known such software existed. Inside her room she rested her hands on the bed, and bent over, breathing fast.

She hated Mark, hated every molecule of his being. Would she ever be free of him? Had he saved the footage, waiting to blackmail her with it? Would she wake one day to find naked videos of herself all over the internet?

She focused on her breathing, taking long, slow breaths to calm herself. She wouldn't let him win. This was another nail in his coffin. When he was caught, he would go away for a very long time. She had to believe it.

"How are you holding up?"

She spun around at Kim's voice. Tears pricked her eyes. She brushed them away. She wouldn't shed tears over Mark any longer. "I trusted him. I gave my life to him and this is what he did with it." How could someone be so cruel?

Kim stepped inside the room, out of the doorway but kept his distance. Good. She couldn't deal with a man crowding her.

"Want me to give you some space? I can take the laptop to Humphries."

She gestured to the computer. "Please."

Kim gave her a small smile, collected the laptop and left.

She huffed. What did she do about him? From a man who never listened to her, to one who did whatever she asked. The differences were all too confusing, but she should focus on those differences, such as Kim knowing her favourite flower. She closed her eyes. It would be so easy to lean on Kim, to let him take over, to take care of her.

But she couldn't.

Not if she ever wanted to respect herself again. She would break that habit, have faith in her own ability. He was simply a friend who supported her. It couldn't be more than that, not now, not yet. She shouldn't have kissed him.

She glanced up and spotted the smoke detector, the only place to hide the camera. Humphries was probably watching her. Alyse stood on her bed to examine the device. A black dot she'd mistaken for dirt was the lens. Bastard. She'd been so pleased when Mark had insisted on installing smoke detectors throughout the house and sheds, had seen it as proof he could change, that he'd turned over a new leaf, that he cared. The first time she'd asked, he'd refused because it would cost too much.

She should have known there'd been something in it for him. Did the damn things even work? She wanted to rip it from the ceiling and throw it on the ground. She clenched her hands. It was all evidence, additional ways to put Mark away.

She picked up a beeswax candle and rubbed it between her fingers. The sweet scent calmed her as did the waxy texture. She'd survived Mark. She wouldn't let this, or anything else the police discovered, break her.

She was strong.

***

Kim held his anger in check until he left Alyse's bedroom.

He gritted his teeth. It would be a pleasure to see Mark right now. He had a few choice things to say to him.

Kim shook his head. Alyse had gone white as a sheet which was an impressive feat considering her skin was pale already. The horror on her face made him want to punch something.

He jammed his hand into his pocket.

When Kim handed Humphries the laptop, Humphries asked, "How is she?"

"Angry," he said. "Did you find anything on the phone?"

Humphries nodded. "It's pretty sophisticated, much better than your standard software."

"Mark has a lot of money."

Humphries pursed his lips and one of his technicians entered the office. "We're done in the rest of the house."

"Can Alyse clear out the master bedroom?" Kim asked. Maybe it would make her feel better.

Humphries raised an eyebrow at his technician.

"We've got everything we can. Aside from the two cameras, there's nothing but clothes and Mark's personal things."

"I'll double-check with the detectives," Humphries said.

Kim entered the kitchen and sat at the table. He didn't like the idea of Alyse being on her own, but she needed space.

To distract himself, he flicked through his phone, uninterested in social media or any of the usual websites he visited. The things he'd purchased today were still in a bag on the table. Perhaps he should do some drawing.

He sighed. What he should do was focus on his graphic design business. It had always been easy to do it in his spare time and not have to worry whether he made any money. But seeing how Alyse had kept her apiary running despite all the shit Mark threw her way made him realise if he wanted his business to be a success, he had to put the work in. It wouldn't just magically succeed. And if he wanted flexibility in his work so he could help Alyse with her bees, then he really should focus on his graphic design.

He opened the notes app and typed. He needed to increase his portfolio of work and brainstorm where to find potential customers. Plenty of marketplace websites advertised jobs. Some didn't pay well but he could bid for a bunch of jobs, build his portfolio.

He'd talk to his father about cutting back his hours and training someone else to do the business side of things. His father had been adamant when he'd started the restaurant he wanted as little to do with administration as possible. None of Kim's younger sisters would be interested. Eden and Sarah were still at university and Leanne had a job in Perth. The other staff seemed happy in their roles, but he'd ask them if they wanted a change. Sometimes people hid what they wanted.

Just like he was hiding how he felt from Alyse. She'd kissed him.

It had taken all of his control to let her set the pace, choose how far to go. But he'd been dreaming about kissing her since high school and hadn't been disappointed.

Alyse's warning about being a mess was easy to ignore because he loved her anyway. But if he wasn't careful, his heart would be broken. He might be her rebound guy.

He had to be happy to have her back in his life again.

Kim opened the drawing pad and started doodling. What kind of logo would Beatrice's Beekeeping Supplies have? He played around with a few ideas, enjoying the flow of the idea to the page. He already had a couple of rough designs when Alyse entered the kitchen.

"What are you up to?"

"Just messing around." Nerves dancing in his stomach,

he showed her the logos.

She grinned. "These are great! Do you think you could modernise the apiary logo for me?"

Pleasure swept through him. "Sure. What do you want?"

She grabbed a jar of her honey from the pantry. "A new font and something a little less cartoony, but that still has the feel of the original."

He examined the existing logo and then sketched his idea while Alyse put the kettle on. By the time she'd made a cup of tea he had a rough example. "Something like this?"

She studied it and his nerves jiggled again. Then she smiled. "It's perfect."

Relief filled him. "Great. I'll refine it and find some fonts for you to approve."

Humphries walked into the kitchen. "We've finished with the master bedroom," he said. "You can clean it out."

Alyse's grin was wicked and lit up her whole being. "Let me get the bin bags."

***

Alyse stood at the doorway to the master bedroom. It was unrecognisable as the warm and loving place it had been when her parents had been alive. Now it was messy and masculine and smelled like Mark, dark, dangerous and a bit off. When she was finished, she'd burn some beeswax candles to remove the stench. She strode over to the window and opened it. The cold air blew in, but it revitalised her. She was getting rid of Mark.

"Where do we start?" Kim asked.

She handed Kim a bin bag. "His clothes."

"Are you throwing them out?"

It was so very tempting, but she wouldn't be the bad guy here. Even in hiding, Mark would find some way to twist her actions and make her seem unstable. "I'll call Craig to pick them up." Or maybe not. She'd forgotten about the business accounts. "I'll be back in a second."

She found Bosch in the office and handed her the list of transactions.

"What's this?" Bosch asked.

"A list of transactions both Mark and his brother Craig made on my business account. Craig shouldn't have had access to it."

Bosch scanned the list. "Thanks. Have you spoken to Craig about this?"

"Not yet. I was going to call him to pick up Mark's clothes."

"Hold off on that until I tell you," Bosch said.

Alyse nodded. If Craig was involved, she wanted him caught as well.

"Alyse, I need to talk to you about some of the documents in here," Bosch said.

Nerves sprang to her skin. "I told you Mark had me sign some contracts after my parents died."

Bosch nodded. "Why don't you take a seat?"

Alyse left the office, exhaustion dragging her feet. Bosch had taken her through everything she'd signed. The contract Mark had shown her was the worst of it, but there were a couple of smaller ones for companies which apparently existed only on paper. It would be her word against Mark's about how involved she'd been. Bosch said they might be able to get data off the tracking software Mark had put on her phone which would prove she'd made no contact with the companies.

It was a lot to hope for.

Kim sat on her bed, doodling in his notepad. He put it aside and rose as she walked in. "Everything OK?"

She shrugged. "As good as it can be." She really needed

something to cheer her up. "Ready to get rid of Mark?"

He grinned. "Absolutely."

His smile lifted her spirits and she walked into the master bedroom and flung open the wardrobe doors, grabbing a bunch of clothes on coat hangers and throwing them onto the bed. Already it was an improvement. She slid the clothes off the hangers and shoved them into black plastic bin bags. Every time she added an item, a little part of her felt lighter, freer.

It took very little time to clear out the wardrobe. Kim gathered the empty clothes hangers and hung them back in the cupboard. He seemed content to let her do the discarding. She appreciated it. She opened the dresser and took handfuls of clothes, shoving them in another bag. Within about twenty minutes she was done. The empty drawers and cupboard reduced the weight on her soul.

"Where do you want them?" Kim asked.

"By the front door."

While he carried them out, she started on Mark's personal effects—combs, aftershaves, deodorants. She piled them all into a bag and tied it off. Now to clean. She would scrub every speck of Mark from this room. Alyse fetched a bucket of water and cleaning products from the laundry and scrubbed the walls, the doors, every surface Mark might have touched. Kim joined her and they worked side-by-side, not speaking but both determined to finish as fast as possible.

With only one door to go, Kim asked, "Do you want me to vacuum?"

She nodded. "It's in the laundry."

Alyse had never seen Mark pick up a vacuum, but Kim knew what he was doing. It soothed her.

She went to find Humphries. "Can I do the lounge room?"

"Yes," he said. "The only room we still need is the

office."

"Thanks."

The vacuum switched off, and Alyse took one of her candles into the bedroom where Kim was packing up the machine. She closed the windows and lit the candle, placing it in the centre of the dresser where nothing could catch alight. The candle was in a cute glass container so there was no danger of any wax spilling.

"What's next?" Kim asked.

"The lounge room." She had boxes in her shed which would be the right size for all Mark's DVDs and games. "I'll fetch a few containers."

Clouds had gathered, and the air wasn't as crisp as it had been this morning, but it smelled sweet. She wanted to dance, sing and laugh. Across by Mark's shed, another team of technicians were labelling evidence and packing it into a large van. When they had finished, she was removing the building. She could donate the shell to the motocross club and they could turn it into a toilet block. She grinned.

When she returned to the house with the boxes, she handed Kim one. "Everything in here is Mark's."

His eyebrows lifted as he took in the bookshelves filled with DVDs but didn't comment. Instead he asked, "Is someone coming to get his stuff?"

"Not yet. I can store it in the shed for now."

They began, working side-by-side to fill the containers. Then all that was left were the devices. Alyse unplugged Mark's gaming machine and threw it into a box.

"Hey, Aly, these are yours, right?" Kim held two MVP basketball trophies.

Her heart squeezed. "Yeah." She took one from him. "I forgot I had them. Where were they?"

"In the cupboard."

She set the trophy on the coffee table. This summer

she'd sign up for a basketball team. She might be rusty, but she could buy a new basketball and use the old hoop by the shed to practise. Excitement simmered in her stomach.

They repeated the cleaning process, scrubbing, dusting and vacuuming until the room was clean. Next time she was in town, she'd buy some incense to burn in here. An exorcism.

Humphries came into the room. "Alyse, we have the camera footage from last night. Can you take a look? You might be able to identify the person who broke in."

"Of course."

She went into the kitchen where they'd taken over the table and watched the footage, Bosch and Kim by her side. A large man, about the same height as Mark, but a little slimmer passed underneath the camera. She frowned. "Is that Craig?" Son of a bitch.

Kim nodded. "Could be."

Her heart beat faster.

He was far more involved than she'd realised. What was he searching for? She turned to Bosch. "What now?"

Bosch pressed her lips together and then smiled. "Are Mark's things ready to go out?"

She nodded. "They're by the front door."

"Why don't you call Craig and ask him to pick them up?"

Alyse loved the idea of Craig being caught in a trap. "I'll call him now."

Craig answered immediately. "Alyse, how are you? Have you heard from Mark?"

It was the first time he'd ever cared about her welfare. She needed to be nice, get him out here. "I've had enough, Craig. I can't do this anymore. If you hear from him, please tell him he's not welcome on my property again."

"Alyse, calm down. Aren't you rushing things?"

Was he kidding? "He's been terrorising me for years,"

she snapped. "I should have kicked him out a long time ago." Craig had stood by and done nothing to help.

Bosch touched her arm, motioned for her to ask. Of course.

She swallowed her anger and made her tone contrite. "I've packed his clothes and things. Can you come and pick them up? I can't bear to see Mark again."

"Of course. I'll be right there."

"Thank you, Craig. I really appreciate it." She sighed. The years of practice seeming sincere were coming in handy. "Park by the front door. That's where all his stuff is." She hung up.

"He's coming?" Bosch asked.

"Yeah, he's on his way."

"I'll get my men to shut Mark's shed and move the cars out of sight. We don't want to give Craig any reason to run."

Alyse was really beginning to like this woman. "I'll watch for him in the lounge."

She and Kim returned to the lounge and she opened the window to let in some fresh air. The black leather couches had to go. They loomed in the space, taking up almost all of the room, declaring dominance. She'd move them out to the shed until she could get rid of them. A beanbag would be preferable. And that obnoxiously large TV just reminded her of Mark, so it had to go too. Maybe she could donate them to a homeless shelter or a refuge.

The trophies on the bookshelf caught her attention. Kim must have dusted them and put them back.

"How are you feeling?" Kim leaned against the doorframe watching her.

"Good." She smiled. "Great even. I know Mark's still out there, but I'm optimistic. Maybe Craig even knows where he is." She picked up one trophy, remembering the joy and pride she'd felt when she'd won it. "I'm going to start playing basketball again and I'm taking control of my business. It's going to be a new phase for me."

His smile warmed her heart. "I'm happy for you, Aly. And I'm here for whatever you need."

She moved to him and slipped her arms around his waist, hugging him. "Thank you." A slight whiff of the frangipani cleaning product they'd used tickled her nose, but she ignored it, resting her head against his chest.

Being in his arms felt so right.

Someone behind Kim cleared their throat. Alyse stepped back, her face warm as Adam stood in the hallway, looking out the front door.

She moved back into the lounge and asked, "What do you need, Adam?"

"We need to go over what to do when Craig arrives," he said. "We want you to invite him in here. I'll be outside in case he runs, and Lincoln is down the hall. Ask him to take a seat and offer him a drink and then leave him here." He turned to Kim. "I need you to stay in the kitchen."

"What are you worried about?" Kim asked.

Adam grimaced. "We don't think Craig will have a weapon, but just in case he has, we want as few people around as possible."

"No," Kim said.

Alyse placed a hand on him. "I'll be fine. Craig doesn't suspect anything and I'm good at hiding my fear. He won't have time to think it's a trap."

"I don't like it," Kim said.

"You don't have to," Adam answered. "But it's either the kitchen, or out in the shed." He stared Kim down.

Kim swore. "All right."

At the crunch of tyres outside, Alyse hurried to the window. Craig parked his four-wheel-drive by the front gate. "He's here." He must have been in town for him to arrive so fast.

"Come on." Adam grabbed Kim and hurried him away.

Alyse let out a breath. She could do this. As Craig walked up the steps, she opened the door. "Hey, Craig."

Concern crossed his face. "I'm sorry my brother hurt you again."

She stepped back to let him in. "Me too. Come into the lounge so you can see how much stuff there is."

She closed the door behind him, relief filling her. He was inside. "Can I get you a drink?"

He stared at all the boxes. "You're really kicking him out."

Why did he sound so surprised? "Yeah. Can I get you a coffee?"

He nodded. "That would be great." He poked around in one of the boxes.

Alyse strode down the hallway and passed Lincoln whose expression was grim. Behind her, he said, "Hey, Craig. We'd like to ask you a few questions about what you did last night."

She smiled.

Chapter 18

Alyse's phone rang as she reached the kitchen. She looked at the phone and continued down the hall. "Hi, Zamira." Her words faded, but in the lounge room Craig's voice was raised in a slightly panicked tone. Kim smiled. He deserved whatever was coming to him.

"When Alyse returns, you two should probably go out to her shed," Bosch said.

The police had taken over the lounge and kitchen, so there wasn't anywhere for them to sit. "All right." Maybe he could help Alyse with some work out there.

Alyse walked back in. "That was Zamira," she said. "The Malay women have been in touch with their families and are getting counselling."

"That's great."

Alyse nodded. "She invited me for coffee tomorrow afternoon."

"Are you going?"

"Yeah. We decided it would be safer to meet at the bakery."

Good idea. With the police almost finished, Alyse's safety was at the forefront of Kim's mind. Maybe he could convince her to stay in town with him until Mark was caught.

"How about we hang out in the shed while they question Craig?" Kim said. "You can put me to work."

She grinned. "You may regret the offer, but all right." She asked Bosch, "Do you need me for anything?"

"No. We'll come and get you when we're finished."

The sun was low in the sky as they walked across to the shed and the lack of clouds meant there was a particular bite in the air. Over by the man cave, the doors were open again and the lights were on.

There was a certain amount of satisfaction knowing Mark and Craig wouldn't get away with what they'd done.

Alyse flicked on the large overhead lights. Her van was parked with the new bed still inside. He'd get Adam to help him carry it inside after they were done with Craig. "What can I do?"

She studied him with a small smile that made his blood warm. "You're pretty good with a paint brush, aren't you?"

He nodded. "What needs painting?"

She pointed to several dozen wooden boxes across the shed. "Those."

He followed her over. "Are they hive boxes?"

"Yeah. They're called supers. I have some that need replacing and I want to put a few new ones out too."

"OK, show me what to do."

Some time later, Bosch entered the shed with a couple of police officers. Outside, night had fallen. They'd been painting for longer than Kim had realised.

"We're done for the day. These two will patrol the grounds overnight." Bosch introduced them and Kim shook their hands.

"Is there much left to do?" Alyse asked.

"We should be done tomorrow."

Alyse tapped her thigh. "When you catch Mark, he'll go

to jail, won't he?"

"For a very long time," Bosch assured her. "I'll talk to you about testifying in the morning."

Alyse hunched her shoulders.

"Are Adam and Lincoln still here?" Kim asked.

"No. They arrested Craig and took him in."

They'd have to move Alyse's bed into the house later.

"I'll see you tomorrow." Bosch left the shed with the officers.

Alyse sighed. "Let's call it a day. I need food and a shower."

Kim finished the side he was painting and then cleaned the brush. When Alyse turned off the shed lights, it plunged them into darkness, though someone had turned on the porch light. He took Alyse's hand and heard her sharp intake of breath.

"Sorry." He hadn't even thought about what he was doing. He tried to release her hand, but her fingers tightened around his.

"Don't be."

He couldn't make out her expression in the dark.

They walked across to the house and walking hand-in-hand with Alyse at the end of a day's work felt so right.

In the kitchen, Alyse pulled two microwave meals out of the freezer and held them up. "These do for dinner?"

"Yeah." But first he wanted a shower. "Do you know if Ryan dropped off my things?" It would be nice to change into something he hadn't been wearing for two days.

"No."

Kim rang his friend.

"Sorry, mate. I didn't get a chance," Ryan said.

Damn. He should have bought some clothes while he was in Albany. "It's fine. I'll pick them up tomorrow." He could do that while Alyse was with Zamira.

"No luck?" Alyse asked.

He shook his head.

"How about we wash your clothes tonight? I have a dressing gown that should fit you." She hurried out of the kitchen and returned a few minutes later with a fluffy navy blue dressing gown and a pair of shorts with a drawstring waist.

He tried the gown on. It fell to about calf length on him but he managed to belt it up. As long as he made no sudden movements, he shouldn't expose himself. "Thanks."

"Go have a shower. I'll heat dinner."

"Have you locked the doors?"

"I'll check them now."

Kim waited until she returned and confirmed the house was secure, then he went into the bathroom. At Alyse's request, the investigators had removed the surveillance cameras. He showered quickly, not wanting to leave Alyse alone. Then he slipped on the shorts and the fluffy gown, adjusting the belt to make sure it wouldn't come undone. He'd have to be careful he didn't spend the evening flashing his chest at Alyse. He gathered his clothes and took them through to the laundry. Before he switched on the washing machine, he called to Alyse, "Do you have any washing?"

"I'll leave mine for the morning."

He added the detergent and put the machine on the washer/dryer setting. As he walked into the kitchen, the microwave dinged.

"Great timing," Alyse said. She switched the meals, placing the steaming container on the table and set the microwave going again. Then she turned to him and her grin was like a supernova. "Love the outfit." Her chuckle sang to his heart and Kim resisted the urge to pull her close.

"I make it look good." He posed.

She shook her head. "I'll have my shower. Don't wait for me to eat."

Kim poured them both a glass of water. The curtains were closed, reminding him Mark was still out there, still a threat. What could he do to protect Alyse?

He sat in front of his limp corned beef and vegetable meal. He picked at it and debated whether to call Adam. No, he would still be with Craig, and Adam couldn't tell him about the case. Until Mark was caught, Alyse was in danger.

Perhaps he should booby trap the doors and windows, figure out an escape plan if Mark showed up. Kim's car was still parked outside, but he could move it next to Alyse's bedroom window.

The microwave finished and he took Alyse's meal out. How could he protect her from a man with a gun? He was useless. His presence wouldn't prevent Mark from attacking her, it would more likely encourage him.

The simple truth was they needed to find Mark and put him behind bars for good.

Could they lure him out somehow?

Not without a way to contact him, and he'd heard Bosch say they couldn't trace Mark's phone.

Alyse returned, her long red hair towel-dried, and wearing black tracksuit pants and a grey hoodie. It wasn't anything special, but it still looked good on her—the pants tight enough to hint at her lush bottom and the jumper not so baggy he couldn't glimpse her rounded breasts. He shouldn't be admiring her body. She didn't need that kind of attention right now. He sipped his water. "Have a nice shower?"

"Yes. Thank you." She sat across from him and started eating.

Kim forced himself to eat some of the bland meal. "Are you happy with what you achieved today?"

She grinned, a beam of sunshine, and Kim's breath left him.

"Yes. Today has to go down as one of the best days ever. I cleared Mark out, went on a boat without having a complete meltdown and I kissed..." Her face flamed and she glanced at her food. "You."

He cheered inwardly, but he stayed outwardly calm. "The kiss was a highlight for me too."

Her smile captured her pleasure. He wanted to kiss her again.

Slowly. Everything with Alyse had to be slow and careful so he didn't frighten her.

"I'm glad." She cleared her throat. "I thought tomorrow we'd finish the work in the shed."

"Sounds good." Staying at home while the police were still here would be safer for her. He hoped she didn't need to check any of her isolated hives anytime soon.

Kim threw the meal container in the bin and put the kettle on. He yawned, covering his mouth, exhaustion hovering over his body.

Alyse laughed. "Sounds like you're as tired as I am. How about we go to bed early?"

The vision of sleeping next to Alyse was appealing, but it wasn't what she meant. "Sounds good to me. Will you sleep in the master bedroom?" He got two mugs out of the cupboard.

She shook her head. "Not with that bed in there."

Kim closed his eyes. It killed him to think of what Alyse might have endured. He made two cups of tea and gave one to Alyse. "Finished?" At her nod, he disposed of her container. When he turned back she was studying him with her head tilted to the side, eyes wide.

"What is it?" He checked to ensure the dressing gown was still belted.

"You don't even realise you've done it, do you?" Was it

amazement in her voice?

"Done what?" His mind raced.

"You made me a cup of tea without asking and then cleaned up from dinner."

He frowned. "Sorry, I should have asked if you wanted a drink."

She stood, walking over to him. "Don't apologise. You knew I'd want one." She grasped his hands. "You did it without thinking, the kindness automatic. It's a beautiful thing." She kissed his cheek. "Thank you."

He slipped his hands onto her waist. "Aly…" She shouldn't be thanking him for a simple act of kindness. Hadn't Mark done anything nice for her? "You deserve it." He longed to kiss her, show her how much he cared. Their eyes met. Alyse slid her hands up his chest and over his shoulders, shifting closer, brushing against his front. The shorts he wore wouldn't hide his reaction for long. Heart thumping, his lips met hers. Her eyes fluttered closed, but he wanted to take in this moment, make sure he didn't go too far.

Her lips were so very soft and the touch of uncertainty made his heart ache. He kept his hold on her hips light even though he wanted to hold her tight and not let go. His hormones raged to take over, but he ignored them as her lips parted and her tongue slid over his.

Sweet heaven.

She tugged him closer and he shifted, but his erection pressed against her and she gasped, taking a step back.

Heat filled his face. "Sorry, I don't have a lot of control over what he does."

She bit her lip, and he clenched his hands to stop himself from hauling her into his arms again.

Her cheeks flushed, and she opened her mouth, but closed it again without saying anything.

"Out with it, Aly," he said.

She shook her head. "It's too much. I can't ask you."

He took her hand. "You can. We're friends."

"See, that's the problem," she groaned. "You view me as a friend who needs help and I want to have sex with you."

Kim's mouth dropped open.

He hadn't seen that coming.

Chapter 19

Alyse cringed at Kim's shocked expression. The heat in her face could have warmed her whole house. She threw up a hand and turned away. "Forget it. I shouldn't have said anything."

"Wait!" Kim grabbed her hand, stopping her.

She couldn't look at him. She'd let the daydreams she'd had in the shower get the better of her. Images of christening the new bed with Kim, of finally freeing herself of the fear she associated with the master bedroom, with sex. But the new bed was still in the van.

She'd started reclaiming her house, now she wanted to reclaim her body and there was no one she trusted more than Kim. It had been years since she'd felt any desire and now lust filled her body like a bubbly wine, dancing and giddy, wanting release.

"Aly." He lifted her chin. "Look at me."

She took a deep breath and raised her eyes. The intensity of his gaze made her heart race.

"You're so much more than a friend to me," he said. "I would love to have sex with you, but I don't want you to do anything you're not ready for."

Her chest squeezed and she could barely breathe. Never had a man been so willing to put her needs first. How could she not feel more for Kim? "I'm ready." She didn't want to explore the depth of her feelings for Kim right now. That was too scary.

His smile was slow and a little wicked as he pulled her towards him. "Stop me if I go too fast."

Their kisses until now had been nothing compared to this. Kim plundered her mouth, tasting and taking, and she groaned as heat flooded her. Yes. This. She kissed him back, squeezing his butt like she'd been wanting to do all afternoon. His erection pressed against her and she shifted, rubbing it.

Kim moaned. "Aly, bedroom." He lifted her up, and she wrapped her legs around his waist as he carried her down the hallway. He hesitated outside the master bedroom.

"No. My room."

He kicked the bedroom door shut behind them and set her on her feet.

The dressing gown came undone and his nipples were erect. She slid her hands over them, liking his hiss of pleasure. Pushed off his shoulders, the gown pooled on the floor. She'd never really admired the male form before, but now she took her time, running her hands over his muscles, bending her head to taste his skin.

Kim's hands tightened on her hips, his head tilted back, eyes closed.

"Is this all right?"

His nod was sharp.

Concern filled her. "Are you sure? I don't want to do something you don't like."

Kim's laugh was strangled. "Aly, you're killing me."

She stepped back, doubt filling her. "I'm sorry. I'm kind of new at this. Tell me what you like."

His eyes shot open. "I like everything you're doing," he growled. "Don't stop."

"But—"

"You're killing me in a good way. I'm trying to stay in

control."

Comprehension dawned. "Oh." Smugness filled her. "So you like it when I lick your nipples?"

"Yes."

She licked and sucked first one and then the other. His heart raced under her fingertips.

She pushed him back onto the bed and followed him down. Straddling him, she slowly explored his chest and then moved up to his collarbone, tasting and teasing until she nibbled his neck and he groaned again.

The control and power of knowing she aroused him, pleased him, was heady.

"Aly, can I touch you?" He gripped the quilt cover.

Still controlling himself. Still giving her control. Her heart sang. "Yes."

He slid his warm hands under her hoodie, up her back, his touch firm but gentle. She arched into them as tingles spread over her skin. His thumbs brushed her breasts and she gasped, closing her eyes in pleasure. Not even when things between her and Mark had been good had it been this amazing. He'd always been in a rush, only interested in his own pleasure.

Her body was so hot she stripped off her hoodie and the cool air kissed her skin.

Kim swore and brushed the bruises on her stomach. "Maybe we shouldn't do this. You must still hurt."

"I do, but your touch makes me forget." She wanted this, wanted him.

He searched her eyes.

"Unless you'd prefer not to. I know it's not pretty." Perhaps he didn't want reminders of what she'd been through.

Kim shook his head. "Aly, you're so beautiful." His gaze full of wonder made her feel like a goddess. He shifted and sat, adjusting her on his lap and took her breast into his mouth. Hot sparks of fire seared her as he tasted her. She gasped for breath as emotion and sensation swirled inside her, whipping around in a frenzy.

"Kim," she cried, her head flung back as the sensations overwhelmed her body. So much pleasure, so much joy.

"You're a goddess." Kim's fingers circled her other breast. He nibbled at a spot just under her earlobe.

She twitched, the pleasure so close to the surface.

"I want to see all of you, Aly. Can I finish undressing you?"

"Yes." She lay on the bed and Kim knelt beside her, slowly drawing her pants down her legs. His touch was so slow and steady and she savoured it.

"Can I taste you?"

The direction of his gaze ensured she understood exactly what he meant. Mark had never gone down on her. She nodded.

Kim settled between her legs and the moment his tongue met her skin, all thoughts left her mind. She gasped, arching into him, needing more and he required no further encouragement. He licked, sucked and tasted her until she was writhing beneath him. She'd never known it could be this good, never known she could feel like this. Joy washed over her along with her orgasm.

Tears pricked her eyes and her heart pounded as she got her breath back and Kim settled next to her, pulling her into his arms, kissing her forehead.

"You OK, Sweetheart?"

She nodded frantically, unable to form words.

He pushed her hair away from her face, concern in his eyes. "Did I hurt you?"

"It was amazing." She shifted and his erection pressed into her. Lust still filled her. Apparently a lifetime without decent sex had turned her into a sex maniac. She touched his penis, wanting to return the pleasure he'd given her.

Kim stopped her. "You don't need to, Aly."

She frowned. "I want to. I want you inside of me." His penis twitched under her hand.

"We don't have any condoms."

She hadn't considered that. "I'm on the pill." She'd taken it religiously for years. Mark had refused to use condoms, and she hadn't wanted to end up pregnant. But there was the box of condoms her mother had brought her all those years ago. "Give me a second." She reached down and opened the bottom drawer of her bedside table. Yep. They will still there. She checked the date. "It's expired." Damn. Kim looked so sexy lying half-naked on her bed. Could they risk it? Pregnancy wouldn't be an issue, but… "When I discovered Mark having an affair, I had all the tests. I'm clear and I haven't had sex since."

"I've never had unprotected sex." Kim pulled her back to him. "An expired condom is better than nothing." He kissed her, his passion pouring into the kiss. "Do you trust me?"

She did. As an answer, she slid his shorts off and opened the condom packet. Crap. The last time she'd used one was in a high school sex education class. What was she supposed to do?

"Let me." Kim took the condom and slid it on. Then he shifted so he was on top of her, his penis nudging her entrance. "Are you sure?"

"Yes." She opened her legs and he slid into her. She moaned. Bliss.

He moved slowly, his arms shaking as he held himself above her, not squashing her. She moved with him, the sensations building as he filled her again and again.

"More," Alyse demanded. This was what sex was supposed to be like, pleasuring each other, being in control, wanting everything he could give her. She squeezed her eyes closed, savouring the moment, lost in the sensations building in her body. Kim moved faster. He was close. She wanted to share the moment with him.

"Aly," Kim cried, and her name on his lips filled her heart and she shattered once more.

It was several minutes before Alyse could form any coherent words. "That was…" What word could she use? "Incredible. Mind-blowing. Out of this world."

Kim chuckled and pulled her against his chest. "Careful. You'll give me a big head." He kissed her forehead. "It's never been that good for me either."

She glanced at him. "Really?"

He smiled. "We make a good team."

Her heart warmed. Is that what she wanted? A team, a partnership? Yes, she wanted what her parents had, a best friend to share her life with.

His hand brushed her side and she leaned into it.

"Will you share my bed tonight?" It was too small for the two of them, but she didn't want to let him go.

"I'd love to." He kissed her and then yawned, covering his mouth. He winced. "Sorry."

Alyse grinned. "Don't be. I'm tired too." She switched off the light. It was nice not having to worry about offending Kim. He wouldn't read the worst into any of her actions.

Kim pulled her into his arms. She was safe and warm.

Alyse smiled and fell asleep.

***

Kim woke with a start as someone pounded on the door. It was light outside and next to him Alyse stirred, her red hair spread over her pillow. His heart swelled. Last night had been incredible and he could barely believe he was here with her.

Alyse groaned and reached for her phone. "It's eight

o'clock. It must be the police."

"I'll answer it. Why don't you have a shower? I'll see if my clothes are dry."

"OK. Thanks."

Pleased she was letting him do something for her, Kim dressed in the shorts and dressing gown and hurried down the hallway to the front door where someone was knocking again. He checked the peep hole before opening it to Detective Bosch.

Her eyebrows raised. "Did I get you out of bed?"

He ran a hand through his hair. "Yeah. Alyse and I needed the sleep after the past few days."

"Sorry. I just wanted to tell you we're back, and should be done within a couple of hours."

He grimaced. Not long until Alyse was on her own. "What does that mean for Alyse's safety?"

"We'll have to discuss it. Is she up?"

"She's in the shower."

"All right. I'll discuss options with her, but if she's not willing to leave her property, there's not much we can do for her." Bosch shrugged apologetically. "I'll be back later." She headed around the house to the man cave.

Kim closed the door. He understood Alyse's reasoning, but her safety was more important than her property. Somehow he'd have to convince her to either hire a bodyguard, or go to a safe house. She wouldn't like either option. He sighed and went to the laundry to get his clothes out of the machine. The jeans were crinkled, and his jumper and T-shirt appeared smaller. Frowning, he tried on the T-shirt. It clung to him like it was made of Lycra. Crap. The jumper had also shrunk. No way he could wear them. Maybe he could convince Alyse to run into town with him this morning to get some clothes.

He put the dressing gown back on and headed for the kitchen. Breakfast first.

He played some upbeat music on his phone. It suited his mood—happy and optimistic. He had no doubts about how he felt about Alyse. He loved her with all of his heart and wanted her in his life.

He should be cautious though.

It might have just been sex to her. Another way of exorcising Mark from her life. Kim couldn't get his hopes too high. But he wouldn't back away from the challenge.

Alyse entered the kitchen, her hair tied back in a bun exposing her luscious neck he'd nibbled on the night before. "Are your clothes dry?"

"Yeah, but I ran into a problem." He showed her the T-shirt.

She laughed. "Did you wash it in hot water?"

He shrugged. "I chose the automatic washer/dryer setting."

"Are they all that small?"

"I haven't tried the jeans yet. Thought I'd shower before I do." He took a pot from the cupboard. "I was about to make porridge. Do you want some?"

"I'll make it," she said. "Go shower so you can get out of that gown. I'll find you something to wear."

He stroked the lapels. "Isn't this a good look for me?"

She laughed. "I prefer you out of it." Her eyes darkened and her face flushed as she glanced away.

Lust shot through him. "Your wish is my command." He shed the dressing gown and stalked towards her, kissing her hard. Though he would willingly take her in the kitchen, she was probably sore. "I'll be back in five."

Her breathless, "Sure," made him smile as he walked out the door.

The jeans were obscenely tight, but they would do for a trip into town. Kim made a note always to check the temperature on a washing machine in the future. He returned to the kitchen shirtless and Alyse's eyes widened.

She grinned, her whole face alive with joy. "I like the look."

He chuckled. "Thanks. Do you have a big jacket I could borrow?"

"Yeah." She gestured to an apiary jacket on the table. "Try it on."

It was a little snug. "After breakfast can we head into town? I don't think I can wait until this afternoon for a change of clothes."

Alyse hesitated. "I wanted to work today. Why don't you go now while the police are still here?"

He hated leaving her alone, but she would be safer here with the armed police officers. "OK." He ate some of his porridge. "What will you do?"

"I'll finish building the frames."

"OK, I'll finish the painting when I return."

She smiled. "That would be great."

Kim finished his breakfast and grabbed his keys from the bench. "I'll be less than an hour. I'll let Bosch know I'm heading out."

Alyse kissed him. "See you when you get back."

Kim spoke to Bosch and then drove into town, stopping at the police station for the bag Sarah had left him. As he parked, one of the police cars sped out of the yard, Lincoln behind the wheel. Kim hurried inside and Ryan's eyebrows lifted. "Nice jeans."

"Laundry mishap. What's going on?"

Ryan firmed his lips. "I can't say. You after your stuff?" He reached below the counter for a bag.

"Thanks. Can I get changed before I go?"

Ryan opened the door into the interrogation room and Kim changed into a different pair of jeans and a warm jumper. He went through the bag. He could do with some more things. While he was in there, the police station phone rang.

Kim exited the room as Ryan picked up his keys from the table. "We have to go. There's been a car crash on the highway."

Hopefully it wasn't anyone he knew. "I'm done. Thanks, mate. Take care." Kim returned to his car and drove home, going through the main house to say hello to his sisters. Eden was heading out the door dressed for work. She stopped. "Are you back now?"

He shook his head. "Just picking up a few things."

Her shoulders slumped. "Damn." She stomped out the door.

In the lounge room, Sarah was stretched out on the couch watching a reality TV show featuring drag queens. "Hi, Kim."

He waved. "Glad you're making the most of your holiday."

She pouted. "Don't judge. Uni was brutal this semester."

She was right. He didn't know what university was like.

"Have the police found Mark yet?" Sarah asked.

"Not yet."

"Be careful. Didn't you say they found guns and sex slaves in his shed?"

"I can take care of myself." He headed for his granny flat. The door was unlocked. Sarah must have forgotten to lock it after herself. He was halfway across the room when he registered the mess. Couch cushions on the floor, the coffee table on its side and paper everywhere.

"I knew you'd come home eventually."

The voice made him whirl around, heart pounding. Mark stood in the doorway of the bedroom, clothes grubby, hair a mess and pointing a gun at Kim. Fuck. Kim's heart lurched and he stepped back.

"Don't move," Mark growled.

Kim resisted raising his hands. Think. Be calm. Talk your way out of this. "Mark. Nice to see you." He dug his phone out of his pocket, fingers shaking as he dialled the police.

"Put it down!" Mark stormed over and ripped the phone out of his hand, disconnecting the call. He threw the phone across the room.

Worth a try.

"You think you're smart," Mark snarled. "But I'm smarter. You'll pay for stealing my woman."

Now wasn't the time to antagonise Mark. His gaze was full of fury. "What do you want, Mark?"

"I want my life back and I want Alyse to love me."

Kim's hands clenched. The door was only a couple of metres away, but Mark wouldn't miss if he made a run for it.

"Kim!" Sarah's call stopped his heart. He whirled around as she strode over the grass towards the granny flat.

"If she sees me, she's dead." Mark shifted back into the bedroom. "If you warn her, you're both dead."

Kim opened the door, blocking the entry so Mark couldn't shoot her. "What's up?"

"Dad rang," she said. "Wants to know if you're free for a family brunch tomorrow morning. He says you can bring Alyse."

Mark growled.

Sarah frowned, glanced behind him. Damn. Kim ran his hand through his hair, moving to block her view. "Sure. What time?" He didn't dare speak in Vietnamese and tell her to call the police.

"About eight-thirty."

"All right. I'll see you then."

Sarah tilted her head. "Is everything all right?"

"Yeah. I'm just getting a few more things. My clothes

had a fight with the washing machine and the washing machine won." He waved and moved back into his flat, hoping she wouldn't come any closer.

"OK. Later."

He let out a breath as she returned to the house.

"How dare you invite her to a family event," Mark said as Kim closed the door.

"We're friends," Kim said.

Mark glared. "We'll see about that. See if she comes running when she knows you're in trouble." He called someone and said, "We'll be there in ten," and then gestured to the door. "Here's what we're doing. We're going out the side door and around the back of the flat. If anyone sees us, I'll shoot them, got it?"

Kim nodded, his heart pounding. The property backed onto bush. Chances were high, Mark had come from there. Did he have a vehicle? At least it would give Kim a chance to get away. They'd have to climb the fence and Mark couldn't hold the gun on him the whole time.

He wasn't letting Mark use him as bait to get to Alyse.

No way.

He scanned for something to use as a weapon. He couldn't overpower Mark, but he was fast.

Nothing.

He hurried through the laundry door and ducked behind the granny flat, the distance between the wall and the fence only a metre. Mark was right behind him, making the space suffocating. "What now?"

"Climb it."

Kim laughed. "You overestimate my upper body strength."

"Do it or I'll shoot you, then I'll go inside and show your sister what a real man is like."

Chills spread through Kim, followed by red hot rage. He gritted his teeth. The gun was only centimetres away from him. Without a word, Kim grabbed the top of the fence and hauled himself over. With Mark's threat playing in his mind, Kim didn't dare run, but he scanned the bush for a heavy stick. Nothing. Frustration filled him. He'd find another opportunity when they were further away from home. When Sarah couldn't be hurt.

Mark landed with a thud next to him and shoved the gun into Kim's back. "That way."

Not far away, an old white ute was parked at the edge of the bush. Mark gave him the keys. "Get in and drive where I tell you."

Kim leapt inside but couldn't get the engine started before Mark joined him. He reached for the seat belt.

"Keep it off," Mark said, strapping himself in.

No chance of crashing the car and getting away. He followed Mark's directions along the outskirts of town, rain spitting against the windscreen. Yesterday's beautiful weather had been an anomaly. He turned towards the ocean. The beach road was quiet and the rain now fell in sheets, making the turns slippery and requiring all of Kim's attention.

"Turn left."

Kim frowned as he slowed, looking for a road. A small track, barely distinguishable amongst the bush. "Here?"

"Yeah."

They were about five kilometres from town, and not many would be out in this kind of weather. The track ended, and the ocean was visible through the trees.

"Get out."

By Kim's calculations they had to be around the point from town where large granite boulders met the ocean. No one came this way because there were more accessible swimming and fishing spots along the coast. Kim pushed open his door, the rain soaking him. Could he wait until Mark got out and then jump back in and drive away? No.

Mark would have an easy shot.

Kim pocketed the keys and pushed his hair back, wiping the rain off his face. Maybe he could run for it. There were enough trees to give him some cover.

Mark picked up something from the tray of the ute and tossed it at Kim. Kim caught the heavy metal chains.

"Put them on," Mark said.

What the—? Leg shackles—similar to the type prisoners wore. Had Mark used them on the kidnapped women? If Kim put them on, running wouldn't be an option. He'd be more at Mark's mercy than he already was. His gaze caught on Mark's moon boot. Of course. With a broken foot, Mark wouldn't be able to chase Kim if he ran. No wonder he had the chains.

"Hurry up."

What options did he have? Run and risk being shot, or hope he could outsmart Mark later.

Even if Kim got away, Mark could still call Alyse, and lure her here before Kim found a phone to call her.

"Now." Mark pushed the gun hard into Kim's chest. He wasn't playing around.

Slowly Kim squatted and attached the first cuff. His best chance was getting back into the car, but Mark stood between him and it.

He was screwed. Kim clipped the second cuff and stood. The cuffs rattled and the short chain made it difficult to walk.

"That way." Mark gestured to the ocean, the waves noisy as they crashed against the rocks. Kim inhaled the salty air, and stepped through the low bush, hoping an idea would come to him. By the time he reached the granite rocks, he had nothing.

"Up you go."

The rain washed down the dark grey surface making it slippery. Maybe if he pushed Mark, he'd hit his head. His first step rejected the idea as he slipped and fell heavily onto his hands. Mark's laugh bellowed behind him.

Kim climbed to his feet, wiping his stinging palms on his wet jeans. At the peak of the rock he had a clear view of the ocean. Someone stood at the tiller of a boat anchored not far offshore and between the boulders was a channel leading onto a small beach. Damn.

"Keep going." Mark shoved him in the back and Kim caught himself before he sprawled down the rock.

What was Mark's plan? The boat would have to gun it to get through the narrow channel without getting pushed against the rocks. Kim scanned the ocean to see if the waves were coming in sets.

"Down there." Mark gestured to the beach and then waved to the boat.

As Kim reached the sand, the boat sped through the small gap, surfing the wave. It slowed and gently brushed against the beach. They'd done this before. The skipper jumped off the boat and Kim recognised Mark's nephew, Don. His eyes were full of fear and fury.

Mark grabbed him. "Remember, you tell anyone about this and I'll kill your little brother, got it?"

Don nodded. He walked past Kim, shoulder checking him and murmured, "Flare gun." He climbed the rock not looking back.

Kim blinked. Was Don helping him?

"Get in," Mark said.

Kim's boots squelched as he climbed awkwardly into the boat searching for the gun. The orange safety device was on the dashboard. Before he could reach it, Mark shoved the boat back, and the movement caused Kim to trip on his chains and sprawl onto the wet carpet. He struggled to stand and by the time he did, Mark was at the wheel.

Mark shifted the boat into reverse and backed the boat

out of the channel. Yeah, this wasn't the first time he'd used this spot. Kim eyed the flare gun and then the gun Mark still held in his hand. He'd have to time it perfectly.

Mark pulled his phone out of his pocket and dialled. "I've missed you, Alyse." The pure malice on his face made Kim sick. "I can change your mind," he said. "I'll trade your Asian whore for you. Take my dinghy and meet me off Old Man's Blowhole."

Kim's heart froze. No. Over his dead body. "You're crazy. She won't get on a boat in this weather."

"Fear is a great motivator." Mark grinned.

No. He wouldn't let her. "Tell Bosch, Alyse," he yelled.

Mark pistol-whipped him and Kim slumped against the wet, smelly marine carpet, his head spinning. Darkness claimed him.

Chapter 20

"We're finished now, Alyse." Bosch stood at the entrance of the shed.

Alyse placed the paintbrush on the can and joined Bosch at the door. "Already?" Kim wasn't back yet.

Bosch smiled. "We have everything we can use. It will keep the lab busy for the next few weeks."

Alyse shivered and hugged herself as the wind blew around her. The clouds were low and dark, and the trees shook back and forth. Over by Mark's shed, the technicians were packing up. "So what now?"

"Now we keep looking for Mark. Have you thought further about going into a refuge?"

Maybe she was crazy not to. "I'll call them." Mark was dangerous, but if he couldn't get to her, he might target Kim. Better if she was the bait.

"Great. Is Kim back yet?"

"No. He shouldn't be long." He'd been gone forty minutes already, but he was probably catching up with his family.

"I don't want to leave you here by yourself."

She wasn't keen on the idea either. "I'll call Kim and if he's going to be much longer, I'll go over to Jeremy's."

Zamira had said to drop around any time. She dialled Kim's number, but he didn't answer. She frowned. Perhaps he hadn't heard it. Unease crept into her stomach as she called Zamira and explained the situation.

"Sure, come around. I'll put the kettle on."

Alyse hung up. "I'm going next door," she told Bosch.

The police vehicles were packed and Khan waited for Bosch in the car. Alyse shook her hand. "Thank you for your help."

"Thank you for yours," Bosch said.

Alyse climbed into her van. This was it. When she returned, she'd have to be alert, constantly on the lookout for Mark. Nausea swelled in her stomach. She was an idiot. Her life would be constant paranoia, constant tension. Going to a refuge, even for a week while the police actively searched for Mark, would be sensible and Kim could go away as well. She'd call the refuge when she arrived at Jeremy's.

As she reached the road, she waved to the detectives in front of her and they drove away.

She was about to pull out after them when her phone rang. "Hello?"

"I've missed you, Alyse."

Mark. She tightened her grip on the phone and glanced around. Was he watching her? Had he seen the police leave? She forced herself to speak. "I haven't missed you."

Mark's next words shot her heart into her throat. He had Kim. Fear trampled her, and she gritted her teeth, focusing on what he was saying. He wanted her not Kim. All she had to do was board a tiny boat in terrible weather and motor offshore near the blowholes. Bile rose in her throat. The dinghy still sat in the open doorway of the man cave and she did a U-turn and drove towards it. The wind buffeted the car and she bit back the urge to scream. "Prove you have Kim."

In the background, Kim yelled, "Tell Bosch, Alyse."

Shit. Kim was there.

"If I see the police, I'll shoot him," Mark growled. "You have twenty minutes, then I use Kim for target practice." He hung up.

Alyse squeezed her eyes shut, clutching her stomach to stop from vomiting. This was her punishment. He'd taken Kim and made it virtually impossible for her to save him. Even as panic threatened to take control, she checked the time and then backed the van to the dinghy and connected it. One step at a time.

She couldn't lose Kim. Not now. Not ever.

Though she doubted Mark would stick to his word about doing a trade, she had to try. She scanned the boat. It had been so long since she'd prepared a boat for a day out. What did she need to check? Fuel first. She tried lifting the fuel tank, but it was too heavy. The cover was back over the engine, so she assumed Mark had fixed the issue. The drain bung was in and then her gaze caught on the life jackets sitting on the bench next to the EPIRB beacon and flare gun Mark's father had bought. Alyse's heart jumped and she threw them into the boat. Perfect.

She leapt back into the car and tore out of her property. The rain, which had been threatening all day, suddenly unleashed, blurring the windscreen. She'd already wasted precious minutes preparing the boat. As she sped past Jeremy's place, she hoped Zamira would realise something was wrong when she didn't turn up. Seconds later her phone rang.

"Where are you going?" Zamira asked.

"Mark's taken Kim."

"What?"

Alyse took a breath to calm herself. "He'll trade me for Kim. We're meeting somewhere off Old Man's Blowhole." Though she doubted she'd still be alive when Mark made it to shore, the police would catch him. "Don't let the police come after me," she said. "Mark will shoot Kim if he sees them. Have them monitor from the shore." Even if they commandeered a boat in time, she had a head start. "I have an EPIRB in the dinghy. I'll turn it on when I see Mark's boat so the police have my position."

"Alyse, you can't do this. It's too dangerous."

"If I'm not there in twenty minutes, Mark will shoot him." Her heart squeezed. "Please, Zamira. I can't let Kim die."

Zamira groaned. "I'll call them now. Be careful." She hung up.

Alyse yelled, the pain and frustration ripping out of her like a wounded animal. She'd finally found friends, people she trusted and Mark wanted to rip them from her. Enough was enough. She wouldn't let Mark beat her. He'd taken too much already.

She and Kim would be alone on the ocean with him. Mark had a gun, and he had a boat—either stolen or his father's—but it would be better than hers. Even if she got Kim on the dinghy, Mark could run them down, or shoot Kim from a distance.

The gun was her first hurdle. Perhaps the rain would render it useless. Disarming Mark would be impossible, and she might not have the opportunity to shoot the flare gun. What kind of speed and accuracy did it have?

She pulled up at the boat ramp and her heart froze. The ocean was choppy, dark, menacing. The waves weren't as big as they were last week, but it wasn't the smooth glassy surface of yesterday. Nausea rose, and she swallowed hard.

She forced her hand to move, to put the van in reverse and back down the ramp, not bothering to take off the rear lights. Mark wouldn't be using it again if she had anything to do with it. Rain drenched her as she got out and the wind blew through her. Quickly she loosened the cable and pushed the boat off.

She clenched her hands as the dinghy bobbed in the waves. Time to get in and go. She waded knee deep into the water. Where was the life jacket? She grabbed it from the bottom of the boat, and put it on. It gave her a measure of comfort.

She checked the time. More than ten minutes since she'd left her property. She visualised Kim's deep brown eyes, his patient gaze and the tension in her body lessened. She could do this. She *would* do this.

Waiting for a break in the waves, she leapt onto the dinghy and started the motor. It purred to life. Relief filled her. She accelerated, one hand rested on the tiller while the other gripped the metal side.

Kim. Keep thinking about Kim, about his rescue, not about the depth of the dark ocean, or the soaking waves, the salt stinging her eyes. The pressure in her chest made it difficult to breathe. She sucked in short sharp breaths. Focus on something else. Old Man's Blowhole was still a fair distance away and speed wasn't an option in this weather, in this boat.

After she motored past the break, she turned east, keeping as close as possible to the shore. If anything happened, she could swim to the beach.

No, she had to rescue Kim.

She scanned the empty ocean for another boat. They must already be around the point.

Was Kim still alive?

The EPIRB caught her attention. She uncoiled the rope and tied one end to the fuel tank.

Her phone vibrated in her jeans and she slowed while she tried to dig it out of her pocket.

"Hello?" She rested the phone between her ear and her shoulder.

"You're late."

"I'm almost there," she pleaded. "I'm coming around the point now." Or would be shortly.

"I knew you were faking it. You didn't want to go fishing with me." She wanted to vomit at his flat tone. This was furious Mark, unpredictable Mark.

She prayed for Kim's life, tears welling in her eyes. "I'm terrified," she sobbed. "You gave me no choice."

"Sure I did. You could have stayed at home."

"Please, Mark. I couldn't let anyone die."

"Who said anything about dying?"

She closed her eyes. What had he said? "You said you would use him for target practice."

Mark laughed. "Yeah, I did. I should punish Kim for your tardiness."

Anger spiked. He'd set her up to fail. Getting there in twenty minutes was impossible. She bit her tongue to stop lashing out at him. Placate, don't antagonise. She swallowed and lowered her voice. "Please, Mark," she begged. "I'm sorry. I'm not as fast as you." She used the tone he liked, that made her sound cowed.

"Kim has chains on his ankles," Mark said. "If I push him overboard, do you think he'll sink?"

Chains? Terror blocked her throat. She pushed the boat faster, the roar making it difficult to hear the phone. "That wasn't part of the agreement. We were going to trade."

"Maybe I'll push him in and come to you."

She wouldn't ever win against him. "No! I'm here now." She cleared the point. Nothing. No boat as far as she could see. "Where are you?" She slowed to hear his reply.

Mark's chuckle chilled her bones. "About a kilometre offshore."

She retched as she stared towards the dark horizon, empty of everything except ocean. Bastard. "I can't. Please, Mark. Don't make me do it."

"You don't have to. I can leave Kim here."

"How do I know you're really out there?"

"Are you calling me a liar?"

She gritted her teeth and wiped the rain off her face. "No."

"Kim will tell you where we are." A scuffle, then Kim's voice.

"Alyse, don't come. Call the police."

Tears pricked her eyes.

Kim grunted and Mark growled, "Tell her where we are, or I'll shoot you."

"No."

The gun shot made Alyse shriek. Kim yelled in pain and Mark came back on the line. "Better hurry or he might bleed to death." Mark hung up.

Alyse's hands shook. She couldn't do this alone. Kim needed medical help, he might already be dying. Mark wouldn't get away with this. She dialled triple zero and told the operator she needed police and ambulance. "My name is Alyse Wilson. My ex, Mark Patton is wanted by the police. He's kidnapped my friend and taken him on a boat about a kilometre out from Old Man's Blowhole. He just shot my friend, and he's demanding I trade myself for Kim."

"Where are you?"

"I'm at the blowhole, about to head out to meet them."

"Ma'am, I don't advise that. I've notified the police and ambulance. It's best if you let them deal with it."

"I can't. Please tell them to hurry. I'm turning on my EPIRB now so they can find me." She prayed they were already on the way. She tucked her phone into her bra and switched on the EPIRB. Determination swept over her as she opened the throttle. Kim couldn't die. She loved him. She wouldn't let Mark take him away. The ocean wouldn't take another loved one from her.

She pushed the dinghy as hard as it would go, crashing down over waves, jolting off the seat, but her terror of losing Kim dulled her fear of the ocean.

Was Kim bleeding out? Was he already dead?

She scanned the horizon. A lump over there. She changed course. After Kim was on board, she'd head back to the blowholes. It was the closest car access for an ambulance.

So how could she overpower Mark, disarm him and get an injured Kim to safety?

Maybe if she tucked the flare gun in the back of her life jacket and faced Mark, Kim could grab it.

But what if he was restrained, or unconscious? There was nowhere else to hide it. She placed the gun in her lap. Until she saw where Mark was, where Kim was, she'd have to play it by ear. Mark was already angry, and he'd be simmering over all the wrongs she'd done him.

Would begging help? He always liked it when she begged.

Her phone rang.

She slowed, her heart racing. "Hello?"

"Alyse, it's Sergeant Zanetti. Where are you?"

"About half a kilometre south of Old Man's Blowholes."

"Can you see Mark or Kim?"

"The boat's about six hundred metres away," she said. "Where are you?"

"On our way. Stay there until we arrive."

She shook her head. "I can't. Mark will kill Kim if he sees the police."

"We have a hostage negotiator on board," Lincoln said.

Alyse laughed. "That won't help."

"Alyse, please. Don't put yourself in danger. We're trained to handle this."

She wished it would help. "You don't know Mark like I

do. I'm Kim's best chance." The truth of the words resonated. She'd had years of studying Mark, interpreting his every mood, his every twitch. She would have a split second warning before Mark made his move. It might be enough. "I've activated an EPIRB, Sergeant. You should be able to find us." She hung up.

She would distract Mark long enough for the police to arrive.

She tucked the phone back into her bra and accelerated again. As she drew closer, she recognised Richard's blue boat with *The Vale* painted on the side. Only Mark was on the deck. Her heart stopped. Had he already thrown Kim overboard?

She scanned the water nearby. Nothing.

She stopped about five metres away. "Where's Kim?"

Mark hauled Kim to his feet one-handed, the gun in his other hand. "Right here."

Kim's face was pale, and he shivered in only a T-shirt, his blood-stained jumper tied in a tourniquet around his left thigh. "Don't come any closer, Alyse."

She didn't need to fake her horror. If the bullet wound didn't kill him, hypothermia would. Act fast.

Mark studied her, assessing, waiting. She had to get him on her side. Somehow. Play to his beliefs. Make him feel important.

Though the words hurt, she scowled at Kim. "You let Mark beat you?" She let the disbelief flood her tone. "Did you put up any fight?"

Hurt flashed across Kim's face and his mouth dropped open. She ignored it.

Mark laughed. "Nope. He was weak as piss. He followed my every command."

Laughing was good. The tension in Mark's shoulders was replaced by a puffed-up chest.

Work with it.

Alyse bit her lip. "Maybe I was wrong." She pulled alongside the boat and threw Kim the rope. "I was so scared. You hurt me." Her eyes stayed on Mark's and she wiped the rain from her face as if wiping a tear. He shifted, unsure. Behind him a life jacket hung over each seat and on the dash was another EPIRB and flare gun. Thank you, Richard.

Mark smiled, smug satisfaction on his face. "I knew you'd come back. I could have killed you yesterday when I shot at you, but you made Kim sleep on the floor."

She wanted to be sick. He'd been watching them on the cameras in her room. Thank God they'd discovered them and removed his access.

"You shouldn't have lied to me," he continued.

Alyse didn't correct him, didn't look at Kim. "I'm so sorry." She thought about how she would feel if Kim died and tears sprang to her eyes. "Will you forgive me?"

Mark still pointed the gun at Kim, but he relaxed his hold. She wouldn't be fast enough to use the flare gun on her lap. She fell forward as a wave rocked the boat and let the gun fall off. Carefully she climbed to her feet. "Can I please come aboard?" She waited for his nod before climbing onto Richard's boat. Get between Mark and Kim.

Mark hesitated and then shook his head. "You're weak, Alyse. Are you going to run back to him the next time we fight, the next time you're scared?"

Did he seriously believe he would get away from the police?

Kim grabbed her arm. "What are you doing? You can't go back to him."

Her heart ached that Kim believed her act.

"Shut up," Mark yelled. "It's your fault it's come to this."

Damn it. He was getting mad. Alyse stumbled and fell against Kim. "Trust me," she whispered. "Get to the dinghy."

His hands tightened on her arms.

She stepped back and prayed the chains on Kim's ankles weren't too heavy—though he still held the dinghy tow line too. "You're right. He's weak. We don't need him." She pushed Kim hard in the chest. His eyes widened as he flailed backwards and fell over the side into the water.

Mark gaped at her.

Now. She grabbed the life jacket which hung over the passenger seat and flung it towards Kim who struggled to stay afloat. He lunged for it as she picked up the flare gun on the dash and spun around pointing it at Mark's chest, her heart pounding. "Drop the gun."

"You lied to me." He swung the gun towards her, his eyes dead.

Her breath caught.

This was it. He would kill her. She closed her eyes and squeezed the trigger.

Chapter 21

Kim heard two shots almost simultaneously and then glass shattered. His heart stopped as he gripped the side of the dinghy and twisted. Mark stood at the back, clutching something smoking on his chest. A flare. With a scream of pain, Mark dived into the water.

Where was Alyse?

The chains made it difficult to swim and the salt in his bullet wound stung beyond belief, but determination buoyed Kim as he hauled himself into the dinghy and started the engine. "Alyse!" Heart pounding, he brought the boat alongside and cut the engine. She was curled in a ball, her red hair over her face blocking her expression. "Alyse." Fear punched him in the gut.

She had to be alive.

He climbed back into the boat and pulled Alyse up. "Aly, talk to me." He swept back her hair. "Are you hurt? Did you get shot?"

She groaned. "I think so." She held her arm, and he pulled away her hand, examining her. The bullet had burned her skin, but not pierced her. The windscreen had shattered.

Relief swept through him. "You're OK."

She flung her arms around Kim. "So are you." She shook.

He hugged her, breathing in her sweet scent. She was really here, safe. She'd come all this way, by herself, in a boat. Mark's yells pierced his consciousness. The water had probably done little to soothe the chemical burn of the flare. "Aly, we need to call for help. Can you stand for me?"

She nodded and pulled herself to her feet. "The police are on their way."

Kim helped her onto a seat. Though he had no desire to help Mark, leaving him to drown wasn't an option. He threw the other life jacket to Mark and then picked up the gun. He held it pointing downward. "Do you know how to remove the bullets?"

Alyse shook her head and then pointed. "The police are coming."

The Marine Rescue boat sped towards them. Kim smiled. He was tempted to meet them halfway, but Mark might really be hurt. The man had hold of the life jacket and was swimming towards the boat, pain and fury on his face. Kim lifted the gun, pointing it to the right of Mark. "You can stay in the water until the police arrive."

Behind Mark a movement caught Kim's eye. A fin.

Fuck.

"Shark," Alyse said.

Mark's eyes widened and he twisted around. "Where?"

"Behind you." Kim scanned the choppy water for another glimpse. The blood from his bullet wound must have attracted it. He couldn't leave Mark in the water with a shark. He handed Alyse the gun. The police were almost there.

Mark kicked hard and reached the ladder as the fin came to the surface only metres away, circling the boat. The Great White was about five metres long. Kim reached out to help Mark up, but a glint in Mark's eye made him step back, away from the ladder. Mark hauled himself aboard, his chest bleeding and shirt blackened.

Alyse held the gun steady, aiming at Mark. "Don't come any closer."

Mark raised his hands as the boat arrived, Lincoln behind the wheel and several officers on board, all aiming their guns at them.

"Drop your weapon," one of them called. He didn't look familiar to Kim, so he must be from Albany.

"Not until Mark's detained," Alyse said, her voice steady.

"Lincoln, there's a Great White circling," Kim said. "Be careful with the transfer." He hugged himself and shivered, the wind icy cold.

"Are you both all right?" Lincoln asked.

Kim nodded. His leg hurt, but the bleeding had slowed. "We could do with the thermal blankets." His teeth chattered.

The officers ordered Mark to board the Marine Rescue boat. He hesitated long enough for Kim to think he wouldn't give in, but then he moved across. Alyse sighed and lowered the gun. An officer read Mark his rights while Adam climbed onto *The Vale*. He took the gun from Alyse, and removed the bullets, then handed them both a blanket. Kim sat on one chair, his head a little light and pulled Alyse into his arms, wrapping a blanket around her shoulders. "Thank you for saving me."

She kissed him. "I'm sorry for what I said—"

"It's fine, I understand why you said it."

"What happened to your leg?" Adam asked.

"Mark shot me."

"There's an ambulance waiting at the boat ramp," Adam said.

Alyse wrapped the other blanket around Kim's

shoulders and he leaned into her, drawing warmth from her body. She was fine, they both were, and Mark would go to jail for a very long time. "Can we go now?" Alyse asked. "Kim's freezing."

"Give me a second." Adam had a brief conversation with Lincoln and came back. "Yeah. We'll need to interview you both when we get to shore."

Kim was fine with that.

Adam put the boat into gear.

They were going home.

***

Less than an hour later, the ambulance doors opened, and Kim was wheeled into the emergency room at Blackbridge Hospital. Alyse followed him inside where he was surrounded by family. Lincoln must have called them. She hung back, not wanting to get in the way as the nurse, Fleur took over from the paramedics and wheeled Kim out the back. Mai whirled to Alyse and Adam. "What happened?"

Exhaustion flooded Alyse and she sank into the nearest chair, clutching the thermal blanket around her shoulders. Kim was safe. The doctors would take care of him. He'd be fine.

"Alyse?"

She blinked and looked into the expectant faces of Kim's parents and sisters. "Mark shot him in the leg."

Mai shook her head. "How did he end up on the ocean?"

"I don't know. He went into town to get some things and then Mark called me to say he had Kim." Her chest tightened at the memory.

One of Kim's sisters spoke. "Mark must have been waiting in the granny flat. I thought Kim was acting weird. I should have known something was up."

Her father hugged her. "Don't blame yourself."

Alyse nodded. "Mark had a gun."

"So what did Mark want with him?" Mai asked.

"He wanted to trade Kim for me. I had to meet him off Old Man's Blowhole."

"I thought you were terrified of boats," Mai said.

Alyse shivered, pulling the blanket tighter around her shoulders. "Mark didn't give me a choice. If I didn't go, he was going to kill Kim."

"Thank you." Kim's mother hugged her and then stepped back. "You're wet. You need to get into some dry clothes before you catch cold." She walked to the triage counter and asked for some scrubs for Alyse.

Tears pricked Alyse's eyes. "I'm sorry. If it weren't for me, Kim wouldn't be injured."

Mr On sat next to her, put an arm around her shoulders. "Nonsense. If it weren't for you, Kim would be dead."

She leaned into him.

The exterior doors opened and Zamira and Jeremy rushed in. Zamira made a beeline for Alyse. "Are you OK?" She hugged Alyse. "I was so scared."

"Kim's going into surgery now," she said. "Mark shot him because I took too long."

"And Mark?" Jeremy asked.

"I shot him with a flare gun," Alyse said. "The police have arrested him." He couldn't hurt her anymore.

Mai whooped. "You go, girl." Her enthusiasm made Alyse smile but she could still smell Mark's skin burning as the flare hit him. She was lucky she hadn't killed him, but he'd twisted at the last moment.

Fleur came out with some scrubs. "Kim's in surgery now. He should be out in an hour. Why don't you all get a coffee?" She turned to Alyse. "Can you come with me?"

Adam helped her to her feet, and they followed Fleur

out the back into a cubicle. Fleur handed Alyse the scrubs. "Get changed and then I'll get the doctor to examine you." Fleur shut the curtain behind her and spoke quietly to Adam.

Alyse's body felt like lead. She peeled off her wet clothes, leaving them in a pile on the floor while she dried herself and dressed in the yellow scrubs. Her phone was a little damp, and she dried it off. There was no one to call. The police would inform the Pattons. She opened the curtain and the nurse entered.

"Any injuries?" Fleur asked, getting the blood pressure cuff. "Did you hit your head at all?"

"No. Mark didn't touch me." And he wouldn't ever again. She winced as Fleur placed the cuff right on the bullet graze.

"What's wrong?"

"Mark shot at me, but it just grazed the skin."

"Let me look at it." She continued examining Alyse and then said, "The doctor should be here soon."

It didn't take long for the doctor to check her and discharge her.

"We'd like to ask you some questions now," Adam said.

Alyse hesitated. She didn't want to leave the hospital until she knew how Kim was.

"I can take you home so you can get into some warm clothes," Adam continued.

Kim's family would want to see him first. She might as well answer the million questions from the police while she waited. "OK."

She followed Adam out of the hospital and Jeremy and Zamira gave them a lift home.

***

Kim woke to see Fleur peering down at him. "Wake up, sleepy head." She smiled.

He blinked, trying to clear his head. Fleur was wearing scrubs, so he was in hospital—he'd been shot. "Everything go OK?"

"Yeah. The doctor will be in shortly to give you the details." She checked his vitals. "Your family is dying to see you."

"Alyse?" He sat, wincing at the pain in his thigh.

Fleur placed a hand on his arm to steady him. "Adam's taken her home to get changed and so the police can ask questions. I'm sure she'll be back soon."

Disappointment filled him. She hadn't waited for him to come out of surgery. No, she would have been freezing. "Did the doctor check her over? Is she all right?"

"She needs rest, but she's fine."

Good.

The doctor arrived and shortly after Kim's room was filled with his parents and sisters, all talking at once. He held up a hand. "I'm fine. The doctor says I need to stay off my leg for a couple of weeks, so I'll be on crutches."

"Ugh, does that mean I have to work at the restaurant for even longer?" Eden asked.

Mai shushed her.

It was another couple of hours before a flash of red at the door caught his attention. Alyse hovered in the hallway, as if unsure whether to enter. "Aly." He gestured her in. Her hair was dry, and she was rugged up in a thick woollen jumper, jeans and boots. Her skin had a flush of pink, but dark rings shadowed her eyes. She needed rest.

She bit her lip and entered, giving his family a small smile, but keeping her distance. He wanted her in his arms.

"How are you?" she asked.

"Better now you're here," he said.

"Sorry I didn't come sooner. The police wanted to talk to me."

"I guess I'll get a turn soon."

She nodded. "Bosch and Khan are right behind me."

So he didn't have much time with Alyse. He shot Mai a look. Luckily she understood.

She stood. "We should give Kim time to rest. Do you need a hand doing prep in the restaurant, Dad?"

His father smiled. "That would be great."

They said their goodbyes and left. Alyse turned to go too. Mai stopped her. "Not you."

Kim patted the edge of the bed. "Sit with me a while."

She hesitated. "How's your leg?"

"It'll be fine." He stroked the back of her hand with his thumb. "Thank you for rescuing me. It was so incredibly brave."

She shook her head. "I couldn't let Mark take you away from me." She gazed into his eyes. "I… care for you too much to lose you."

His heart twinged. She might not be able to say the words, but her actions spoke far louder than she realised. Nothing less than love would have got her on a boat to save him. He would be patient, would show her how he felt and wait until she was ready.

He wasn't losing her.

"I care for you too, Aly. A whole lot." He kissed her hand and tugged her forward.

She sighed and settled next to him on the bed, her head on his shoulder. Right where she belonged.

It would take time.

But they'd made it through the worst part.

It would only get better from here.

Epilogue

Alyse checked the time. Kim was running late. He'd said he'd be there by four so they could get to Albany for an early movie. She smiled.

They were dating. Although Kim always couched it in terms of being friends, she wasn't stupid. He was courting her, patiently, slowly, with no pressure. But she felt his love in every phone call, every time he dropped by to say hello, in every stolen kiss over the past fortnight.

At the knock on the front door, a grin spread over her face. Finally.

She hurried down the hallway and pulled open the door to find Don staring at his toes. She stepped back. She hadn't seen him since Richard's funeral, but Kim had told her about the part he'd played in Kim's kidnapping and Adam said they'd had an anonymous tip about Mark's whereabouts before Zamira called. That's why they'd arrived so fast. Don shuffled his feet.

"Hey, Don. This is a surprise."

"Yeah, ah, well… I wanted to say sorry." He glanced at her. "For helping Mark kidnap Kim," he blurted. "I didn't want to. He said he would kill Tyrone."

Alyse placed a hand on his shoulder. "You're not at

fault here. Mark is." And he was behind bars where he wouldn't be able to hurt anyone again. "Why don't you come in, have a cuppa?" Kim would understand.

"OK."

Don followed her into the kitchen. "This place looks different—nicer."

"I painted." Another way of exorcising Mark. The house now felt like hers again. Memories still cropped up when she least expected them, but little in the house was the same as when Mark lived there. She'd chosen pastel colours and had cleaned out the office, replacing the furniture with her own and turning it into a business hub.

She poured two cups of tea and placed one in front of Don. "How's your family?"

"Everyone's pretty angry. Mum's furious I didn't tell her about Uncle Mark and she's angry about Uncle Craig breaking in here."

Craig was out on bail and would go to trial later. The police suspected Craig was the ringleader of the whole crime ring, but they didn't have enough evidence yet.

Don shrugged. "I stay out of the way."

The poor kid. It couldn't be a pleasant environment. "If you need to get away, you're always welcome here."

He stared at her. "Why would you let me?"

"Because you helped me every time we had a family dinner. Spending time with you and Tyrone made me happy for a short time." She smiled at him. "Besides, despite Mark's threats you called the police anyway, didn't you?"

Fear crossed his face and then he nodded.

"Thank you."

His face flushed and his hands curled around the mug. "I'm sorry I didn't know how bad Uncle Mark was."

"It doesn't matter. It's better now."

"With Kim?"

"Yeah."

A knock on the back door. "Can I come in, Aly?" Kim called.

"We're in the kitchen."

Don pushed back his chair so fast it fell over. "I'd better go."

Kim walked in and as soon as he saw Don, he strode to Alyse's side. "Everything OK?"

Alyse stood, held out a placating hand to both of them. "It's fine. Don came to apologise for his part in your kidnapping." She squeezed Kim's hand.

"Oh." Kim relaxed. "You're not to blame. Mark's scary."

Don's lips twitched. "Yeah." He looked Kim in the eye. "I'm really sorry."

"I forgive you." Kim smiled.

Don's shoulders slumped. "Thanks." He picked up his chair. "I'd better go. You look like you're going out."

"We're going to the movies," Alyse said.

"Cool."

She walked him out. "I meant what I said, Don. You and Tyrone are welcome here any time."

"Thanks." He threw his arms around her and hugged her for a split second before jogging to his car. Alyse's heart broke for him. She would have to keep an eye on him, stay in touch. He had little emotional support. She returned to the kitchen where Kim had tidied the cups.

"That was unexpected," he said.

"Yeah. Don's a good kid though."

Kim pulled her into his arms. "And you have a big heart." He kissed her slowly. "I missed you today."

She laughed. "You texted me twice, and you were busy doing those logos for the new shop in town."

"Still missed you." He kissed her again and her heart sang. "You still want to go to the movies?"

"Yeah. I'm looking forward to popcorn and choc bombs."

"Then don't let me disappoint you." He held her hand. "Let's go."

He could never disappoint her.

Their life was just beginning.

Thank you for reading!

I hope you enjoyed the book. It would be super awesome if you could leave a review wherever you bought it, because I love to hear what you thought of the story.

Acknowledgements

I want to thank all the people who helped me with this story. Derek Stone from the Denmark Marine Rescue showed me around and answered my questions, Sergeant Matt Hartfield helped me with the policing details and I had several people help with the beekeeping information I needed. So thank you to Leilani Leyland from the Bee Industry Council of WA, Daniel, and Shelly Bodin from SKK Honey.

I want to also thank Jess Hill who wrote *See What You Made Me Do* (Black Inc Publishing), a book about Power, Control and Domestic Abuse. I read this book in order to understand the situation Alyse was in. The stories and statistics are truly horrifying and it really opened my eyes to what is happening in thousands of households across the world. If you are experiencing domestic abuse there are numbers you can call on the next page.

Thank you as always to my editor, Ann Harth, copyeditor, Teena Raffa-Mulligan, and cover designer, Lana Pecherczyk. And a big thanks to my original cover model Jack who was a little uncertain about modelling for a romance book, but who nailed it, and to Shelly Boston from Smile Photography for taking the photos for the original cover.

Domestic Abuse Helplines

There are a number of places you can call if you are experience domestic abuse.

<u>Australia</u>
1800 Respect   1800 737 732
https://www.1800respect.org.au/

White Ribbon has a list of hotlines
https://www.whiteribbon.org.au/find-help/domestic-violence-hotlines/

<u>USA</u>
National Domestic Violence Hotline 1-800-799-7233
https://www.thehotline.org/

<u>Canada</u>
Ending Violence Association of Canada list
http://endingviolencecanada.org/getting-help/

<u>UK</u>
National Abuse Domestic Helpline 0808 200 0247
https://www.nationaldahelpline.org.uk/

<u>New Zealand</u>
The NZ Police list a range of help options
https://www.police.govt.nz/advice/family-violence/help
including
Women's Refuge 0800 733 843
https://womensrefuge.org.nz/

<u>South Africa</u>
The South African Government lists organisations which can help.
https://www.gov.za/faq/justice-and-crime-prevention/where-can-i-find-organisation-offers-assistance-victims-violence

Protect

The Blackbridge Series #8

She'll do anything to defend her family. He must keep her out of a deadly crossfire. Are they destined for love or doomed to die?

Accountant Olivia Demidenko puts her trust in numbers. And her mind for detail is certain there is more to her cousin's death at the hands of drug dealers. So with the cops warning her off, Olivia's intuition tells her this case needs a thorough audit.

Adam Marshall can't shake the guilt from killing a man in the line of duty. Already struggling to feel worthy of his badge, he's faced with a civilian poking around in his dangerous investigation. And just as he starts falling for her, he discovers a vengeful kingpin could have the innocent woman in his sights.

Though she can work the evidence for leads to her cousin's killer, Olivia can't quite decipher Adam's intentions. And when Adam digs up the last detail needed for the arrest, he's terrified he's staring down the barrel of another tragic ending.

Will the digits add up for this unlikely pair of detectives, or is this a fatal attraction?

Protect is the eighth and final standalone novel in the nail-biting Blackbridge romantic-suspense series. If you like emotionally driven protagonists, secretive enemies, and stories of redemption, then you'll adore Claire Boston's edge-of-your-seat thriller.

Buy *Protect* to count down to passion and peril today!

www.ingramcontent.com/pod-product-compliance
Lightning Source LLC
Chambersburg PA
CBHW060921190726
48286CB00002B/588